HEARTLESS

JENNIFER SUCEVIC

Heartless

Copyright© 2019 by Jennifer Sucevic

All rights reserved. No part of this book may be reproduced in any form or by any electronic or mechanical means, including information storage and retrieval systems, without written permission from the author, except for the use of brief quotations in a book review.

This is a work of fiction. Names, characters, businesses, palaces, events, locales, and incidents are either the products of the author's imagination or used in a fictitious manner. Any resemblance to actual persons, living or dead, or actual events is purely coincidental.

Cover Design by Mary Ruth Baloy at MR Creations

Jenny Sims at Editing4Indies

Home | Jennifer Sucevic or www.jennifersucevic.com

Jennifer Sucevic Newsletter (subscribepage.com)

ALSO BY JENNIFER SUCEVIC

Campus Flirt

Campus Heartthrob

Campus Hottie

Campus God

Campus Legend

Campus Player

Claiming What's Mine

Confessions of a Heartbreaker

Crazy for You (80s short story)

Don't Leave

Friend Zoned

Hate to Love You

If You Were Mine

Just Friends

King of Campus

King of Hawthorne Prep

Love to Hate You

One Night Stand

Prince of Hawthorne Prep

Protecting What's Mine

Queen of Hawthorne Prep

Shameless

Stay

The Boy Next Door

The Breakup Plan

The Girl Next Door

SKYE

"Yay! The bitches are back together again, and tonight we ride!" Lanie wraps her arms around me and squeezes tight. "It's been too long, girl! *Way too long!*"

A reluctant smile curves my lips. "I know. It's good to be back." The circumstances surrounding my return are less than ideal, but I'm happy to see Lanie again. She's been my best friend since middle school, and I've missed her. FaceTime and texting are nice, but it's not the same as talking in person. She links her arm through mine as we walk across the open field.

I glance at the cute cowboy boots that adorn her feet. When she told me that we were going to a field in the middle of nowhere, I didn't believe her.

That was my first mistake.

Second mistake?

Not going with sturdier footwear.

Instead, I'm wearing a pair of flimsy sandals. They're cute as hell, but that's not going to do me a whole lot of good across this terrain.

Lanie insisted we celebrate my return by dragging me to a bonfire in a farmer's field. Already, the place is crawling with drunk-off-their-asses, barely legal adults. Shouting and raucous laughter fill the balmy night air.

Even though I know it won't do me any good, my gaze coasts anxiously over the ever-swelling crowd. Nerves dance across my spine as I silently pray Hunter will be absent from the revelry. Or, if he is here, we'll somehow be able to avoid one another.

If I know Lanie—and I do—she'll be up my ass to cut loose and have fun. How can I do that when Hunter and I now attend the same college? At any given moment, I could turn a corner and smack right into him.

The thought of that happening makes me nauseous.

As much as I want to play it cool and act like my ex-boyfriend doesn't matter, the words slip from my mouth before I can stop them. "You don't think he'll be here, do you?" I shoot her a look that's rife with concern.

Lanie doesn't bother to ask who I'm referring to. She doesn't have to. She's all too aware of my past. She had a front row seat to our relationship and its demise.

"I don't know." She pauses and pops her shoulders into a careless shrug. "Maybe."

"What?" My feet grind to a halt as my mouth dries, turning cottony. I'm barely aware of the blades of straw poking my feet through the leather sandals. "But you said—"

Her expression hardens, transforming into one of impatience. "Even if he *is* here, the chances of you running into him are slim." She waves an arm toward the massive group of students who have gathered to mourn the end of summer by drinking themselves into a stupor. "Look around. Half the university is here. There's no way you're going to see him, Skye, so stop worrying about it and live a little."

My teeth sink into my lower lip before I suck the fullness into my mouth. No matter what Lanie says, I'm going to worry.

When I remain silent, my best friend plants her hands on her hips and glares. Here comes Lanie's version of tough love.

"Would you rather sit home by yourself on a Saturday night

because you're too chickenshit to show your face? Afraid that you *might* run into Hunter Price?"

I'm sorry, is that really a question?

From the annoyed expression that flickers across Lanie's face, I decide to keep those thoughts to myself.

"Skye Elizabeth Sinclair!"

I wince as my full name cracks through the air. It brings an unpleasant image of my mother to mind. This is what I get for living with someone who isn't afraid to call me out on my bullshit. Maybe I should have taken Dad up on the offer to live with him.

I decide to go with something close to the truth. "I was hoping to avoid him for a while," I mutter. "That's all."

And when I say a while, *what I really mean is forever.*

Is that really too much to ask?

Lanie sighs as her expression softens. Marginally. "I know, but you're going to run into him on campus or at a party eventually. It's inevitable. Accept it and move on."

I snort.

Easy for her to say. Lanie doesn't have any ghosts from her past that are ready to jump out and scare her.

I have a carefully constructed plan in place for the year. It involves lying low and flying under the radar, so Hunter doesn't even know I'm here. "Yeah, I guess…"

Unwilling to let me backslide, Lanie loops her arm through mine and pulls me toward the growing group of partiers. "It'll be fine. I promise."

Unfortunately, my bestie isn't in a position to guarantee me anything, and we both know it.

The closer we get to the party, the more my anxiety ratchets up. At least night has fallen. The only light emanates from the bonfire that flickers in the distance and the stars that twinkle across the dark velvety sky.

For the time being, I'll remain vigilant. There's really nothing more I can do.

I inhale a deep breath before carefully blowing it out.

Maybe Lanie's right, and I'm making a big deal out of nothing. It's been three years since we've seen each other, and a lot has happened since then. We've both moved on with our lives. I'm sure he's forgotten all about me. As those thoughts circle through my head, my shoulders loosen from around my ears, and my heart stops thumping a painful beat.

The moment we reach the outer ring of people, Lanie is swept off her booted feet and spun around in a tight circle like a rag doll. Her short floral dress flies around her thighs. Laughter rings throughout the air as her arms slip around her boyfriend's neck.

Jaxon Conway has a typical football player's physique. He's a mountain of a man—tall, broad in the shoulders, and muscular. He looks like he could easily bench press Lanie's VW Bug. I would be intimidated by him, but he's quick to laugh and has warm brown eyes. He's like a teddy bear—big and gruff on the outside but tender and mushy on the inside.

"Missed you, babe," he growls.

"It's only been a couple of hours since we saw each other!"

"Doesn't matter," Jax complains. "I still missed the hell out of you."

"Aww." Lanie's voice softens, becoming dreamy. "I love you so much."

"I love you more," he responds with enough heat to melt the panties off Lanie's body.

Ugh.

Make it stop.

These two are so sickeningly sweet that I get a toothache every time I'm around them. Although, if anyone deserves a good guy, it's Lanie. Like most girls in their early twenties, she's dated her fair share of assholes. Jaxon is almost too good to be true. Kind of like a mythical unicorn that sprang to life. He's an athlete who isn't interested in screwing as many girls as he can get his hands on.

Ever since I rolled into town a few days ago, Jaxon and Lanie have been glued together at the hip. I get the feeling he'll be our unofficial third roommate for the year.

Know what's been getting a lot of use?

My noise-canceling headphones.

Most nights, those two sound like they're auditioning for a porno. Let's hope it calms down soon.

Jaxon and Lanie coo at each other before their mouths fuse, and they start going at it like a pair of cats in heat. I clear my throat and glance everywhere but at them. If we were hanging out at the townhouse, this would be my cue to exit stage left. But we're not at home; we're in the middle of a field a few miles from town. There's nowhere for me to go, and no one for me to talk to.

Awkwardness descends as I flick a piece of straw from my shirt.

Maybe I should take this opportunity to grab a beer. There must be a keg around here somewhere. You can't have this many college kids congregating in one spot and not have alcohol. That would be considered sacrilegious, right?

With any luck, by the time I return, Jaxon and Lanie will have stopped mauling each other long enough for us to move on with our evening. It's not like he's being shipped off to war tomorrow and they'll never see each other again.

Sheesh.

My gaze meanders to them in hopes that they've gotten their fill of each other.

Nope. The face sucking has become even more intense. Any moment, clothing is going to spontaneously combust from their bodies.

I don't really want to be around when that happens.

So…a beer it is.

Not that either of them is paying me the least bit of attention, but I point toward the mass of bodies that have multiplied in the fifteen minutes since we've arrived. "I'm going to grab a drink." When my words are met with kissy noises, I say, "Try not to miss me too much while I'm gone."

Lanie waves a hand absently in my direction as they continue to get it on.

"Okay then," I mumble before reluctantly taking off on my own.

The number of people gathered here is a little overwhelming.

Lanie's right; half the university must have shown up. Everyone is talking, laughing, and drinking. In other words, they're having a great time.

Me, not so much.

It takes a good ten minutes to find the keg. Or maybe I should say *kegs* since there are six of them next to the back end of a midnight black pickup truck blasting music from massive speakers. I can barely hear myself think over the thumping bass. Then again, maybe that's for the best. It's a relief to get out of my head, even for a few minutes.

I locate the line for the beer and take my place at the end of it. I'm not much of a drinker, but I need something to smooth out all of the rough edges so I can relax and enjoy myself.

My flesh prickles with awareness, and I run my hands over my arms to banish the disconcerting sensation. I glance around, scouring the crowd for one face in particular but don't see him anywhere. That alone should alleviate my anxiety, but it doesn't.

My parting with Hunter wasn't what one would call amicable. I don't blame him for being hurt and angry. Whether Hunter understands it or not, I did what needed to be done. As painful as it was, I'd do it all over again. I loved Hunter more than life itself.

A part of me still does.

Probably always will.

If everything I've read online is true, then my sacrifices have been well worth it. Hunter will get snapped up in the NFL draft before graduating this spring. Ever since I can remember, that's been his goal. If one person deserves for all his dreams to come true, it's Hunter Price. Unwilling to dwell on my ex, I shove him from my mind and take in the scene before me.

People are gathered together in groups, greeting one another as if they're long-lost friends who haven't seen each other in decades. It's surreal to be surrounded by so many people yet feel so removed from it all. As if I'm more of an observer than a participant. Other than Lanie and Jaxon, I don't know anyone else. I'm sure people from high school attend CU, but I lost touch with most of them after I moved away.

By the time I make it to the front of the line, I'm antsy and ready to head back to my friends. Even if they're still going at it. Which is really saying something. I'd much rather stand around as a third wheel than be an island onto myself. I dig through my front pocket and hand over a couple of bucks in exchange for a blue plastic cup before it's filled to the rim with golden liquid.

The cute guy manning the keg flashes me an easy grin as his eyes drift over my body. When he's finished with his perusal, his gaze once again settles on my face. Kudos to this guy for not gawking at my boobs like he's never seen a pair of D cups before.

"Here you go, beautiful," he says, handing over the cup with a gallant flourish.

This little bit of silliness lightens my mood. "Thanks."

Our fingers brush as I take the Solo cup from him.

"Next time, cut to the front of the line." He gives me a flirty wink. "I got you covered."

I flash him a grateful smile. Maybe tonight won't be so bad after all.

With my drink in hand, I'm ready to make my way back to Jaxon and Lanie. Only now does it occur to me that they could have moved from the spot where I'd left them.

Who's to say I'll even be able to find my way back?

A knot of unease settles at the bottom of my belly. My fingers go to the purse slung across my chest. It's big enough to hold my phone, but that's about it. I could always shoot Lanie a text, but who knows if she'd hear it. And I have no idea how to navigate my way back to our apartment. The unsettled feeling that had taken up residence in my gut turns into full-on nausea.

Only now do I realize that walking away was a bad idea. I should have stuck to Lanie and Jax like glue. But standing around and watching them make out felt pervy.

And not in a good way.

With those thoughts swirling through my brain, I spin around and slam into a wall of impenetrable muscle. The impact knocks me off-balance, and I stumble back a step. Before I can fall, strong hands reach out and grab my shoulders, yanking me forward. My breath catches, and my heart pounds at the narrowly avoided tumble.

I shake my head to clear it as beer sloshes over the rim of my plastic cup and spills onto the ground at my feet. I'm lucky it didn't end up down the front of my top or the shirt of the unsuspecting person I plowed into.

How humiliating would that have been?

Ugh...I don't even want to think about it.

"I'm so—"

My voice falls off as I glance up, my gaze colliding with narrowed blue eyes. Hunter quickly sets me free as if his fingers have been burned. Neither of us breaks eye contact. All of the raucous noise of the bonfire dies away until it's just the two of us standing alone in the middle of a dark field.

This is the moment I've been dreading.

My eyes roam over his face, cataloging the myriad of changes that time has wrought. When I walked away, Hunter had still been a boy, his lean muscles beginning to thicken. Now the transformation has been complete, and he's a full-grown man. Hunter has always had size on his side, but somehow, he's managed to grow both taller and broader. He must be somewhere in the vicinity of six three or four. I have to crane my neck to hold his gaze. The graphic T-shirt he's wearing stretches tautly across the wide expanse of his chest and hugs the chiseled strength of his biceps. It's enough to make my mouth dry and my knees soft.

If I have one weakness, it's for thickly corded arms. All that tightly harnessed power waiting to break free...

A shiver of desire scampers down my spine before I stomp it out.

Unaware of the effect he's having on me, Hunter's deep voice cuts through my thoughts.

"What are you doing here, Skye?"

It's the harshness of his tone that has my gaze snapping back to his as heat floods my cheeks. I can't stop myself from staring. The little bit of cyberstalking I've done over the years has in no way prepared me for coming face-to-face with my ex-boyfriend. He's grown into his dark looks, becoming even more of a heartbreaker than he was in high school.

My tongue darts out to smudge my parched lips as nerves dance along my skin. I search Hunter's eyes, looking for any hint of softening, but there's none to be found. His gaze is as frigid and detached as I imagined it would be. The tiny kernel of hope that our time apart would be enough to heal our past wounds shrivels and dies inside me.

There is no forgiveness in his heart.

But then again, did I really expect there would be?

Maybe. It would have made coexisting on campus for the next year so much easier.

It's obvious from his terse behavior that Hunter would prefer to pretend I never existed in the first place. As much as I would love to give him that, I can't. Unforeseen circumstances have forced me home.

I straighten my shoulders and attempt to keep my voice level. I don't want him to hear the slight tremble that is working its way through my body. "I transferred to Claremont for my senior year."

His shadowed jaw ticks as he clenches his teeth. *"Why?"*

The way he bites out that one word leaves me wincing.

I take a quick step back and lift my chin, not wanting him to see how much power he still holds over me. Time has done nothing to diminish it. "That's none of your business."

Whether Hunter realizes it or not, he still owns a piece of my heart. It's better for both of us if he never suspects the depth of my feelings.

His hands tighten into fists as he closes the little bit of distance that I've managed to put between us. Instead of scrambling back the way every instinct is clamoring for me to do, I hold my ground until we're standing toe-to-toe. My heart pounds a painful staccato against my breast as his harsh breath feathers across my parted lips.

There was a time when I couldn't get close enough to Hunter.

Now I can't get far enough away.

Sorrow floods through every fiber of my body that it has to be this way between us. Next to Lanie, Hunter was my best friend. He was my first everything.

Date.

Kiss.

Love.

Heartbreak.

Everything we once shared has been blown to pieces, and we're nothing more than strangers. Actually, what we are is much worse. His animosity is palpable. It radiates from him in suffocating waves that threaten to choke the life out of me.

"You shouldn't have come back," he growls. "You don't belong here anymore."

That may be true, but there's nothing I can do about it. I'm here. And I'm not going anywhere.

I shift my weight and force myself to say, "Claremont is big enough for the two of us."

"No, it's not. Stay the fuck out of my way, Skye." His eyes flash with barely suppressed hostility. "You won't like the consequences if you don't."

Before I can summon up a retort, he stalks away. Rooted in place, I track his movements until he fades into the crowd. Not once does he turn around and acknowledge my presence. I've been dismissed. Relegated to the black hole that is our past.

Once he disappears from sight, my knees weaken as the pent-up breath rushes from my aching lungs.

I haven't been on campus for a full seventy-two hours, and in Hunter's eyes, I'm public enemy number one.

HUNTER

This night has turned to total shit, and there's no way to salvage it.

Not even the two gorgeous girls tucked under my arms are enough to pull my attention back to them. Although, they're trying their damnedest. Their hands stroke over my chest as they press their firm titties close to my body. If this were any other night, I'd be kicking back and enjoying the female adoration that comes with being QB for the Claremont Cougars.

With Skye in the vicinity, that's not possible. I'm ridiculously aware of her on every level. If she shifts a muscle or inhales a breath, I'm cognizant of it. Worse than that, I can't stop myself from watching her. Every so often, our gazes will lock before she quickly jerks hers away.

If I'd thought I was mentally prepared to see my ex after all this time, I was mistaken. Catching my first glimpse of her was like getting tackled from my blindside. My chest tightened, and for a heartbeat, the time, distance, and hurt fell away, and I was staring at the girl I'd once loved beyond all reason. Even though it's been more than an hour since she slammed into me, I still feel off-kilter. My world has tilted on its axis, and there's no way to right it again.

Skye fucking Sinclair.

A million unbidden memories flood through my mind. It was Skye's golden blond hair that first caught my attention freshman year of high school. Once she looked at me with those bright green eyes, I was a goner.

It's disconcerting to realize that the attraction I'd always felt for her was just as powerful. If Skye had been pretty as a teenager, she'd grown into her looks, becoming drop-dead gorgeous. Her body had always shown signs of curves, her breasts more than a handful, but now her waist was nipped in and her hips lush.

And I wasn't the only one noticing. All I had to do was glance around to see how many guys were checking her out. She was attracting way too much attention. It took every ounce of my tightly leashed control not to stalk over and chase every single asshole away from her.

Instead of staying as far from Skye as I could get, I'd positioned myself to watch her. Every time she shrank away, trying to melt into the crowd, I stalked closer. There were times when her anxiety would ease, and she would flash a smile at whoever she was talking to before her gaze would unexpectedly collide with mine. In the blink of an eye, her happiness would dissolve, and she'd attempt to slink farther away from me.

I haven't allowed her to get far. It's as if there's an invisible string connecting us.

Where she goes, I follow.

Whether I want to or not.

With my attention locked on Skye, I don't realize that one of my teammates has sidled up to me.

Uncaring of the girls pressed against me, Lucus points at Skye. "Who's the chick with Jaxon?"

I bite off the frustrated growl that aches to slip free. I know who he's talking about, but it pisses me off that he's zeroing in on Skye. There are plenty of chicks at this party. Can't he sniff around one of them instead?

"His girlfriend, Lanie."

Lucas frowns before scoffing. "I know who Lanie is." He jerks his head in Skye's direction. "I'm talking about the blonde honey with the big titties. Haven't seen her around before." He smacks his lips together and leers. "Damn, but I love me some fresh meat."

You know what *I'd* love?

To punch this joker in his fucking mouth. Instead, I flex my hands to keep them from curling into fists and doing exactly that.

"Skye," I grunt.

"Huh?"

"Her name," I reluctantly grumble, "is Skye."

Lucas strokes his chin as a shit-eating grin slides across his face. "I don't know about *sky*, but I'm willing to bet there's a little piece of heaven between those gorgeous thighs."

Motherfucker!

"Whoa!" Lucas's voice turns panicky. *"What the hell, dude?"*

It takes a moment to realize that I've dropped my arms from around the girls and am advancing on Lucas until he throws up his hands to ward me off. My jaw is so tightly clenched that I wouldn't be surprised if it cracked under the pressure.

"Sorry, dude. Didn't know you had interest in that direction. I'm not trying to step on any toes." When I don't take the conversation any further, his muscles gradually relax, and he snorts while giving me a bit of side-eye. "Not like there isn't enough pussy to go around."

Fuck. I shouldn't give a damn about him or any other guy who wants to get in her pants. Unfortunately, that knowledge doesn't alleviate the anger pumping through my veins. "Stay away from her. Got it?"

"Loud and clear, Price." Lucas claps me on the shoulder and takes off like his ass is on fire. I blink and realize that the two girls who had been groping me have also scattered. I plow a hand through my hair.

You know what's not helping this situation one damn bit?

Standing around watching Skye like a love-sick teenager. I need to stay as far away from that girl as I can get. And even that wouldn't be far enough.

Why the fuck did she have to return now?

I need to get out of here, but I'll be damned if I leave this party alone. All I'll end up doing is sitting around and stewing over the past. Much better to have a distraction for a few hours. Maybe then I'll be worn out enough to fall into a dreamless sleep.

My gaze roves over the crowd until it lands on a couple of chicks who are watching me with hungry looks. I know exactly what these girls want, and luckily for them, I'm in the mood to give it. It takes effort to smooth out my features before forcing a smile to my lips. As soon as I do, they start in my direction.

I don't have to lift a finger. It's almost too easy.

When they're close enough, they say in unison, "Hi, Hunter."

"Hey." I give them each a chin lift in acknowledgment.

One's a brunette, and the other is a redhead.

Perfect.

Both are toned and athletic-looking.

Even better.

They look *nothing* like the girl I've spent three years trying to evict from my head.

"You ladies want to get out of here?"

Their eyes light up as they nod.

"Great." I wrap an arm around each girl before tugging them close.

As I'm about to walk away, I glance in Skye's direction. It pisses me off that I'm unable to resist the temptation. I already know that her presence on campus is going to be a problem.

It's Skye fucking Sinclair.

How can it not be?

Sadness flickers in her eyes right before she rips her gaze away.

Once upon a time, I gave this girl my heart, and she stomped all over it. If she knows what's good for her, she'll stay the hell out of my way.

SKYE

Unsure if I should knock, I hesitate at the front door.

Technically speaking, it's Dad's house. His name is on the mortgage, but he shares it with his third wife. She moved in a couple of months after they started dating and pretty much took over the place, making it her own. Ever since then, it hasn't felt like my house. I'm treated more like a guest, which sucks, but there's nothing I can do about it. If I want to have a relationship with my father, then I need to paste a smile on my face and pretend we're one big happy family.

Decision made, I rap my knuckles lightly against the wood and hold my breath. When the door swings open, I'm relieved to find my dad standing on the other side of the threshold.

His lips lift into a smile when he sees me. "Hey, why didn't you just walk in?"

I shrug. My father enjoys living in a little place called denial. He wraps it around himself like a warm cloak. It's not worth the trouble it'll cause to insert reality into this situation. Especially now, given the circumstances. There are more important issues to contend with other than my feelings regarding his spouse.

Instead of commenting, my gaze runs over the length of him, taking stock of his appearance.

"You look good, Dad." It's not a total lie. He doesn't look bad.

"Thanks," he says, "I'm feeling pretty good."

That's the ironic thing about cancer. You can be dying on the inside but look perfectly healthy on the outside. Dad was diagnosed with stage four colon cancer about twelve months ago. It's the reason I transferred to Claremont for my senior year. His illness is probably the only thing that could have forced me home.

The prognosis isn't good. Let's just say cancer doesn't have a stage five and leave it at that.

Even though he keeps reminding me that people beat this every day, I've done enough research to understand that the chances of that happening are nothing short of miraculous. A colonoscopy ten years ago—at stage one or two—would have made all the difference in the world.

The fact this disease was preventable is a bitter pill to swallow.

Dad waves me to the kitchen at the back of their sprawling, five-thousand-square-foot house. "I was about to make myself a bowl of soup."

Soup?

Seriously?

Please tell me it's at least the homemade variety. Something hearty with vegetables and protein.

"You're having soup for dinner?" I glance around the kitchen, taking in all the changes Brandi has made. Four years ago, she did a complete renovation. Out with the dark cabinetry and tan granite and in with high-end white cabinets and gray marble countertops. More like, out with all the decorating choices Dad's second wife had made, so Brandi could erase her predecessor's fingerprints from the house. The master bedroom, closet, and bath were the first rooms to get a facelift.

"Sure, I love soup. You know that." He shrugs as if it's no big deal before going to the cupboard and pulling out a can of bean and ham.

"Dad," I protest as anger bubbles up inside me, "you need to eat healthy. I just read a book about all these foods that help your body fight cancer." I wave toward the can he's holding in his hand like its poison. "Put that garbage away. I'll make you something else."

"You don't have to do that."

"I know, Dad." I sigh.

But someone needs to.

And the woman who *should* be taking care of him is conspicuously absent. Which, from what I've witnessed over the years, is fairly typical. Other than sucking up resources, I have no idea what Brandi does. All right, that's not completely true. She's into working out, shopping, and Botox.

If Brandi cared about my dad's health, she would be here making him a proper meal.

So what does that tell you?

Exactly.

"Put the can away." I pull open the doors to the fridge and consider the options. There's a shit ton of yogurt, which is what Brandi subsists on. Another Brandi favorite—meal replacement shakes. My guess is that she's trying to stay in fighting shape for husband number three. While this is Dad's third marriage, it's her second. From what I've been able to piece together, Brandi doesn't like to be on her own. She needs a man to take care of her.

I tap my foot and narrow my eyes as I rummage through the fridge. Wedged in the back, I find a carton of eggs, a bag of shredded cheese, and a small container of mushrooms.

All right, I can work with this.

"How about an omelet?"

"Sure." He settles at the oversized marble island as I pull out a sauté pan and fire up the stove. "Are you going to join me?"

I throw a pat of butter in the pan and dump in the sliced mushrooms. Once they've browned up, I pull out a large glass bowl, crack the eggs, and add a splash of milk before whisking the mixture. "Yup. I haven't had time to shop for groceries this week."

"Are you settling in okay?" Before I can respond, he adds, "You could have always stayed at the house."

If it were just my father, that's exactly what I would have done. But with Brandi in residence…no thanks. When she's around, it's all-Brandi all the time. It's almost impressive the way she can make everything that happens—even Dad's cancer—about herself. The woman is thirty-five years old and needs constant attention. The way Dad fawns over her only makes it worse.

So, no…I was never going to stay here.

Once I have Dad's omelet prepared, I slide it onto a plate and serve it to him at the counter. Five minutes later, mine's ready to go. I turn off the burner and drop onto the stool next to him with my plate in hand. He's halfway through his eggs as I lift the first bite to my lips. It might not be the dinner of champions, but it's a hell of a lot better than a can of soup.

"It's really good, kiddo. Maybe you should reconsider a career in counseling and think about culinary school instead."

"I don't think so. I'm fully aware of my own limitations. Omelets are about as fancy as it gets." I point my fork at him. "And you know it."

"Well, your efforts have been appreciated." There's a pause as we dig into our meal. "You know I didn't want you uprooting your life for me, but I'm grateful you're back." He clears the emotion from his throat. "I'm glad we have this time to spend together."

The egg and cheese concoction turns to ash in my mouth. It takes everything I have inside to choke it down and keep the tears that prick the back of my eyelids at bay. A few moments slide by as I wrestle my emotions back under control. "Me too, Dad."

As I pop the last bite of omelet into my mouth, the back door swings open, and a high-pitched voice cuts through the silence.

"Hello, I'm home!" There's a pause. "Dean?"

And that would be my cue to leave.

I jump to my feet and grab both of our plates before setting them in the sink.

I'll let Brandi clean up the mess.

It's the least she can do.

SKYE

Great.

It's the first day of the fall semester, and I'm already late for my nine o'clock class. Had I been smart, I would have walked around campus to familiarize myself with it. Claremont University has a sprawling property that covers more than two thousand acres.

I'm now paying the price for that decision.

Everything that could have gone wrong this morning has.

Not only did I sleep through my alarm but I've also managed to end up at the southern tip of campus instead of the northern end. I should be at Hastings Hall, the health sciences building, at this very moment. Not Grover Hall, where the engineering classes are held. I'm as far from an engineer as you can get. Now I'm stuck backtracking, trying to haul ass across campus.

By the time I reach Hastings for my required health class, I'm out of breath, and my shirt is clinging to my sweat-dampened back.

Have I mentioned that it's already eighty degrees outside, and it's only nine o'clock in the morning?

Welcome to late August in North Carolina.

I drag myself up the staircase and locate the lecture hall. My footsteps stutter when I find the door already closed, which means there won't be any quiet sneaking in for me.

Could this day get any worse?

I wince.

Asking the universe to continue screwing with me probably isn't the wisest idea.

With my fingers wrapped around the knob, I carefully twist the handle and push open the door. The less attention I draw to myself, the better. As soon as I step over the threshold, the professor pauses. My wide eyes shoot to the woman standing ramrod straight behind the podium. Her lips thin as she glares at me.

And the hits keep on coming.

Silence rains down upon us before she clears her throat. Loudly. "As I was saying," her steely gaze stays locked on mine, "tardiness is unacceptable and will not be tolerated."

I flinch as everyone swings around to stare.

"Sorry," I mumble, face radiating with heat.

"Please take a seat." When I remain rooted in place, searching the sea of occupied desks for an empty one, she snaps, "Quickly! We haven't got all day. This is a fifty-minute class, and right now, you're wasting everyone's time, including my own."

When my gaze lands on familiar brown eyes, I huff out a relieved breath before swiftly moving in that direction and sliding onto the seat next to Jaxon.

"Hi," I whisper. "I didn't realize you were in this class."

He flashes me a grin. "Just transferred this morning."

I smile, grateful for a friendly face.

"No talking! This isn't high school, people. Don't make me treat you like it is."

My eyes widen as I shoot Jaxon an alarmed look. One brow lifts as a smile hovers around the corners of his lips. Not wanting to be singled out again, I hastily pull out my laptop and fire it up.

"In an effort to conserve paper and help save the planet from the overuse of sustainable resources, the syllabus will only be available online. You'll find all tests and assignments listed in chronological order. Everything is to be turned in by email at the beginning of each class period. Late work will not be accepted under any circumstance."

I pull up the syllabus and peruse it as Dr. Bennet goes in-depth regarding key components of the course. CU requires a three-credit health class to be fulfilled before graduation. I had to scramble to fit it into my schedule. Four sections were available, but this was the only one that fit with everything I needed to cram in this year.

This woman seems like a hard-ass, but the class itself should be interesting since it covers various health issues human beings face from birth to death. Plus, it should be fairly easy and will hopefully balance out the statistics course I'm taking. Stats is like a foreign language, and I'm not looking forward to it.

I glance at the professor again and realize I might have to readjust my thinking. At first, this class seemed like it would be a blow-off, but now I'm not sure that will be the case. I'll reserve judgment until after the first assignment has been graded.

Jaxon leans toward me and whispers, "Is there a reason Hunter Price is staring at you?"

That name has my head snapping up, and I forget to keep my voice pitched low. "What?" A few people in the nearby vicinity turn and stare. Jax jerks his head to the left. Almost immediately, I become ensnared by Hunter's blue eyes. It's as if I'm powerless to look away.

"Skye?" Jaxon nudges my shoulder to reclaim my attention.

I clear my throat and rip my gaze away from my ex. "Oh. Um, we know each other from high school."

Jaxon nods and says from the corner of his mouth, "That's cool, but why is he staring at you like that? Do you two have a problem?"

Yeah...you could say that. Although I'm not going to.

I slouch farther onto my seat, wishing I could disappear through the floor. Does Hunter have to make his hatred for me so obvious? Why can't he pretend we don't know each other? Would that be so difficult?

Apparently so.

"Ummm, something like that." I made Lanie pinky promise that she wouldn't mention my past relationship with Hunter to her boyfriend. It's old news and not worth talking about. Plus, they're teammates. Jaxon is a tight end for the Claremont Cougars.

I refocus my attention on Dr. Bennet.

"Since this course includes a twenty-page paper, I'll be assigning partners today to ensure an adequate amount of time to compile research and complete the project. Even though it's clearly stated on the syllabus, I want to remind all of you that this will be worth forty percent of your semester grade. I suggest you get together with your partner by the end of the week, decide on a topic of interest, and work diligently throughout the semester to complete it in a timely manner."

"Too bad we can't pick our own partners," Jaxon murmurs. "It would be so much easier if we could work together."

I nod in agreement.

That would be ideal.

Jaxon is always hanging out at our apartment, so finding time to work on this project wouldn't be an issue. Plus, from what I've learned over the past week, Jax is a pretty smart guy. He has the brains to match all that brawn.

Dr. Bennet rattles off the first couple of names, and I realize with a sinking heart that she's going in alphabetical order down the class list. Jaxon and Tasha Adams, a girl a few rows away from us, get partnered up. She turns and flashes him a full-wattage smile. It's like she just won the lottery. Jax lifts his chin in acknowledgment.

By the time Dr. Bennet makes her way to the P's, a swarm of angry butterflies have winged their way to life in my belly. It feels as if they're trying to flee by any means necessary. My body breaks out in a cold sweat as I wait. Roughly a third of the class still remains, and Hunter is one of those students.

"Hunter Price." Dr. Bennet's gaze fastens on him, and she does the unexpected. Her lips lift into a smile. It's the first one I've seen this woman crack in the twenty minutes since I walked through the door.

Why am I surprised?

If any guy's capable of thawing a woman's cool demeanor, it would be Hunter. For as long as I've known him, women have been putty in his hands. Even when we were in high school, they would stare at him with lust-filled gazes. And I'm not just talking about the girls, but the female teachers as well. They would eat him up with their eyes and find reasons to graze his arm or shoulder with their hands. I used to tease him about it all the time, and he'd reassure me that I had nothing to worry about.

I still worried.

Anxiously I glance around the lecture hall. At this point, I don't care who I'm paired up with as long as it isn't my ex-boyfriend. That empty desk in the corner would be more preferable than—

"Skye Sinclair."

Damn.

Reluctantly I glance in Hunter's direction to gauge his reaction. His expression darkens as his lips sink into a scowl. My hand shoots into the air.

The smile Dr. Bennet had bestowed on Hunter disappears as she glowers at me. "All partner assignments are final. There will be *no* altering them. Nor will you be allowed to work independently. Welcome to the real world, people. Deal with it."

My hand drops back to the desk with a heavy thud.

I've only been home for a week, and I've already had a run-in with him at a party, and now we're partnered up for the health project. There's no way we can work together. Nausea churns in my stomach as I consider my options. Perhaps if I explain the situation to Dr. Bennet, she'll take pity on me and make an exception.

I glance at her in contemplation. The woman is buttoned up to her chin, and her hair is scraped back into a tight bun at the nape of her neck. She holds herself so rigidly that it wouldn't surprise me to learn she has a broom shoved up her ass.

This woman is the very definition of repressed.

I could probably tell her Hunter Price murdered every person in my family, and she would refuse to assign me a new partner. My shoulders slump at the realization that Hunter and I are stuck working together for the duration of this semester.

I flick another glance in Hunter's direction. His brooding gaze pins mine in place. An unwanted shiver of awareness slithers down my spine. If time and distance haven't softened Hunter's disposition toward me, then it's doubtful anything will.

Once class is dismissed, I shove my computer in my bag before Jaxon and I get swallowed up by the flow of traffic in the corridor. I need to put as much distance between Hunter and myself as possible. The less our worlds collide, the better off we'll be.

Jaxon fills me in on the upcoming football game this weekend. It's the first one of the season. When I was in high school, football on a crisp autumn Friday night was a given. I would have died before missing one of Hunter's games. It didn't matter if it was at home or away. My ass was glued to the stands, rooting for my man.

Even though I was halfway across the country in Wisconsin, I couldn't bring myself to attend any of the college games. They reminded me too much of the guy I'd left behind in North Carolina. Breaking up with Hunter had been one of the hardest things I'd ever done. It was like severing an appendage. Even after the relationship had been cut off, it continued to throb with phantom pain.

A few girls do their best to catch Jaxon's attention as we push through the glass doors of Hastings into the bright, late summer sunshine. He gives them a polite chin lift in response but not anything more. Certainly nothing that could be misconstrued as flirting.

Now that I'm nowhere near Hunter, the pressure in my chest has loosened, making it easier to breathe. My lips lift into a smile as I tease, "It must be difficult to be so wanted."

He shakes his head and rolls his eyes.

I hope Lanie realizes how awesome her boyfriend is. A lot of guys in Jaxon's position would want to keep their options open, but Jax is the total opposite. His focus is solely trained on Lanie. I don't think he's aware of other girls flirting with him. I try not to dwell on the fact that I had a guy just as devoted to me, and I cut him loose.

As we hit the last step of the building before hitting the sidewalk, a deep voice cuts through the chatter that surrounds us.

"*Skye.*"

Everything in me seizes up as I turn and reluctantly meet Hunter's gaze.

HUNTER

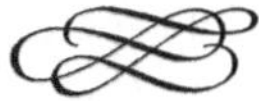

Once Skye's attention is locked on me, I jerk my head to the side, away from the busy pathway as people rush past, jostling us as they flee the building. "Let's talk over here."

Jaxon's feet stall as he stares at me with curiosity. Out on the field, Jax and I are always in sync. Clearly, that's not the case since he doesn't budge from Skye's side.

Why that should irritate me, I have no idea.

"Alone," I add pointedly.

Instead of taking his cue to leave, Jaxon pokers up and shifts his stance. "What do you want with Skye?"

I'm not used to my teammates questioning me. Out on the field, I'm the one in command, calling the plays. Everyone else falls in line.

"That's not any of your concern, bro," I snap. "Move it along."

His eyes narrow before he gives Skye a considering look.

Tension fills the silence between the three of us before she clears her throat and her hand flutters to his thickly corded forearm.

I glare at the place where her fingers settle.

"It's okay, Jax." She gives him a tentative smile. "You should get to class."

"Are you sure?" Uncertainty flashes across his face. It's like he's leaving her alone with an ax murderer. "I don't mind sticking around." He flicks a hard look in my direction. "And making sure you're all good."

I grit my teeth to keep from biting his head off. Jaxon is the last person I want to have an issue with. I don't understand why he's involving himself in this situation. It has nothing to do with him.

"Yeah, I'm sure. Go ahead and take off," she encourages.

"I'll see you later." Jaxon jerks his head into a tight nod, giving me a suspicious look before reluctantly leaving.

As he disappears through the thick crowd, I turn my back to Skye and head toward a large oak tree where there's a little bit of relief from the sweltering sun. I swing around and find Skye hesitantly trailing me. The moment I stop, she skids to a halt. It's obvious from the eight feet that separate us that she wants to keep her distance.

My gaze licks over her body before I can stop it. She's wearing tiny white shorts that reveal far too much sun-kissed skin, along with a tight navy shirt that hugs her generous curves. Her thick blond hair has been pulled up into a ponytail at the back of her head. I'm tempted to reach out and pull the band from her hair so I can watch the silky mass tumble around her shoulders. It's something I've done a hundred times before. My hands tighten into fists, so I don't do exactly that.

How the hell did I ever delude myself into believing I was over this girl?

The thought is almost laughable.

From the first moment I saw her freshman year of high school, I knew she would be mine. It's disheartening to realize that nothing has changed where Skye is concerned even though everything is different. I want her with the same intensity I did when we were in high school. If there were a way to cut her out of my memories, I'd do it in a heartbeat.

Unwilling to stand here and resurrect the past, I fold my arms across my chest and get down to business. "You need to drop this class."

Caught off guard, she inhales a sharp breath before forcing it out and straightening her shoulders. "No."

"I'm sorry, what did you say?" It's disconcerting when she doesn't do the expected and fold under the heavy weight of my stare.

"No," Skye reiterates, her voice gathering strength. "I can't drop this course. I need it for graduation, and this is the only section that fits into my schedule."

Her tongue darts out to moisten her lips, and I'm momentarily distracted by the movement. Who am I trying to kid? I'm distracted by every damn thing about her. And that's a fucking problem.

"If you don't want to be in the same class with me," she continues, "then *you'll* have to drop it."

I blink and reconsider the girl standing in front of me. The Skye I knew in high school was malleable and agreed easily with every word that came out of my mouth. This one...

Not so much.

I'm not going to lie. Most people at Claremont quickly acquiesce to my demands, no matter how outlandish they are. It's one of the many benefits of being a high-profile athlete at this university.

The challenge in Skye's voice has my cock stiffening. It's perverse as hell, and I damn well know it. I'm tempted to yank her into my arms and kiss her into submission, but that's not going to happen.

It can't *ever* happen.

I need to keep this girl at arm's length no matter how much I want to disregard the past and pull her close. She's as deadly as swallowing a mouthful of broken glass. She'll slice you up inside and not think twice about leaving you to bleed all over the floor.

Maybe I'm being a bit melodramatic.

But you know what?

Once burned, twice shy.

And the last time I was burned, it nearly killed me. So I'm not taking any chances.

"I can't move it around in my schedule either," I ground out. "Everything for the year is locked in tight. There's no wiggle room."

"Then it looks like we're stuck together."

That's not the answer I wanted.

I move in her direction, expecting her to scramble back a few steps. We both know that deep down, her bravado is nothing more than a shaky house of cards. Instead, she holds her ground, refusing to budge an inch. There's a stubborn tilt to her chin when she raises it, maintaining eye contact the entire time. The defiance flashing in her green eyes only makes me harder. My dick is throbbing in my boxer briefs as hot licks of desire punch my gut.

"I'll make this class hell for you." I have no idea if it's an empty threat or not. I haven't gotten that far yet. What I do know is that seeing Skye for fifty minutes a day, three times a week for the rest of the fall semester is going to be hell. And then there's the project...

"I wouldn't expect anything less from you," she acknowledges quietly as if she's already come to terms with my anger and the subsequent retribution I'm intent on doling out.

The urge to kiss her roars through my blood. It takes everything I have inside to tamp it down. Without another word, I stalk away before I do something we'll both regret.

Skye Sinclair is a distraction I can't afford.

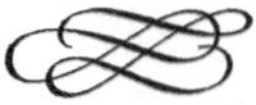

*L*anie and I are parked at a table on the second floor of the library. We started out studying at the apartment, but there were too many distractions, so we relocated.

It hasn't been a whole week of school yet, and I'm already buried beneath an avalanche of reading material. This is what hitting the ground running looks like. Maybe it's better this way. The busier I am, the less time I have to dwell on my dad's prognosis.

Or Hunter.

Being at the same school is more difficult than I anticipated it would be. Everywhere I go, I catch sight of him. It's like we can't get away from one another. Maybe it's only for a moment or two, but it's enough to force him to the forefront of my brain.

Lanie lifts her arms with a groan and stretches. "This chapter on carbon-containing ligands and molecules is going to be the death of me."

When I give her a blank stare in response, she laughs. "It's for inorganic chem."

And here, I thought statistics was hard. Inorganic chem sounds like the stuff nightmares are made of.

She glances at the books splayed out in front of me. "What are you working on?"

"Health."

"That's the class you have with Jax, right?"

"Yup." The thought of facing Hunter three times a week without backup is enough to leave me shuddering. If it weren't for Lanie's boyfriend, I might have buckled under Hunter's pressure to drop the class. It's important for me to graduate this spring so Dad can see me reach that milestone. I don't want to think about the ones down the road that he will miss.

Her expression turns sympathetic. "It's crappy luck that you got stuck working with Hunter."

Ugh. I don't even want to think about it.

"I know." Reluctantly, I admit, "We're getting together next Tuesday to hammer out some of the details." I point at the book in front of me. I've been perusing the chapters to find topics that seem interesting. "I'm trying to do some of the legwork now so we can spend as little time together as possible."

"Did you talk to the professor? Maybe you can get reassigned a different partner."

"I don't think so. Dr. Bennet doesn't strike me as the flexible type."

"Oh…you have Bennet?" Her grimace reconfirms all my thoughts about the woman. "I had her sophomore year, and she failed a guy after he was diagnosed with mono. She wouldn't allow him to turn in late work."

Yup, I believe it. A student could die in that class, and she would probably have an F stamped on his transcript.

"I've come to terms with it." I sigh.

Sort of.

Which is precisely why I'm doing all this research now. That way, I'll be able to give Hunter a few options, we can divvy up the tasks, and never get together again. That's my plan moving forward.

And it's a good one, right?

Hunter doesn't want to be partnered up with me any more than I want to be with him. I'm trying to make this situation as easy as possible for both of us. It would be nice if he met me halfway instead of trying to make the circumstances more difficult.

I glance at my phone surprised to find that two hours have already slipped by. Maybe Lanie and I should study at the library more often. The last time we tried working at the townhouse, my bestie took a break midway through a study session to make snickerdoodles. And a pan of brownies. Then we scarfed them down. Sure, Jax helped, but still...

It was bad.

When Lanie stresses, she goes into baking mode. Unfortunately, she's really good at whipping up cookies, cupcakes, and brownies. I've already packed on a couple of pounds.

Would you like to guess who's a stress eater?

Yup, this girl. I'm going to have to start working out on a regular basis if Lanie and I are going to live together.

I pick up my silver water bottle and bring it to my lips before realizing it's empty. Maybe a walk to the drinking fountain is exactly what I need. Every step counts, right?

That's what my fitness tracker keeps telling me.

As I push away from the table, I shake the container in my hand. "I need a refill. I'll be back in a few." Maybe I'll do a lap around the second floor to get a few more steps in.

"Okay," Lanie mutters, staring at her book. "You really should have tried harder to talk me out of a chem degree. These classes are no joke."

"Hey, I'm not the one who wants to be a veterinarian."

She scrubs a hand over her face. "Think it's too late to switch majors? I don't know how I'm going to make it through vet school if every class kicks my ass like this."

Lanie is the smartest person I know. She graduated valedictorian of our high school class. If anyone can make it through vet school, it's this girl. I'm so proud of her. She's going to do amazing things with her life.

"Sure, you could switch to something else if you want to tack on another two years of school." I laugh. "Your parents would love that."

"Actually, they would kill me."

"Let's be real. You would never give up your aspirations of being a big animal vet and owning a barn with a dozen or so horses."

Her lips quirk at the corners as her dark eyes brighten. "You remember that, huh?"

"Of course I do. That's always been the dream, right?"

She nods, looking less stressed than before.

"Take a deep breath," I tell her. "And focus on one chapter at a time."

"Good advice, but I'm still making cupcakes when we get home."

"No!" I groan. "I can't deal with any more baked goods. I'm going to have to buy bigger shorts if you don't knock it off."

"Hey," she says with a shrug, "no one's force-feeding you."

"Like I can resist your cupcakes," I grumble.

"They *are* pretty tasty."

"Too damn tasty!" I point at her book. "Now get to work. I'll be back in a couple of minutes."

"Fine." She sighs as I take off.

A few moments later, I'm weaving my way through the tables scattered throughout the second floor. The drinking fountain and bathrooms are located at the far end of the building. Instead of cutting through the stacks, I decide to walk around them. I wasn't exaggerating about my shorts feeling snug. I've been stuffing my face with way too many of Lanie's tasty treats. And that needs to stop.

Now.

Tables and study carols line the perimeter of the spacious area. Hushed tones break the silence. Normally, I would tune out the noise, but a deep chuckle catches my attention, and my body goes on high alert. A shiver of unease scampers down my spine.

Only one person is capable of soliciting that kind of reaction from me. My gaze lands on Hunter's dark head, and I quickly realize he's not alone. There's a pretty redhead perched across from him. Even though her back is to me, it's easy to tell she's straining toward him as if she can't bear the distance that separates them.

A shaft of heartache slices through me, nearly cleaving my body in two. I tell myself Hunter is free to be with whoever he wants, but that doesn't help. Watching him flirt with other girls cuts deep. I have no right to feel that way, but it doesn't stop the pain from throbbing through me.

Every time I catch sight of him, he's with a different girl. They follow him around campus like love-sick puppies. They crowd around him in class. I'm sure they fill the stands and watch him at practice just like they used to in high school. Even when he was mine, jealousy would eat away at me.

Now that I have no claim on him, it's much worse.

From a distance, I watch as Hunter flashes a panty-dropping smile at the girl across from him. I can almost hear the sigh of pleasure as it falls from her lips.

It's disheartening to realize I'm still in love with him. There doesn't seem to be anything I can do to kill these feelings. The best I can hope for is that at some point in the near future, I'll be able to look at him and feel nothing.

I'm jolted from those thoughts when his gaze cuts to mine. I squeak in mortification before stumbling back a step and ducking behind a tall bookshelf. My back hits the stacks with a loud thump, and I wince in pain as the spine of a book jabs my right shoulder blade. I squeeze my eyes tightly closed, wishing I could disappear. I need to get out of here before I humiliate myself any further.

When I open my eyes again, prepared to slink back to my table, I find Hunter looming in front of me. I stifle a gasp. He's so close that I have to crane my neck to hold his gaze. If I didn't know him, his size coupled with the ever-present scowl that mars his features would have me shaking in my shoes.

"What are you doing, Skye?" He cocks his head and narrows his eyes. "Stalking me around campus like a jersey chaser?"

"Of course not!" I moisten my lips and point in the direction of our table. "Lanie and I are studying by the doctoral dissertations. I had no idea you were here."

One dark brow rises as if he doesn't believe me. "Then why were you staring?" He leans closer, and his voice drops, becoming silky. "Is that what you're into now? You want to watch me with other chicks?" One side of his mouth hitches. "Hey, that's cool. I don't mind an audience."

Even though his barbed words are meant to wound and embarrass, his physical proximity makes my head swim. I want to shove him away and tell him to go to hell, but I don't.

Can't.

"I wasn't staring," I protest weakly. That's a lie, and we both know it.

Hunter smirks and edges closer, forcing me to flatten against the shelf. I flinch as another book digs into my back.

"Sure, you were." Before I can refute his words, he reaches out and trails his fingers against the side of my face. "Know what I think?"

With my lips pressed firmly together, I shake my head.

His mouth curves into a nasty smile. "I think you still want me."

"No."

The truth is that I never stopped wanting Hunter, but I'll be damned if I admit it to him. I've had a few boyfriends since our breakup, but none have come close to touching the place he once owned.

He presses closer, caging me in, before his lips ghost over mine. My nipples harden into stiff little points as he invades my personal space. I'm desperate to conceal the response. No matter how wrong my brain knows it is, my body still wants him.

I stifle the groan that is desperate to break free, determined to keep the sound buried deep inside. Hunter is probably aware of the effect he's having on my body, but I refuse to confirm it. If I've learned anything in the weeks since my return, it's that Hunter will use whatever weakness he can find against me.

"Are you sure about that, Skye?"

With an excruciating deliberateness, his lips stroke over mine without ever quite touching them. The air between us stirs with his movement. It takes every shred of my self-control to remain still.

"Yes," I force myself to whisper, "I'm sure."

I blink as his warmth disappears, and there's once again an ocean of distance separating us.

"One of these days, I'm going to prove what a little liar you are." He takes another step away. "But it won't be this afternoon." He jerks his head toward the table he's been studying at. "As you can see, I've already got my hands full. You'll have to take a number and get in line."

With that last parting shot, he strides away. Even after he disappears around the corner, I remain frozen in place. What I can't decide is if I've been let off the hook or not. One thing is for certain, whatever is happening between us is only getting started.

HUNTER

I pull up the long gravel driveway on the outskirts of town. Even though it's after eight o'clock in the evening, I bypass the house my brother and I grew up in and head straight to the garage. With the amount of time Mason spends there, he should set up a cot and just be done with it already.

I step through the wide door and into a space large enough to hold three vehicles. There's a car hoisted on a lift and another with its hood popped open. My brother slides out from beneath the cherry-red Camaro when he hears my approaching footsteps.

"Hey, what are you doing here?" he asks, voice filled with surprise. There's grease smudged on his cheek, and his fingers are covered in it. Even when he scrubs them at the end of the night, they never get completely clean. Guess that's one of the occupational hazards of being a mechanic.

I shrug and head to the dinged-up fridge off to the side and grab a beer. "Want one?"

"Sure. I've put in a twelve-hour day. I deserve it."

I pull out two Miller Lites and pop the tops before handing one to my brother. He sits up and takes a thirsty swig.

"Damn." He sighs. "That hits the spot."

I jump onto the long stretch of counter before bringing the bottle to my lips and taking a long pull.

Mason watches me for a moment and tilts his head. "You got that look on your face, little bro. Spill it."

My mouth quirks. I never could get anything past him. The guy knows me too damn well. For the past six years, it's been the two of us. Our parents died in a boating accident when I was fifteen years old. Since there had only been a small life insurance policy, Mason had to drop out of college at the beginning of his junior year and work full-time. He had spent most of high school employed by a local auto mechanic doing small jobs like changing the oil and tire rotations. Over the years, he's learned how to do everything from repairing a busted radiator to rebuilding a transmission. Two years ago, Mason branched off on his own and set up shop in the garage on our property. The money has been decent, and since I had athletic scholarships to pay for school, we've been able to squeak by financially.

A part of the deal was that once I turned pro, Mason would be free to do whatever he wanted with his life. He could go back to school and finish his business degree.

I owe everything to my brother. Without his support, I wouldn't be in the position I am today. I wouldn't have NFL teams knocking down my door. It was a major pisser when I tore my ACL midway through the season last year. Instead of entering the draft my junior year, I had to put it off and rehab my knee. If I injure it again this season, I'm fucked. No pro team will touch me, and I'll have to kiss my football career adios.

Not ready to drop the Skye Sinclair bomb just yet, I ask instead, "What are you going to do next year? You gonna go back to college and finish your degree?"

Mason has sacrificed all his dreams so I could have this opportunity. A lot of times, that guilt eats away at me. I want my brother to be happy, and I don't think he is. How can he be when I'm off at school, playing ball, while he's stuck in a garage twelve hours a day, fixing other people's cars?

He breaks eye contact and tilts the bottle to his lips again before shrugging. "Nah. I got a good thing going here with the business. Once you get drafted and the money starts rolling in, maybe I'll buy a legit place and hire a couple of people. A few mechanics and someone to run the office. You know damn well I hate paperwork."

That comment brings a smile to my lips. But still...

Before my parents died, owning an auto mechanic shop wasn't even on the radar. He couldn't wait to finish up school and get a real job. Working at the garage was nothing more than a means to an end. It was something he did after school and in the summers to earn cash.

Now it's his future?

I don't buy it. Mason is settling. I hate that I'm the reason he didn't finish college and isn't chasing down his dreams. He lives and breathes this garage. Over the years, I've become his number one priority. Women have come and gone from his life. They never stick around for too long once they realize how far down the totem pole they are. I may not understand everything there is to know about the opposite sex, but I'm pretty sure they want to be more than the hole you fuck at the end of a long day before rolling over and falling asleep. And for Mason, that's what his love life amounts to. A couple of women have given him ultimatums. It didn't work out so well for them.

I drain the remainder of my beer and pick at the label with my thumbnail. "Yeah, I know. All I'm saying is that maybe you should keep your options open. Go talk to someone at the university and see what you'd have to do to graduate."

Mason scrubs a hand over his face. "I can't see going back to school after all these years."

I snort. The guy is twenty-five years old. "It hasn't been that long."

"Trust me, it's been long enough."

Before I can say anything more on the subject, Mason throws up a hand to stop me. "You don't need to worry, bro. I'm good. Let's wait and see what happens down the road. For now, I'm going to stick with this."

My shoulders slump. I have the feeling he's telling me what I want to hear so I'll shut up. "But you don't have to. That's all I'm trying to tell you."

"Right," he says, a hint of bitterness creeping into his voice as he pops to his feet. "The world is my oyster and all that bullshit. I got it. Now, tell me what's going on with you. There's a big game coming up."

I nod. The only time Mason takes a break is when his ass is at the stadium, watching me on the field.

We're playing Kentucky on Saturday, which is exactly what I need to focus on. I should be watching game film and mentally running through plays. Instead, all I can think about is Skye. For years, I've been able to push her to the back of my brain. Now she's front and center where she doesn't belong, and I can't do a damn thing about it.

"Hunt?"

My head snaps up, and I refocus on Mason, who is now frowning at me. "Yeah?"

"I asked if you've been watching game film."

"Yup. Watched an hour after practice this afternoon."

"You better watch out for number eighty-two. Not only is he big but he's also fast. And he likes to take down the QB as often as he can."

"I know."

"Conway better do his damn job out there and protect your ass."

"He will, Mase. Don't worry about it."

"Can't help but worry." He looks pointedly at my knee. "The last thing we need is another injury."

My mouth thins at the reminder. It's my single greatest fear and what keeps me up at night. There's still a twinge of pain if I move it the wrong way, but I'll be damned if I say one word about it to my coaches or trainers. My focus is getting through the next couple of months and showing the scouts that I've made a miraculous recovery during the offseason. Then my career will be back on track where it belongs. "That won't happen again."

We fall into silence before Mason shifts his weight and crosses his arms over his chest. "If you're not worried about Kentucky, then what's the problem? Spit it out already. I have a solid three hours of work left before I can call it a night. I need to get back to it."

I huff out an exaggerated breath and realize there's no point in procrastinating. "Skye is back in town."

Mason stills as his eyes widen. Whatever he was expecting me to say, that wasn't it. I almost feel bad for him. The guy looks like he's been smacked in the face with a two-by-four. *Skye Sinclair?"*

For the first time in weeks, a chuckle rumbles up from my chest. "You know another girl named Skye?"

He scowls. "Unfortunately not."

After Mom and Dad died, Mason got it in his head that Skye was nothing more than a distraction. I was focusing too much energy on her instead of channeling it into football. He was ecstatic when she left town after graduation.

Me, not so much.

"You haven't talked to her, have you?" Suspicion laces his words.

"Nah." I came here tonight intending to tell Mason everything, but his reaction has me reconsidering that decision. Concern is already brimming in his blue eyes. And I don't need my brother any further up my ass.

"Good." He nods. "Make sure you keep it that way. You've got enough going on without getting wrapped up in her again."

"Yeah, I know."

He gives me a skeptical look before stabbing a finger in my direction. "I mean it, Hunter. You stay away from her. She's bad news."

Skye?

Bad news?

Give me a break.

I roll my eyes. "No, she wasn't." Mason didn't like that Skye was my number one priority. Even more than football. In his mind, nothing came before football.

"The best thing she ever did for you was leave. Don't screw things up when you're so close to making all your dreams a reality."

"I'm not going to screw anything up," I snap. "You need to chill out."

Mason rolls his shoulders in an attempt to wrangle his temper back under control. "Skye fucking Sinclair." He shakes his head as his lips twist with bitterness. "She should have done us all a favor and stayed away."

Anger bubbles up inside me like a geyser, and the words are shooting out of my mouth before I can stop them. "I *loved* her, Mase. She's the only girl I've ever felt that way about."

"Fuck that." He waves a hand in disgust. "There'll be other women. Plenty of them." He plows a hand through his mussed hair. "You already get all the pussy you want. What the hell are you complaining about?"

"I'm not complaining," I mutter, glancing away, embarrassed by my outburst. The truth is that Skye was never just a piece of ass. Mason wouldn't have had such a problem with her if that's all she'd been. "I wanted to give you a heads-up. It's not a big deal."

The guy is getting bent around the axle, and there's no damn reason for it.

Before he can say anything else, I jump off the counter and land on my feet in one smooth movement. "I gotta get back to school. I wanted to stop over and—"

"Give me the good news in person?"

My shoulders slump. "Yeah, I guess."

Clearly, that was a mistake.

If my feelings haven't changed for Skye in three years, neither have my brother's.

SKYE

It takes two weeks before I'm able to navigate my way around campus without getting lost or turned around. When I make it to statistics with a few minutes to spare, it feels like a major accomplishment, and I'm tempted to pat myself on the back. Instead, I pull out my stats book. It slips from my fingers before landing on the floor with a loud thud that reverberates throughout the lecture hall. A few people swivel on their chairs and stare.

I reach down to pick it up and realize someone has beaten me to it. Our heads bump, and we both groan.

"Sorry," we say in unison before chuckling.

"Here, allow me." When the guy sitting next to me bends over for a second time to retrieve the book, I take a moment to check him out.

From what I can tell, he has long blond hair that grazes the nape of his neck and strong shoulders. His T-shirt molds to his muscular back. When he sits up to face me, mocha-colored eyes meet mine. His lips curve, and a set of dimples pop. He's definitely handsome.

With an outstretched hand, he passes off the textbook. As soon as he releases it, I grunt under the heavy weight. This has to be the heaviest book known to man.

"Not exactly light bedtime reading material, is it?" he asks with a grin.

"Oh, I don't know about that. It puts me to sleep every time."

"Let me guess." He laughs. "You're looking to explore your career options as a statistician?"

Good lord, no. The very idea leaves me shuddering.

"That's not going to happen. I'm only taking this class because it's a requirement. Otherwise, I would be steering clear."

"Come on." He scoffs. "It's not that bad."

"Trust me, it is."

"You know, this book can be put to other uses. It just takes a little creativity." He picks up his own heavy tomb. "For instance, this makes an excellent weapon. You could always carry it around for self-defense."

"So what you're saying is that if someone tries to attack me, I should pull it out and bore them to death with equations?"

He snaps his fingers and points at me. "Precisely." When he grins, his eyes crinkle at the corners. I get the feeling he's quick to laughter. "I'm Josh, by the way."

I grab my notebook and pencil from my backpack. "Skye."

He tilts his head and studies me more carefully. "Are you a freshman?"

"Nope, a senior." I hesitate before tacking on, "I just transferred to CU this fall."

He nods. "Yeah, I thought you might be new. I would have definitely remembered seeing you around campus before."

"I've been studying at the University of Wisconsin, but I grew up in Claremont."

"That's cool." He angles his body toward me. "So this place is home."

"Yup." Even though that's technically true, it hasn't felt like home in a long time.

Dr. Clarke, our stats professor, takes his position behind the podium and gets the lecture underway. From the few classes we've had so far, he seems like a good teacher. He's slow and methodical when working out problems. He also has a dry sense of humor which I like. Occasionally, he'll crack a really bad math joke. Everyone will groan, and he'll light up like a Christmas tree. It's kind of an endearing quality.

While I appreciate his attempt to bring levity to the fifty minutes I spend here three times a week, he can only do so much to make it enjoyable. If there's one subject that I've always struggled with, it's math. I've already come to terms with the fact that I'm going to have to study my ass off just to eke out a solid B. I'd been hoping that health would be an easy A and would help balance out this class, but I now have my doubts.

After enough formulas and solutions to make my head explode, Dr. Clarke dismisses us for the day. I gather up my book and notepad before taking off. My next class meets in ten minutes, and it's clear across campus, so I have to hustle to make it on time.

"Skye, wait up!"

I turn as Josh jogs to catch up with me. Together, we navigate the crowded hallway.

"I wanted to mention that there's a party at the beach on Saturday after the game. Feel free to stop by."

"Thanks for the invite." My lips curve into a smile. "Maybe I will."

"Awesome. It's kind of a tradition around here to party at the beach after a football game. There'll be a ton of people hanging out, playing volleyball, and stuff like that. It's a chill time."

"That sounds fun."

We push through the doors and into the balmy afternoon air. Even though the campus is a few miles from the ocean, you can still smell the salt wafting on the breeze. It's one of the things I missed most when I was living in Wisconsin.

The first winter I spent there was a shock to the system. In the South, you can get away with wearing a light jacket in January. There's no need for a parka and insulated boots. Or snow pants, depending on how much has accumulated. And if you're not looking to get frostbite, you'd better not forget about hats, mittens, and scarves. Basically, you're wrapped up tight from head to toe.

Wisconsin winters are no joke, and don't let anyone tell you differently.

Sure, the Carolinas may have to deal with tropical storms, hurricanes, humidity, and high summer temperatures. But I'll take my chances with all of that rather than survive another blustery Midwestern winter.

"No problem." He flashes me another flirty grin. "Hope you can make it."

Now that he's walking beside me, I realize how tall Josh is. With his shaggy blond hair and laid-back personality, he has that whole surfer-boy vibe going for him.

A spark of attraction hums between us. It's not a full-on inferno ready to burn the house down, but that's okay. It's probably better that way. With everything that's going on, the last thing I'm looking to do is dive headfirst into a relationship. But there's an easiness about Josh I find attractive. After putting up with Hunter's intensity for the past couple of weeks, it's a refreshing change of pace.

We come to a fork in the concrete pathway that winds its way through campus, and I point at the route that will take me to Brighton Hall. "I'm going this way."

Josh jerks his head in the opposite direction. "I guess this is where we say goodbye." He gives me a wink. "For now."

An easy smile springs to my lips. "I guess it is."

He walks backward so our gazes can stay connected. "It was nice meeting you, Skye from statistics."

"You, too."

When he flashes another grin, his dimples wink. His voice carries over the distance that now separates us. "So…have you decided if I'm going to see you again on Saturday?"

"Nope." I shake my head. "Not yet, but I'll give it some thought."

His eyes widen. "Seriously?"

For the first time in a while, I laugh. It's a light and happy sound. I'm almost bewildered by it. But you know what? It feels good.

Josh flexes his biceps, and the muscles in his arms bunch and pop.

"Does this sway you at all? Do you really want to miss all this at the beach? FYI, I'll probably go shirtless."

Another chuckle falls from my lips. He really is silly, but I'm enjoying our lighthearted banter. "I don't think so."

"Wow, you're tough to impress. How about if I do this?" With a smirk, he turns his head until his lips can brush against one bulging bicep. Then he does the same to the other side.

"Now it's definitely a hard pass."

"Aw, come on," he shouts over the crowd. "Aren't you the least bit tempted?"

The farther away he gets, the louder his voice becomes, causing people to turn and stare. First at him, then at me. A few girls whistle and yell his name to get his attention, but his gaze doesn't stray from mine.

I shake my head and raise my hand to wave. "Bye, Josh!"

"See you soon!" he hollers in return.

With a smile curving my lips, I hustle to my next class. Josh is the first guy I've met in a while who has piqued my interest. I might not have mentioned it, but I know all about the bonfires that follow the football games. Even when I was in high school, Hunter and I would hang out at them. Especially when the head coach at Claremont was trying to recruit him to play for the team.

I haven't been to one since senior year.

There's little doubt in my mind that Hunter will be there.

That thought is enough to give me pause. A part of me wants to avoid my ex as much as possible. But I don't want to shy away from getting to know more people. And Josh is definitely someone I'm interested in getting to know.

SKYE

With my phone in hand, I glance at the text message to double-check the address. It wouldn't surprise me if I ended up at 622 E. Prospect Avenue instead of 622 W. Prospect. Being directionally challenged is an ongoing struggle.

But, nope…this is it.

I'm not going to lie. I kind of wish I was standing in front of the wrong house. From the loud music and boisterous voices pouring from the windows, it sounds like there's a party going on inside.

Nerves eat me alive as I walk up the front porch steps. Rotted wood siding and peeling paint mar the façade. At one point in time, this house must have been gorgeous but that's no longer the case. There's a neglected air that surrounds the property. It's sad to see such a beautiful house in run-down condition. Most of the student housing near campus is in similar states of disrepair. Landlords do the bare minimum to keep rent flowing in.

As much as I would like to prolong this moment with a thorough assessment of the house, I don't bother delaying the inevitable. Hunter and I need to get moving on this project. We're already in the third week of school, and time is ticking. What I don't understand is why he insisted we meet at his house. What's wrong with the library?

As soon as I questioned his choice, he cut me off and said it would be easier to work here. Easier for who, is what I'd like to know. Certainly not me. The thought of being alone with Hunter makes me uncomfortable. Up until this point, I've been able to avoid it.

Although, if the noise coming from inside is any indication, we won't be alone.

So…I guess that's something.

I straighten my shoulders and force myself up the last few steps to the front door. I refuse to let Hunter intimidate me. He wants me to drop this class, and I'm not going to do it.

All right. Here it goes.

I rap my knuckles against the door before shuffling my feet. My gaze bounces anxiously around the porch. After what feels like a lifetime, the front door swings open, and a wall of muscle stares at me from the other side of the threshold.

When I remain silent, a slow grin spreads across his face. "Hello there, beautiful." Instead of inviting me inside, he rearranges himself against the door as his eyes take a leisurely stroll of my body.

Heat fills my cheeks at his unapologetic perusal.

"I don't think I've seen you around before." He smacks his lips together. "I love when new talent shows up."

New talent? What does that mean?

I'm about to ask when the guy is elbowed out of the way, and a grim-looking Hunter fills the space. His sudden appearance has me taking a hasty step in retreat.

Umm, can someone bring back the wall of muscle? I'd much rather deal with him than my ex-boyfriend.

By way of greeting, Hunter snaps, "It's about damn time you showed up."

I slide the phone from my pocket and peek at the screen.

I'm four minutes late.

Is he seriously going to bite my head off over two hundred and forty seconds?

Stupid question.

"You said to be here at eight." I straighten my shoulders and hitch my bag higher. "According to my phone, it's eight. If time is of the essence, then maybe we shouldn't stand around and waste more of it by arguing about how late I am."

The mountain of muscle hoots with laughter as Hunter's glare intensifies. "Whatever. Let's go."

He turns away, muttering something under his breath that I can't quite decipher before stomping up the staircase. Unsure if I should follow or stay put, I hesitate. My gaze meanders to the living room, where a dozen or so people are sitting around, drinking and watching the video game playing out across the big-screen television.

"Skye!"

My head snaps at the sound of Hunter's voice. He glowers at me from midway up the staircase. After two and a half weeks of having that expression aimed in my direction, I should be numb to it. But I'm not because a prick of hurt blooms in my chest.

"What are you waiting for? A personal invitation?" Before I can respond, he barks, "Come on!"

I huff out an exasperated breath and trail him.

What does he think I am?

A mind reader?

Instead of snapping back, I keep my lips firmly pressed together and scramble up the carpeted stairs. Maybe I should reconsider begging Dr. Bennet for a new partner. There's no way it could make the situation any worse.

We haven't even started working on this project, and I can already tell this is going to be a nightmare. Mostly because Hunter is dead set on making it hell for me, and there's not a damn thing I can do about it.

He doesn't glance at me again to make sure that I'm following him. As I arrive at the top of the staircase, Hunter turns into a room a few doors down the hall. Once I step over the threshold, I realize I'm exactly where I didn't want to end up.

And that's alone with Hunter.

My mind tumbles back to the past. Believe it or not, there was a time when Hunter and I couldn't be alone enough. We were always devising ways to sneak away from my parents or his brother. The moment we did, his hands would be all over my body. It wouldn't take long before clothing was shed, and he was sinking deep inside—

Nope.

Can't go there.

Preoccupied with those bittersweet memories, I pause. Hunter snaps his fingers in front of my face, and I blink away the past only to find him glaring at me.

What else is new?

"I need to jump in the shower, and then we can get this over with," he says.

Wait…what?

Why was he so insistent that I get here promptly at eight if he's not even ready to work?

When I shake my head, he waves off my concerns. "It'll take five minutes. Start looking over the project options and get an idea of what we should do."

If he would listen to me, I could explain I've already done that.

Instead, he steps around me before closing the bedroom door behind him. Once Hunter disappears, it's as if all the oxygen floods back into the room again. My rigidly held muscles loosen. Only now do I realize how tense I'd become in his presence. Even though I want to get this over with, his absence is a relief. Maybe a little time to regroup isn't a bad thing.

I glance around the space, looking for a place where we can work comfortably. A queen-sized bed dominates the sparsely furnished room along with a tall dresser I recognize from his childhood home. A nightstand is situated next to the bed with a lamp on it.

You know what's missing?

A desk.

How are we supposed to work without one?

This is ridiculous.

As soon as Hunter returns from the shower, I'm going to suggest we head down to the kitchen and work at the table or walk over to the library.

For the time being, I settle on the mattress and grab my textbook before firing up my laptop. Then I pull up the notes I compiled at the library. I've come up with five topics that have a ton of information. If we divvy up the workload, we can avoid meeting up again in person. We can email information back and forth, and then get together right before the due date to integrate our research.

Easy peasy lemon squeezy.

Maybe this won't be so bad after all.

The thought of not having to meet with Hunter again is a huge weight lifted from my shoulders. Sure, we'll be forced to see each other in class three times a week, but that's manageable. Especially with Jaxon by my side.

By the time Hunter returns from the bathroom, all the nervous energy that had been humming through my blood has dissipated. My attention stays focused on the computer screen as I delve a little deeper into the topic of vaccinations. Who knew it was so controversial? And all the info and research out there will make the project a piece of cake. Hunter and I could even take opposing views on the issue.

How ironic would that be?

If Hunter's agreeable to the idea, we can have this wrapped up in fifteen minutes.

Twenty, tops.

Then we can go about the business of pretending the other person no longer exists. At the end of the day, that's all either one of us wants. The less our worlds come into contact, the better off we'll be.

"So, I was thinking—"

My gaze lifts, and my words trail off. I swallow and nearly choke on my own saliva. Other than a thick navy towel slung across his narrow hips, Hunter isn't wearing a stitch of clothing.

Look away!

Instead, my gaze roves over his upper body before greedily sliding over every inch of exposed skin.

Holy monkey.

How is it possible that he's more beautiful than when we were together?

My attention becomes ensnared by a droplet of water as it slowly migrates down the middle of his chest. It follows the arrow of dark, crinkly hair past his six-pack before being absorbed by the plush material loosely fastened around his hips.

The temptation to reach out and trace the same path with my fingers is almost too irresistible to ignore. A thick shiver of longing slides through me before settling in my core as I fight the natural inclination of my body. After a few harsh breaths, I force my gaze to his.

"Where are your clothes?" I croak. It feels like I'm being choked from the inside out.

"I didn't bring them into the bathroom with me." His voice becomes silky soft as he lifts his shoulder in a careless shrug. "What's the problem? It's not like you haven't seen the goods before."

My mouth goes bone-dry, and swallowing becomes impossible.

Technically speaking, this is true. Except the Hunter I knew in high school was still a boy and looked *nothing* like this. He wasn't nearly this defined. The Hunter now standing before me is all man.

A man I shouldn't be staring at.

Or longing for.

The feelings crashing through my veins are dangerous. I need to leave before the situation unravels any further. Why didn't I listen to my intuition? I *knew* coming here was a mistake. But I ignored my gut feeling and allowed myself to be persuaded.

Before I can shove my computer and notebook in my bag, Hunter tugs the towel from his hips and brings it to his dark head to dry his hair. He stands there as if being naked in front of me is the most natural thing in the world.

Don't look!

Don't do it!

This is exactly what he wants!

My gaze drops to his cock.

Lord have mercy...

And just like that, I'm flooded with memories of what it felt like to have Hunter's hard length buried deep inside my body. Heat and desire flare to life in my core. It's been such a long time since I've felt this kind of need pulse through my blood. It's enough to drown out my better judgment.

I bite down savagely on my lower lip to stifle the moan building inside. My mouth dries as I watch his erection grow. When I gasp, Hunter lowers the towel from his face. His burning gaze cuts straight to mine as he continues to dry himself off with unhurried strokes.

A knowing glint ignites in his eyes.

This is nothing more than a game to him. And it's one I have no chance of winning. Not now and probably not ever. I'm in no position to pit myself against him. Not when my emotions have been stripped completely raw.

"Like what you see?" When I fail to respond, he steps closer. His voice dips, sounding as if it's been roughed up by sandpaper. "Tell me the truth, have you missed my cock buried inside you?"

His husky words send a bolt of desire arrowing straight to the heart of me. The effect is like a firework exploding in my core.

My tongue darts out to moisten my lips as his thick erection holds me enthralled. I force my mouth open to deny his words, but nothing comes out. Not even the smallest squeak of protest. My mind has become too tangled up in the memories of what it felt like when Hunter made love to me. How insatiable we were for each other. How I thought there would never be another man in my life.

"Hmm, sweetheart?" Satisfaction drips from his words.

The mocking endearment is what snaps me from my stupor. I rip my gaze from him and quickly shove my book, computer, and notebook into my bag with trembling hands. Before I can spring to my feet, Hunter is there, crowding me with his muscular body. He cages me in with thickly corded arms so that escape becomes impossible. Slowly, he lowers himself, forcing my back against the mattress until I'm fully stretched out beneath him. My wide eyes stay locked on his as my heart pounds against my chest.

"Hunter," I whisper, "move."

Sparks of anger flash from his blue depths when he growls, "Answer the damn question."

I shake my head. It's a slight movement. Given the circumstances, it's all I can muster. "No, I don't miss it."

The lie rolls easily from my tongue. Truthfully, there hasn't been a single day that I haven't thought about or been reminded of Hunter and how much I loved him. But I'll be damned if I admit that to him. He would only turn around and use it as a weapon against me. I refuse to give him any more power. Emotionally, I'm hanging on by a thread.

The heat of his six-foot-three naked frame emanates through my clothing in suffocating waves. His shower-fresh scent batters my senses, sending every cell of my body into chaos. I'm powerless to stop it from happening. My attraction for him and the love I once felt transcends the feelings he now rouses in me.

It's a bitter pill to swallow.

His gaze drops to my parted lips as I pant beneath him. "That's too bad. I sure as hell missed your sweet pussy."

I press my lips together to keep from admitting the truth. My lack of response doesn't stop him from forcing me to the brink.

"I miss the way you used to throb around me when you'd come, choking the life out of my dick. It was the best damn feeling in the world." His eyes grow distant before he quickly sobers. "Make no mistake, I've fucked a lot of pussy since you took off, but none have ever felt as good as yours." Bitterness seeps into his voice.

Just as I moved on with my life, I knew Hunter would do the same. To hear him boast about the girls he's screwed stabs painfully at my heart. All of the hot licks of arousal that had been burning in my core dissipate as I press the palms of my hands against his chest. How can I think clearly when he's this close?

"Please don't tell me it bothers you that I've spent the past three years fucking my way through Claremont," he mocks. "It shouldn't. You're the one who dumped me. Not the other way around. You need to remember that. I don't owe you a damn thing."

I hate the traitorous tears that sting the back of my eyelids because he's right. I have no reason to be upset that he moved on. Contrary to what Hunter believes, it was never my choice to break off our relationship. My hand was forced. No matter what happens between us, that will always be my secret to keep.

Once I have my emotions locked down tight where he can't feed off them like a vampire, I bypass his question with one of my own. "Why would it bother me?" I force out the rest even though each syllable makes me more nauseous than the last. "You can fuck every girl on campus for all I care."

His jaw ticks as he flexes his hips and strokes his hard length against me. Sensation ricochets through my body, waking all of the desires that lay dormant. This time, I'm unable to hold the groan inside.

Hunter lowers his face until his warm breath can float over my lips. "The bitch of it is that no matter how many girls I screw, it's never been enough to obliterate you from my memories. At the end of the day, that's all I want."

I turn my face away as his mouth grazes my cheek. I can't bear for his lips to settle on mine. It doesn't matter if anger and resentment drive his arousal, I'll still be lost.

Hunter chuckles before the heat of his mouth burns a hot trail along my jaw. I squeeze my eyes shut as he presses another caress against the column of my neck before moving lower. His touch leaves me writhing beneath him with a monstrous need that feels as if it could easily consume me. As much as I want him, deep down, I know it's wrong. We're no longer the same naïve seventeen-year-olds we once were. He doesn't love me. His only goal is to inflict as much pain as possible.

If I were stronger, if my feelings for him didn't run so deep, I'd put an end to this madness before it spiraled any further out of control. But I'm incapable of forcing Hunter away. His tongue continues to lave the sensitive skin of my neck before he works his way down my body. He strokes my collarbone before his hands mold against my breasts.

Gahhhhh.

It's been so long since he's touched me like this.

A guttural groan rumbles up from his chest as I arch my body into his hands. His thumbs strum my nipples through the thin cotton of my shirt until they're hard little points that beg for his attention. I moan as he tweaks each stiffened bud between his thumb and forefinger, inflicting enough pain to flood me with pleasure.

In the past, when we made love, Hunter's touch was gentle and full of reverence. As if I were made of spun glass. His hands are no longer worshipful.

"Do you like that?" he rasps, his mouth following the path of his fingers until his lips close around one hardened tip before drawing it into his mouth. Not a stitch of my clothing has been shed, but that doesn't stop me from feeling the pull of him down to my core. Each tug ripples through my body like a stone that has been thrown into a calm pool of water. Before releasing the little bud, he bites down on it, and the arousal smoldering deep in my belly bursts into flame.

Time away from him has done nothing to dull my desire. It's exactly as he claimed. No matter how many people I've slept with, none have ever come close to eradicating him from my memories. It's doubtful anyone ever will.

Hunter shifts his head and draws the other taut peak between his lips as more shockwaves dampen my panties before he releases it. His fingers go to the hem of my shirt and shove it up to my chest. The moment his lips make contact with the bared flesh of my belly, my eyes roll up into my head as pleasure rushes through my veins. He's barely touched me, and I'm going to fall apart at his fingertips.

He inches lower with every stroke of his lips. The velvety softness of his tongue dips into my navel before he reaches the waistband of my jeans. There's no way I'm going to be able to stop him if he attempts to remove my clothing. As wrong as it is, Hunter's touch feels too damn good. Unlike when we were teenagers, unsure of what we were doing, his hands and mouth have acquired serious skills. And he's turned those well-honed weapons against me. It's as if he instinctively knows what I crave and what will drive me over the edge.

Instead of taking off my jeans, he wraps his hands around my legs and pries my thighs apart. His gaze locks on mine as he lowers his mouth to my covered core and bites down, catching my clit and creating a delicious friction as he works his jaw back and forth.

I arch and flex my hips as a wicked deliriousness falls over me. His thumbs press against my outer lips as his teeth grind against my pulsing clit. My panties are completely soaked. Even through the thick material, there's no way Hunter doesn't understand the effect he's having on me.

As if to punctuate those thoughts, he buries his nose against my center. "Do you have any idea how much I've missed your pussy?"

A whimper of frustration escapes as my hands fist the comforter. I want the clothing that stands in his way removed so I can feel the scrape of his teeth against my bare clit and the lash of his tongue against my lower lips.

"Come on, be honest. Haven't you missed me?" His voice turns husky. "Don't you remember how I'd eat you out for hours?"

Argh!

How could I possibly forget?

This is so wrong.

I shouldn't crave his touch.

Especially under these circumstances.

His words may be wrapped in silk, but the undertone is taunting. The pressure inside me continues to build like a storm gathering momentum until a garbled noise breaks free from my lips.

"Sorry, that's not good enough. I want to hear you admit the truth," he growls before biting down on me. "I want you to beg and plead for what only I can give you."

Unable to hold back any longer, the words burst free in a frenzied rush. *"Yes! Yes, I want you! Please!"*

"Please what?"

Satisfaction laces his voice, and it kills me that he's capable of forcing me to my knees so easily. He's barely touched me, and I'm an inarticulate, writhing mess on the bed.

It's nothing short of demoralizing.

"Would you like me to make you come?"

His teeth clamp down on my clit and I suck in a sharp breath as another burst of arousal explodes inside me. When his touch disappears, I'm left feeling needy and unsatisfied.

"Yeeees!" I have zero shame.

"Tell me what you want," he says.

I choke on the idea of begging him for pleasure.

"Please," I whisper, disgusted with myself for giving in. "I want to come. I want *you* to make me come."

"I know you do." He bites down on my clit again and I moan as the sensation explodes in me. "No one will *ever* make you feel the way I do. You need to remember that."

The delicious cocktail of his commanding voice coupled with the firm pressure of his teeth makes me arch off the mattress as my body tightens in response. I keen out my orgasm as he continues to apply the perfect amount of force to my throbbing pussy.

It's only when Hunter releases my clit and buries his nose against me, inhaling a lungful of breath, do I come crashing back to earth with a painful thump.

"You can hate me all you want," he whispers harshly against the juncture between my thighs, "but you still crave what only I can give you."

The smugness in his voice turns the pleasure in my body to bitterness.

During the time we've been broken up, no one has ever come close to making me feel the way he did. That knowledge is enough to bring tears of frustration to my eyes. I've done my best to move on, but it's not enough.

It will *never* be enough.

Still naked, Hunter straightens to his full height. His cock is impossibly long and thick. A purplish hue colors it as blood rushes to the engorged head.

My breath catches when he wraps his fingers around the girth before giving it a few slow pumps. Drops of moisture bead at the slit and make the bulbous head shiny. His eyes lower to the V between my legs as he continues to stroke his dick. I'm mesmerized by the sight of his heavy balls drawing tightly against his body.

Even though he's no longer caging me in, I remain frozen in place. Unable to move. Or breathe. What am I still doing here? I could easily roll from the bed, grab my bag, and escape, but that's the last thing on my mind.

The way Hunter caresses his thick cock is the most erotic thing I've ever witnessed. His knuckles turn bone white as he tightens his grip before picking up speed.

My core clenches as a fresh wave of arousal washes over me.

How can something like that be so sexy?

The growl that emerges from his lips sounds as if it's been dredged from the bottom of the ocean. My core tingles with need as my gaze flies to his. His expression becomes one of intense focus as his jaw locks, and he grits his teeth. My attention returns to his erection in time to witness his ejaculation. Thick pearly ropes jet from the tip of his cock and land on the bedspread between my legs as he groans out his release. His movements become languid as his dick softens in his hand.

"There," he mutters harshly, "now we're even."

As if slowly waking from a dream, I blink out of the trance that has fallen over me.

Oh my God, did that really happen?

I stare at the gleaming white come painted across the dark comforter as if it can't possibly be real.

I need to get out of here.

Heat scorches my cheeks as I'm spurred into action. Rolling to the side, I snatch my bag before scrambling off the bed. I can't look at Hunter. How can I meet his gaze, knowing what I'll find simmering in his brilliant blue depths?

Satisfaction that he was able to get to me with little to no resistance on my part.

The only bright spot is that we didn't actually have sex. Considering what did happen, it's not much, but it's all I have to cling to at the moment.

"Skye, wait—"

Not bothering to respond, I grab the door handle and fly over the threshold before pounding down the staircase and out the front door. Once I've left the house behind, I inhale a deep breath and try to settle the chaos unfolding inside me.

Hunter Price is so much more dangerous than I allowed myself to believe. No matter what, I can't forget that.

HUNTER

I drag a hand over my face before grabbing a pair of boxer briefs from the top drawer of the dresser and yanking them up my legs. By the time the elastic band snaps against my waist, Skye has already ripped open the bedroom door and is racing down the staircase like she's narrowly escaped becoming a human sacrifice. The pounding of her feet echoes off the bare walls before reverberating in my head. I grab athletic shorts, a T-shirt, and shoes before taking off.

What the hell am I supposed to say once I catch up to her?

That I'm sorry?

Well, guess what?

I'm not.

I've had a major hard-on for that girl since she stepped foot on campus. It was only a matter of time before the sexual energy brewing between us exploded. I wasn't lying when I told her that I've used other women to try to obliterate her from my mind.

The operative word being *try*.

Only now is it apparent that I've been deluding myself.

We've always had undeniable chemistry. What I didn't anticipate was that it would have grown in strength. Skye Sinclair has annihilated the willpower I've always prided myself on having. After the way that girl stomped on my heart, she should mean absolutely nothing to me.

Less than that.

Unfortunately, nothing could be further from the truth.

By the time I make it to the first floor of the house, the front door is hanging open on its hinges. None of the fuckwits in the living room seem to notice. They're too busy playing video games and drinking. I barrel through the door, not bothering to close it behind me. As soon as I hit the sidewalk, I see her familiar figure striding toward campus. I'm tempted to shout her name but decide to keep my trap shut. There's no reason for me to alert her to my presence and make this any harder on myself.

The heel of my foot lands on a pebble, and I remember with a yelp of pain that I'm holding my shoes instead of wearing them. With my gaze focused on Skye, I stop long enough to slip them on my feet before setting off at a quick jog. It doesn't take long for me to close the gap between us. By the time Skye realizes that I'm hot on her heels, it's already too late. I'm there.

She might have dodged me once tonight, but she won't get the chance to do it again. I'll turn her loose when I'm damn good and ready. And not a moment sooner.

Heat fills her cheeks, and her blond hair is mussed. Instead of a freshly fucked afterglow mellowing her mood, her eyes spit green fire. I'm almost tempted to lay my hands on her one more time just to prove that even though she's angry, I can still bend her to my will.

She stops and swings around to face me. "Stay away from me, Hunter! I'm not interested in playing any more games with you." Her voice shakes as her hands bunch and tighten.

I can't help the chuckle that breaks free. "Oh, sweetheart, I'm only getting started."

She growls before whipping around and trying to stride away from me.

If only this were a game. My life would be so much easier if Skye was nothing more than a piece of ass I could fuck out of my system before moving on to the next conquest.

But that's not the case. This is the one girl who has always held power over me. And it pisses me off to realize that she still does.

Silently I fall in line with her and try to collect my scattered thoughts. I refuse to apologize for what happened in my bedroom. She wanted it. Hell, she begged for it.

The only sound that fills the quietness is the soles of our shoes striking the concrete. Skye's body vibrates with pent-up tension until it becomes impossible to contain. She gives me a sidelong look before grinding to a halt.

With her hands planted firmly on her hips, she snaps, "What are you doing?"

"I'm walking you home." I may be angry with her, but that doesn't mean I want to see anything happen. It's confusing to feel both pissed off and protective at the same time.

"You do realize that *you're* what I'm running from, right?"

The irony isn't lost on me.

All the unwanted emotion that Skye dredges up inside me was easier to deal with when we had a thousand miles between us. I didn't think about her on a daily basis or see her around every damn corner. It's become a vicious cycle. The more I see her, the more I think about her.

Know what I should be focused on?

I'll give you a hint…it's not Skye fucking Sinclair.

When I remain silent, she adds in a weary voice, "I can't drop this class, Hunter, and it doesn't seem like you can either. The only thing you can do is talk to Dr. Bennet and see if she'll change our partner assignments. If not, we don't have any choice about working together."

Is it possible for me to sweet-talk my way out of working with Skye?

Probably.

Dr. Bennet and I go way back to first semester of freshman year.

She seems to like me well enough. It certainly wouldn't hurt for me to drop by during office hours and talk to her about the situation.

But...

Why should I let Skye off the hook so easily?

The girl had to know what she was getting herself into when she decided to transfer to CU. That decision has wreaked havoc on my life. As far as I'm concerned, she can suck it up and pay the price.

So…am I going to talk with Bennet and try to get us reassigned to different partners?

Not a snowball's chance in hell.

"You heard what Dr. B said," I remind. "No exceptions. I'm not even going to ask."

Skye's shoulders slump as if she was expecting the answer but was hopeful for a different one.

Well, that's too fucking bad.

She glances in my direction before admitting softly, "I wish it didn't have to be like this."

That makes two of us, but nothing Skye can say will soften my feelings toward her. Not after the way she destroyed me. Even though I don't want to dwell on the demise of our relationship, I can't help but mentally sift over the wreckage.

Our breakup had come out of nowhere. There hadn't been any problems or arguments leading up to it. Hell, I'd been busy mapping out our future. It went a little something like this—we'd spend the summer together after graduation, attend Claremont in the fall, I'd enter the NFL draft junior year, and then we'd tie the knot. A couple of years down the road, we'd have a few kids and live happily ever after.

What a naïve asshole I'd been.

Instead, Skye accepted a position as a camp counselor in Wisconsin.

Wisconsin.

She claimed that I would be too busy with football during the summer, and she wanted to spend time with her mother before we started college. I wasn't thrilled about the unexpected change in plans, but she said all the right things and made me feel like everything was okay. This was a favor for her mom's friend who owned the camp, and we'd visit as much as we could.

But that never happened.

Once she got to Wisconsin, she was too busy to talk or even text. And I was swamped with football camp. Before I knew it, weeks had flown by with only a few sporadic messages between us. Unable to stand the separation, I got in my car and drove the seventeen hours to Camp whatever-the-hell-its-name-was. Instead of being happy to see me, Skye dropped the bomb that she was staying in Wisconsin to attend college. Her mother had pulled some strings and got her accepted at UW-Madison.

I thought she was joking.

Who the fuck wants to live in Wisconsin?

She wasn't.

Then she unceremoniously dumped my ass. Something about our lives moving in different directions and us growing apart—blah, blah, blah. My brain clicked off, and I stopped listening to the bullshit excuses since that was what they were. None of it made sense.

How could she throw away our relationship?

I'm not proud of myself, but in a moment of weakness, I told her that if being closer to her mother was so important, I'd transfer, too. I would talk to the coach at Madison and see what could be worked out. So what if I had to red-shirt my freshman year? Did it really matter? I was a hot commodity. I could have gone to any Division I program in the country.

Skye shot down the idea. She wanted a chance to be on her own without anything weighing her down. And just like that, I was cut loose. Confused and angry, I returned home. After a couple of weeks, I tried reaching out again in hopes that she had come to her senses and changed her mind.

Know what she did?

She blocked me.

Can you believe that shit? The girl fucking blocked me from her phone and all social media.

I sulked for the rest of the summer and into the fall. It was Mason, my older brother, who finally pulled me aside and told me that I was fucking up everything I'd spent my entire life working toward. I needed to pull my head out of my ass and play the way I could before someone stole my spot.

It took time for me to find my groove again, but I eventually got there. I learned to enjoy the benefits that came along with being starting QB for the Claremont Cougars. Which means I screwed and partied my way out of the funk I'd fallen into.

After a while, I forgot all about Skye Sinclair.

Or so I'd thought.

I shake myself from those thoughts as my gaze falls to her lips. After a moment, her tongue darts out to smudge them.

"Hunter…" she whispers thickly.

I flick my gaze to hers and angle my head. "Yeah?"

It doesn't escape me that I could have her down on the ground in a heartbeat if I wanted. I could have her begging me to fuck her. That little bit of knowledge assuages the pain buried deep inside me.

"What happened in your room…" She shakes her head. "It can't happen again."

Wanna bet?

All I'd wanted to do tonight was see how far I could push Skye before she crumbled. It had taken fewer than a handful of minutes before I'd had her spread out before me, begging to come. The memory brings a smile of satisfaction to my lips.

"And why's that?"

Her gaze darts away as she mumbles, "We've both moved on with our lives." She swallows and forces out the rest. "We can't be anything more than friends."

Friends?

I almost choke on my laughter.

Is that what she thinks? That I'm interested in friendship?

I step closer, invading her space. Her body jerks when my fingers slip beneath her chin, tipping her face upward until she has no other choice but to meet my steely gaze. "You and I will *never* be friends."

"What?" Her eyes become impossibly wide as hurt flashes in them.

"There's only one thing I want from you, and it sure as hell isn't your friendship. You need to wrap your pretty little head around that."

"No." She breathes out the word as if it's painful.

My lips lift at the corners. "The only thing I want is closure."

When she attempts to shake her head, my fingers bite into her chin to keep her from moving.

"I-I don't understand."

"Of course you do." I step closer until the tips of her breasts brush against my chest. "I want to fuck you out of my system until you're nothing more than a distant memory. Tell me that you don't want the same damn thing."

Even before she opens her mouth, I see the refusal perched on the tip of her tongue and shake my head to silence her. Skye can deny it all she wants to herself, but she isn't going to lie to me.

"You owe me that much." I lift my other hand and tangle my fingers through her hair until she's rendered powerless.

A whimper leaves her mouth.

"Are you really going to deny me?"

She presses her lips together as I bring my face inches from hers. "It destroyed me when you left town." It hurts to give voice to the words, but she needs to hear them almost as much as they need to be vented. "You stole all the light from my world and left me to rot in the darkness."

A sheen of tears brightens her eyes, making them shimmer in the moonlight. "That was never my intention."

"Does it really matter?" I bite out. "It was the result. I want what should have always been mine."

"Hunter…"

"I'll give you some time to think it over."

Before she can tell me no, my hands fall to my sides. "Come on, I'll walk you home. I've still got a shit ton of work to plow through tonight."

She inhales a shaky breath before giving me a sharp nod. I was expecting her to put up more of a fight, so it surprises me when she remains silent.

We walk quietly, each of us lost in our own private thoughts that we're unwilling to share with the other. I have no idea if Skye will give in to my demands. If I'm being completely honest with myself, I don't want her to. At least not right away. I want to give chase before slowly wearing her down. And only then do I want to claim my prize.

SKYE

"*E*xactly who does that bitch think she is?" Lanie seethes as she paces back and forth in front of the bed I sit on.

The bitch in question is Tasha Adams.

"Calm down. They're just working together on a project. It's not a big deal."

Lanie whips around and plants her hands on her hips. I gulp, glad that I'm not Tasha. I don't think I'd want to be on the receiving end of Lanie's jealousy.

"Shows how much you know. Tasha has been trying to sink her skanky claws into Jaxon ever since freshman year." Her eyes cloud before she reluctantly admits, "Maybe I didn't mention it before, but they've hooked up a couple of times."

"Oh."

"It's not like they ever went out or anything," she tacks on hastily. "He's got much higher standards than that. But she had a hard time accepting that it was a casual relationship. She followed him around like a puppy and would show up at the parties he was at."

Well, that definitely changes the circumstances. Now I understand why Lanie is uneasy about her boyfriend working with Tasha. But I don't think she has anything to be concerned about. Jaxon loves her way too much to jeopardize their relationship.

"If it makes you feel better," I tell her, "he didn't ask to be partnered with her."

"I know," she mutters as her rigidly held shoulders collapse. "I hate the thought of them spending so much time alone. Even though we're together, she still hangs on him, and Jax is way too nice to tell her to get lost."

"That might be true, but you're not."

"You're right." She snickers. "I'm not. I'll take that girl down if I have to."

"You need to keep it in perspective. They're working at the library. Not a hotel."

She rolls her eyes before giving me an *are-you-crazy* look. "Do you have *any* idea what happens at the library?" She pauses for a beat. "Last year, I saw some guy get a blowie in the stacks."

"Jax would never cheat. The guy is head over heels in love with you." To the point where, sometimes, I can't stand to be around them. They serve as an in-your-face reminder of what I used to have and let go of.

The heat in her eyes dies down as a small smile curls around the edges of her lips. "I know. But still…I can't stand that girl. You mark my words. She's going to make a play for him."

"And he'll turn her down flat," I reassure. Tasha can't hold a candle to Lanie. Not with her dark Greek looks, lean body, and fierce personality. And she's smart as hell. Hello, the girl is going to be a veterinarian. Everyone knows it's more difficult to get accepted into vet school than medical school. Lanie has nothing to worry about. Tasha is like an annoying fruit fly that you have to swat away.

"He'd better," she mutters darkly. "I'd hate to mess a bitch up." Her eyes flash with renewed fire. "And his ass would be gone."

"It'll be fine," I soothe.

"I want him to get home so we can have sex," she blurts.

"Didn't you two knock boots before he left for the library?"

A confused expression flits across her face. "Yeah, I was marking my territory."

"Hopefully, I'll be gone when you remark it." I can't resist adding, "You two are ridiculously loud."

She grins before throwing herself on my desk chair and spinning from side to side. Lanie has always vibrated with energy. She can't sit still to save her life which is exactly why she ran cross country in the fall, played volleyball in the winter, and ran track in the spring when we were in high school.

"I need something to take my mind off Jaxon and that skank bag." She drums her fingers on the armrest of the chair. "Tell me what's going on with Hunter."

Ugh. I'd prefer to keep talking about the skank-bag. Hunter already occupies too much of my head space, and that's becoming a problem.

I shrug and stare at my lap. "There's nothing to tell."

When she remains silent, I tentatively lift my gaze to hers. As my best friend, I owe Lanie full disclosure. If anyone could give me sound advice on handling the situation with Hunter, it would be this girl.

"Hmm." She twists on the chair, arcing back and forth in a semi-circle with the tips of her toes. "Why don't I believe you?"

Heat floods my cheeks as unbidden memories from the other night crash through my head. I'm embarrassed to admit that I begged him to touch me and make me come. When I had decided to move back home, I'd convinced myself that my feelings for him were part of the past. They were nothing more than fond memories of a first boyfriend. But clearly, that's not the case. My heart still belongs to Hunter. Not only is that a scary prospect, it's a dangerous one.

Maybe I *should* come clean and tell Lanie everything. This isn't a situation I can handle on my own. If it was, I wouldn't have allowed him to touch me in the first place. It barely took him any time at all, and I was putty in his clever hands.

"Skye?"

The Hunter-induced haze surrounding me dissipates as my head snaps up, and I meet Lanie's question-filled gaze.

She leans forward and gives me a meaningful look. "Tell me what's going on."

"There's nothing," I lie. "He stays out of my way, and I do the same."

"How did your little study sesh go?"

"It was fine." My gaze bounces around the room. "We got a ton accomplished." That's another lie. Other than him bringing me to my knees and humiliating me, nothing got done.

"Huh."

I slap my hands a little too hard against my thighs and wince. "Yup. It's all good. Nothing to worry about." Not wanting her to delve any deeper, I swipe my phone off the bed and glance at the screen before reluctantly unfolding myself from the bed. "Brandi's picking me up in ten minutes for shopping and lunch."

That announcement does exactly as it was intended and distracts my best friend from continuing her inquisition.

"*What?*" Lanie barks out a disbelieving laugh. "Are you being serious?"

"Unfortunately," I mutter, not looking forward to the next couple of hours of my life.

"How did you get talked into *that?*"

"Dad." I sigh as if that one-word answer is more than enough of an explanation. "It's a favor to him."

Lanie's surprise dissolves, leaving a sober expression in its wake. "How is Dean doing?"

Unsure how to answer that complicated question, I shrug. "Okay, I guess."

The truth is that Dad isn't *okay*. But that's difficult to admit to myself, let alone Lanie. I don't like thinking about the time stamp on his mortality. I know that everyone dies at some point, but it's a different matter altogether to accept with certainty that the end looms near for someone you love.

There are days when that's all I can focus on, and it makes me sick to my stomach. I want to curl up in a tight ball and sob. There's no one I can talk to about this, which leaves me feeling more alone than I already am.

A couple of days ago, I dropped by the house to see how Dad was doing. The new medication makes him nauseous, and it's difficult for him to keep food down. While I was there, he spent a lot of time in the bathroom throwing up. Afterward, he looked exhausted. When he's not feeling good or doesn't have the energy to get out of his recliner, it's impossible to pretend that he'll beat the prognosis and prove the doctors wrong.

All of this swirls through my head as I slip my feet into my sandals. "All we can do is hope that this treatment will work."

Lanie nods and bites her lip before worrying it with her teeth.

I take a step toward the door and hesitate. The thought of spending a couple of hours alone with wife number three is enough to give me pause. What are we going to talk about for that long?

"Any chance I can interest you in a free meal on Brandi?" I ask. "I'm sure she wouldn't mind if you tagged along." Everyone knows that my stepmother enjoys a captive audience.

"Yeah, I wish I could," she says evasively, "but I've got this thing..."

I spear a finger in her direction and accuse, "You, madam, are a liar." I can't say that I blame her. If there were a way for me to get out of this, I'd do it in a heartbeat. But I made a promise to my dad, and I won't break it. No matter how painful this turns out to be.

A smile breaks out across her face. "No, really. I have a class at two o'clock. Otherwise, I'd come for moral support."

I grumble under my breath.

"Now...if you're interested in coming clean and telling me what's really going on with Hunter, maybe I'll consider blowing off class. 'Cause I'm pretty sure it's not all rainbows and unicorns over there."

Damn. She's much too clever for her own good.

When I remain tight-lipped, she nods her head knowingly. "Yup, there's *definitely* something going on."

I wave her off before vacating the room. There's no way I'm going to discuss Hunter or the closure he's intent on getting from me.

Then I would have to admit how tempted I am to give in.

SKYE

"I'm so glad we could get together and do this!" Brandi gushes from across the table at Poco Loco, a local restaurant with the best Mexican food in town.

Brandi wanted to go somewhere more upscale, but I convinced her to dine here instead. I love the food and haven't had a chance to stop in since I've returned. If I'm being forced to endure her company, I should at least get a good meal out of it.

"Yeah," I enthuse, "me, too." Dad owes me big time for this.

Unexpectedly, she reaches across the table and lays a perfectly manicured hand over mine. I glance down at her slim fingers and fight the urge to pull away.

"Now that you've moved back home, we have a real opportunity to strengthen our bond. I want us to be close, Skye. Especially with everything that's going on with your dad." Emotion gathers in her baby blues as she blinks back the moisture. "Family is the most important thing, and we need to stick together and support one another. Whatever you're feeling, you can share it with me."

As much as I appreciate the sentiment, that's not going to happen. Brandi and I don't have a deep relationship. Neither one of us has ever bothered to skim beneath the surface. I can't imagine what a heartfelt conversation between the two of us would look like. It's impossible to get real with someone you don't trust.

Or even like.

"Thank you, I'll keep that in mind," I force myself to say.

"Good. There aren't many people I can talk to about this." Her fingers tighten around my hand. "Unless you've gone through it, you don't understand what it's like to have a loved one fighting cancer. These treatments have been so difficult on your dad." Her voice drops to a husky whisper. "I'm not sure it's working."

The floor drops out from beneath me. "Why do you say that?"

She shrugs and grows restless. "He's lost a lot of weight. The chemo makes him really sick, and last week, when they checked the numbers, they hadn't moved."

"Oh." I glance down at the table. "Maybe he needs to look at different options. What about one of the experimental studies Dad was talking about?"

"Dr. Waterman wants to give this treatment a little more time before we move on to something else."

"Maybe you should talk to the doctor about the side effects he's experiencing." We both know that my dad doesn't always tell them what's going on. He doesn't like to complain.

Her lips tug down at the corners before she glances away. "I was already planning on going with him to his next appointment. I'll be sure to bring it up if your dad doesn't mention it."

Maybe Brandi isn't so bad after all.

Trust me, it's a painful admittance.

"This has been nice. I hope we can do it more often." Her eyes brighten as she adds, "Your dad was so happy that we were getting together."

Fine, I'll admit it. This lunch hasn't been nearly as torturous as I'd anticipated. Does that necessarily mean we're going to be besties and have a standing lunch date every week?

Nope, not a chance in hell.

But can we get together and do this every once in a while?

I'll give it some serious consideration.

"Yeah, maybe," I say noncommittally.

"How does next week look? Should we get something on the calendar?"

She's kidding, right? This woman needs to slow her roll. It's going to take time for me to come to terms with the notion that my opinion of Brandi might not be entirely accurate.

"Oh, um…" I glance away and try to pull a plausible excuse out of my ass. "I'd love to, but I need to see how everything goes with my classes. I've been slammed with homework lately."

I'm saved from offering further explanations when the waiter arrives to take our order. Once he leaves, I tense, waiting for her to pick up the thread of our previous conversation. Instead, she switches topics and drones on about the Etsy business she's trying to get off the ground and how many orders have trickled in. I make a few noises to express my interest, and it's enough to keep her talking. A steady stream of consciousness pours from her mouth, and a headache begins to brew behind my temples. Thankfully, I came prepared and have a bottle of Tylenol in my purse. There is no way I could do this again next week. Next month would be pushing it.

The good thing about Poco Loco is that the food is always out quickly, and it's delicious. Even as we dig into our dishes, Brandi continues to yap. It's like she's been locked up in solitary confinement, and I'm the first person she's seen in years.

After another five minutes, my head really begins to throb. She doesn't ask me any questions about what's going on in my life. Everything revolves around Brandi. I'm reminded of why I don't like to spend too much time in her presence.

I glance at my phone. There's no reason we can't wrap this lunch up in ten minutes. Then she can drive me back to campus since she insisted on picking me up in her brand-spanking-new Mercedes-Benz GLE-Class. She did her best beauty queen imitation—fake wave included—as we drove down Main Street.

"Hey," she chirps, "isn't that Hunter?"

My fork pauses mid-air before crashing back to my plate with a loud clatter.

"I'm sorry, what did you say?" I fully admit to tuning her out five minutes ago, so I'm really hoping I misheard her.

"*I said,*" she annunciates loudly as if I'm hard of hearing, "*isn't that Hunter over there?*"

Nope. I refuse to accept that my ex-boyfriend is here having lunch. What are the odds?

"Are you sure it's him?"

Brandi hasn't seen him in years, and admittedly, he's changed since he used to hang out at the house. Let's hope my stepmother's eyesight is deteriorating and she's mistaken.

A gleam enters her eyes as she perks up. "Of course, I'm sure. I would know him anywhere. He was always so handsome."

Seriously?

Weren't we just conversing about her husband who is busy fighting cancer?

Ugh.

Not bothering to look for myself, I toss the napkin on my plate and glance around for our waiter. "Do you mind if we grab the check and get out of here?"

"Sure."

Awesome.

Every muscle that had tightened at the mention of my ex-boyfriend slowly loosens.

"Don't you want to say hello?" she asks.

I give her an *are-you-crazy* look before slowly shaking my head. "No, I don't." If Brandi knew anything about me or my life, she'd know our breakup wasn't amicable, and we're not friends.

"In high school, you two were inseparable. I can't believe that you wouldn't want to say hello."

"Well, I don't!" I snap.

Sheesh. What's wrong with her?

"Oh look, he's coming this way!" she says, voice filling with excitement.

I groan and peer over my shoulder.

Damn. It *is* him.

His lips curve as if this was all part of his evil plan to drive me insane.

Guess what?

It's working. I'm teetering on the edge as we speak.

Before that devious smile can stretch fully across his lips, I swing around and turn my back on him. Every time I make a concerted effort to avoid Hunter, he pops up all over the place, knocking me off-balance. It's like fate or a higher power with a really bad sense of humor keeps throwing us together at the most inopportune of times. Clearly, I'm being conspired against. What other explanation is there?

My gaze bounces around the restaurant, desperately searching for our waiter. *Where the hell is that guy?* This is an emergency. We need to get out of here pronto. If Brandi isn't going to ask for our check, I'll do it myself.

"Hunter, hello!" my stepmother gushes enthusiastically.

"Hi, Mrs. Sinclair," a deep voice says from beside me.

Reluctantly, I glance up only to find myself ensnared by his gorgeous eyes. They remind me of the ocean. Deep and vast. If I'm not careful, I'll end up drowning in them.

"Skye." A smirk simmers around the corners of his lips. He is so loving this. Anything that makes me uncomfortable is right up his alley. "Nice to see you."

"Hey," I grunt through clenched teeth.

Ignoring my inhospitable attitude, Brandi rises to her feet and opens her arms wide. "It's been way too long."

He has no other choice but to move into my stepmother's embrace and wrap his arms around her petite form. Brandi's hands glide up and down his back before she pulls him closer.

Leave it to Brandi to cop a cheap feel.

It's almost difficult to believe that fifteen minutes ago, I'd been thinking that this lunch hadn't turned out so bad and I might have misjudged her.

My mistake. She's as awful as I'd always suspected. In one breath, she's crying about Dad having cancer, and in the next, she's feeling up my ex-boyfriend.

It's enough to make me sick.

I don't realize that a disgusted snort has escaped until Hunter twists his head toward me and catches my gaze. Humor flares to life in his eyes, and my lips reluctantly quirk upward.

Is it weird that we're having a moment over this absurd situation?

My heart picks up its tempo as our gazes stay locked. It's only when Brandi untangles herself from him that I'm able to look away. Just when I think my stepmother can't sink any lower, she reaches out and squeezes one of Hunter's biceps.

"My goodness, it's certainly obvious that you've been hitting the weights since I last saw you." She's practically eating him up with her eyes, and her voice has turned breathy. "Everything about you is rock hard, isn't it?"

Oh my God, she did not say that!

Any goodwill that had been forged between us over lunch has gone up in flames. What the hell is wrong with this woman?

I'm half wondering if he's going to flirt with her in return just to get under my skin. He knows how I feel about Brandi.

Instead, his voice remains neutral as he takes a step in retreat so they're no longer close enough to touch. "Playing Division I athletics is like a job. Working out and taking care of my body is part of it, especially with the upcoming draft."

"Whatever you're doing is working." Her fingers flutter to the deep V of her blouse, where they linger. "Keep it up."

I'm seconds away from gagging. The lunch I scarfed down is about to make an unexpected reappearance. And if that happens, I'm aiming directly for Brandi.

Her eyes widen, and she squeals, "Oh, you should join us! I'm sure you and Skye have a lot to catch up on."

What!

Oh, hell n—

His expression turns apologetic as he shakes his head. "Thanks for the invite, but I'm here with a couple of guys from the team." He points at a table filled with football players on the other side of the restaurant. "I should probably get back to them."

"That's too bad. Maybe another time." Brandi pouts before waving a hand at me. "I almost forgot to mention that Skye has moved back home and now attends CU."

"Yup." Hunter's gaze stays pinned on mine. "We actually have a class together this semester."

"You do?" Brandi says with surprise. "How fun is that? I bet it's just like old times."

Is this woman batshit crazy?

It's *nothing* like old times.

The smile on Hunter's face stays pasted in place, but his eyes have darkened. It's as if the same thoughts are running through his head.

He confirms it by saying, "That's exactly what it feels like. Right, Skye?"

"Yup." Sadness fills me. Nothing could be further from the truth.

"Hopefully, the two of you can find time to catch up soon. You were such a cute couple in high school," she muses.

Spending more time alone with Hunter is something I'm trying to avoid like a case of scabies.

When neither of us responds, Brandi clears her throat. "Well, it was certainly nice seeing you again, Hunter. Don't be such a stranger. Feel free to stop by the house any time."

I'm seconds away from picking up a fork and stabbing Brandi in the eye.

"Thanks, I will. Make sure you say hello to Mr. Sinclair for me."

At the mention of Dad, Brandi's expression sobers. "I'll be sure to do that. I don't know if Skye has mentioned it—"

"Hunter really needs to go, Brandi." I gesture toward his table as the waitress appears with a massive tray. "It looks like his food has just arrived."

My stepmother glances over at where his teammates are sitting. "Of course. We'll have to catch up some other time."

"Definitely." Hunter's gaze bounces curiously between the two of us before he gives Brandi a polite smile and takes off.

Once he's gone, I collapse against my chair in relief. I want to get out of here and away from Hunter. Being around him for even a few minutes sets my nerves on edge.

And then there's Brandi…

She was practically drooling. It was so embarrassing.

"Well, that boy certainly grew up nice," she says, interrupting my uncharitable thoughts, "I bet you're kicking yourself for letting him get away."

Really?

"I'm the one who broke up with him," I remind.

I'm annoyed with her but mostly with myself for thinking Brandi was anything more than what I'd always suspected. Again, I wonder what the hell my dad ever saw in her.

Never mind, I know *exactly* what he saw.

Ugh. I may puke after all. The Mexican isn't sitting well.

I crane my neck, searching the restaurant for our waiter. It's as if he's totally disappeared. Does the guy even work here anymore?

Brandi pops a shoulder and grabs her fork before picking at the remains of her salad. "All I'm saying is that it's a decision you probably regret."

There was never a time I didn't regret it. But I keep that tidbit to myself. Brandi would never understand the kind of sacrifice I made for Hunter. There's no way she could conceive of putting anyone else's welfare above her own.

"Your dad still keeps up on news about him. As long as Hunter doesn't injure his knee again, he'll be a top round draft pick this spring." Her eyes turn dreamy. "Think about it, you could have been the wife of an NFL player." She presses closer to the table. "Do you have *any* idea the crazy amount of money he's going to make in the next few years? If you'd been smart, you would have tied that down when you had the chance. Then you wouldn't have to work a day of your life."

I didn't think it was possible, but my disgust for her ratchets up a few dozen notches. Brandi's antiquated thinking sets women back at least a hundred years. Maybe she enjoys being a kept woman, but that's not the kind of lifestyle I want for myself.

It's difficult to keep the anger from vibrating in my voice. "I was never interested in Hunter because of his earning potential." I can't resist tacking on, "That seems really shallow."

Why am I trying to explain myself to this woman?

Brandi shakes her head before giving me a pitying stare. "A girl has to look out for herself. No one else is going to do it for her, Skye. The sooner you learn that lesson in life, the better off you'll be."

I almost snort.

And there you have it in a nutshell…Brandi's personal philosophy. I'm sure she has it stitched somewhere on a pillow.

No matter how much I love my dad, there's only so much I can take of his third wife, and I've reached my limit. I glance at the phone next to my plate and clear my throat. "This has been fun, but I need to get back to campus for a two o'clock class."

"Is it really that late?" She swipes her blinged-out phone from the table, and her eyes widen. "I had no idea!"

Relief floods through me. We're in total agreement that this lunch has reached the end of its lifespan, and I have no intention of trying to revive it. Now we can grab the check and get the hell out of here. It's been at least ten minutes since Hunter sat down at his table. As much as I've tried to pretend that he's not dining at the same restaurant, I'm intensely aware of his gaze burning holes through my back.

Brandi flags down our waiter, who has materialized out of nowhere, and slips him a black credit card without glancing at the check. When he walks away to process the bill, she says, "I have a Botox appointment at two, and it's clear across town. It's going to be nearly impossible for me to get there on time."

Ummm, okay.

"Would you mind grabbing an Uber back to campus?" She digs around in her wallet and pulls out a twenty. "Here. For your trouble."

I stare blankly at the bill she shoves in front of me.

Is she serious?

Brandi is actually ditching me?

For Botox?

I almost laugh.

A twenty doesn't begin to cover the aggravation this lunch has caused me. The woman can add a stack of twenties solely for the psychological damage of watching her grope my ex-boyfriend.

I'm kicking myself for not driving and meeting her here. Instead, I let Brandi talk me into a small shopping excursion and lunch. I didn't even buy anything, so it was a total bust.

All I can say is—

Never.

Again.

"Sure. Whatever," I say flatly. At least I won't have to spend any more time with her. So, there's that.

The words barely make it out of my mouth before she signs the credit card receipt and pops to her feet. "Great!" She rushes around the table and pulls me in for a quick hug. "I'm so glad we could get together! We'll have to do it again real soon! I'll text you!"

Over my dead body.

And then she disappears out the door, leaving a cloud of Chanel perfume in her wake. All I can say is that the woman is un-freaking-believable. Thank goodness it's over. Aggravation bubbles up inside me before I snatch my phone from the table and shoot Lanie a text. I'm about to hit send when I remember that she's in class.

Damn.

I kick around the idea of getting an Uber, but it's only a two-mile walk to campus. And since I've been stuffing my face with baked goods and not exercising, a walk will probably do me some good.

It certainly can't hurt.

HUNTER

"Catch you back at the house." I fist bump Sam Henderson on the way out of Poco Loco before heading to my '69 Ford Mustang parked in the lot. Mason bought it off one of his customers dirt cheap. At the time, it had to be towed to the house because we couldn't get the engine to turn over. We spent the summer before my senior year of high school fixing it up and getting it to run. My brother's friend did a custom paint job on it in exchange for some repair work, and it's been purring like a kitten ever since. No matter how much money I make, this car is my baby, and I'll never get rid of it. I slide onto the butter-soft black leather and start it up. It's music to my ears when the engine growls to life.

"Damn, Price, that Shelby gives me major wood every time I see it," Eric Wixom shouts as he jumps into the pickup truck parked next to me. "Sure you don't want to sell her?"

"The answer hasn't changed from last week, Wixom. You can stop asking."

I pull out of the lot and into the flow of traffic before cranking the music in an attempt to drown out thoughts of Skye. I can't go anywhere without that girl turning up. Tell me how I'm supposed to move on if she's constantly in my face?

Three blocks later and she materializes before my eyes.

What the hell?

It's not a conscious decision on my part to ease the car to the side of the road. It's pure instinct. A deep need to be close to her no matter what my feelings are. If I could sever the connection between us, I would do it in a heartbeat.

As if sensing my presence, Skye glances toward the vehicle. The moment her gaze locks on mine, she frowns and jerks her head forward so I'm no longer in her line of sight. A smile curves my lips. I like Skye best when she's pissed off and feisty. Is it wrong that I enjoy needling her so much?

I turn down the music and yell out the passenger side window, "Need a lift?"

Already I can hear the word *no* sliding off her pouty lips. If given the choice, she'd prefer to be bound and gagged in the back of a serial killer's van than endure ten minutes of my company.

"From you?" The icy look Skye spears in my direction is full of contempt. There's even a slight curl to her upper lip in case I missed her other subtle signs. She forces out a bark of laughter and shakes her head. "I don't think so." Then she hastens her pace as if it's possible to leave me in her dust.

I glance at her footwear.

Sandals.

Strappy silver ones that look too delicate to make it more than a block. She won't get far in those. If she does, she'll pay the price for that decision later tonight.

The Mustang crawls beside her as my fingers tap the steering wheel. "You really going to walk all the way back to campus, Skye?"

"Yup."

A horn blasts, and I glance at the rearview mirror. A line of cars has formed behind me. I step on the gas until the car shoots forward, and I'm once again moving. Two blocks up the street, I find a spot to pull over and cut the engine. Then I slide out of the driver's seat and walk around to the other side before casually leaning against the car while I wait.

It takes about five minutes for her to catch up.

Her face has turned a bright shade of red, and she sounds far crankier when she snaps, "Go away, Hunter."

Yeah…that's not going to happen. Even if I were so inclined, I wouldn't leave her to walk the rest of the way. I'll fully admit to being an asshole, but I'm not *that* big of one.

"Get in the car. You'll never make it back to campus without tearing your feet up." I could strangle Brandi for leaving Skye to her own devices. More than that, it grates against my nerves that I actually give a damn about her welfare. "Look at you, it's only been a couple of blocks, and you're already limping."

She presses her lips together and glares.

"What's the matter? Was Brandi too busy to drop you off after lunch?" I focus on the one thing we can agree on. Our mutual dislike for her stepmother.

"Yup," she admits begrudgingly. "She had a very important Botox appointment that she couldn't be late for."

That sounds about right. I should have guessed it was something ridiculous like that. "Are you really surprised she ditched you?"

She huffs out a breath, and her shoulders fall. "No."

What I'd like to know is why those two were even together in the first place. Sure, there have been plenty of changes over the years, but I don't believe for one damn minute they're now best buddies. Ever since I've known Skye, she could barely tolerate the woman. And now they're going out to lunch together?

It's weird as hell.

Instead of satisfying my curiosity, I say, "Why don't you stop wasting my time and get in the car. I'm not going to let you walk home."

She throws her arms wide. "Why do you even care?"

I shrug. The truth of the matter is that I shouldn't. It's not like I *want* to care.

"Get in the car," I snap, tiring of this conversation.

She sucks her lower lip into her mouth and studies me. Indecision is written across her face. It takes a moment before she relents. "Fine, but I'm only agreeing because my feet feel like they might fall off, and I'm nowhere near campus."

I unleash a smug smile before pushing away from the car and popping open the door. "Whatever you say, sweetheart."

She scowls as I wave her inside.

By the look on her face, this is killing her. I'm sure she doesn't want to be anywhere near me, especially after the other night. Even thinking about the way she begged me to make her come gets me rock hard. I want nothing more than to put my hands on her body again.

If I know Skye, she consoled herself afterward by vowing that it would never happen again. She may not realize it, but that's a lie. At every turn, I'm going to prove that I can break her down and bend her to my will.

And you know what?

I'm going to enjoy every fucking minute of it.

Nervous energy vibrates from her as she slides onto the passenger seat. When she fumbles with the seat belt, I knock her fingers aside and take over. My face hovers close enough to feel her breath feather across my lips. She swallows as I pull the belt across her chest. My knuckles graze the softness, and her nipples pebble under her shirt. I'm so tempted to push the material out of my way and suck the tight little buds into my mouth.

"Hunter," she whispers, "don't."

"Don't what?" I raise a brow. "Don't make sure you're safely belted in?" I give her a wolfish grin before bouncing to my feet and slamming the door.

Her wide gaze stays fastened on me as I saunter around the hood of the car. By the look on her face, she's already regretting this decision. Blistered feet are nothing compared to the threat I pose to her well-being.

Once I'm belted in, I start the engine and pull into traffic. It never occurs to me to fill the silence with music. Tension gathers in the pit of my gut as I glance at her from the corner of my eye. After we broke up, I never imagined she would sit next to me again in this car. When we were seniors in high school, this Mustang meant freedom. We drove all over the place and fooled around on these leather seats hundreds of times. Even when she was wet and sandy from the beach, I couldn't keep my hands off her.

It's as if Skye can sense my silent trip down memory lane. She shifts her body, and a flash of leg catches my attention. My mouth dries as the pretty little skirt she's wearing hikes up her thigh only to reveal more sun-kissed flesh.

If she were still my girl, I'd already be strumming my fingers against her leg, inching higher with every pass until I could stroke the sweetness between her thighs. She would widen them, allowing me to touch her before tossing her head back and closing her eyes. Her breathing would pick up, and she would whimper with pleasure. Back then, touching Skye was as natural as breathing. Maybe even more so.

I give myself a quick mental shake. The girl sitting next to me is no longer mine. She threw our relationship away after high school and never looked back. It's all I can do to clench my jaw and stare straight ahead.

This was a mistake.

My goal had been to push her buttons and prove that her body still ached for my touch. Instead, all I've done is give myself a raging boner with no relief in sight. No matter how pissed off I am, all I want to do is touch her and brand her as mine. Skye is the only female capable of burrowing under my skin and that's the last thing I need right now.

She interrupts my thoughts when she points at the street we just whipped past. "Hunter, you missed the turn."

I blink away the thick web of memories and glance in the rearview mirror.

Fuck. She's right. I blew right past the turnoff for campus.

"Where are we going?" Apprehension threads its way through her voice.

It would be all too easy to explain that I wasn't paying attention, but then I realize it's not true. Muscle memory has taken over, and I'm headed to the beach. The one we used to call our own.

Goddamn, this really *was* a shit idea on my part. I should turn around and head back to the relative safety of campus, but I'm power-less to pump the brakes and jerk the wheel.

"Where are we going?"

I press my lips together, afraid of the answers that might escape. After a mile, I pull into the small parking lot that overlooks the ocean. I cut the engine and allow the saltiness of the air to waft over me. Skye and I used to come here all the time. We'd have bonfires at night with our friends. She'd sit between my outstretched legs, and I'd bury my face in her hair as the wind blew through it.

I can't come here without thinking of Skye. The two will forever be entwined in my mind. She's been a beach girl for as long as I've known her. The ocean has always been a place where she could forget about all the bullshit in her life. She would close her eyes and float on the waves, and I'd tease her about being part mermaid.

An image of Skye walking out of the water with her long blond hair clinging to her sun-darkened skin flashes unbidden through my mind. When we were together, I couldn't get enough of her. One taste and I was addicted. She was like a drug pumping through my system.

A wave of nostalgia washes over me and threatens to suck me under. It feels as if someone is squeezing my heart with their fist, making it impossible to breathe. As soon as I realize that I've become mired in the past, I swear under my breath and clear those thoughts away.

"Hunter?" She stares at the beach before glancing cautiously at me. "What are we doing here?"

All at once, the answer is clear, and I angle my body toward hers. She wrings her hands together in her lap as tension fills the air.

"Have you given any consideration to what I said the other night?"

"I don't understand."

She's just full of lies. The biggest one being that she no longer wants me.

The way her gaze skitters away as her chest rises and falls in rapid succession under the blue shirt she's wearing gives away her inner-most thoughts.

"Who's the one playing games now?" I reach out and drag my knuckles across her cheek. "You know exactly what I'm talking about."

She inhales a sharp breath as the pulse in her throat kicks into overdrive.

Her panicked energy is exactly the balm I need. It smooths out all my sharp edges, giving me far more patience for this pursuit than I thought possible. Instead of pouncing and devouring her in a matter of minutes, I force myself to slow down and enjoy the hunt. Her anxiety flavors the air between us, and I inhale a deep breath to savor.

"Come on, now." I stroke a finger over the fullness of her bottom lip. "I want to hear you say it."

Her throat convulses as she chokes down her discomfort. "Closure."

Yup, that's it. I want to bury myself deep inside her body and pour all of my anger and frustration into her where it belongs. I want her to carry the burden of it around for the next three years. Maybe then, I'll finally be able to find some peace and move on with my life.

She owes me that much.

"Have you given it any more consideration?" I repeat.

"I didn't think you were serious." The way her voice warbles makes me wonder if there's a hummingbird trapped inside her throat.

That's another lie.

My gaze dips to her mouth. It's the perfect cupid's bow. I remember the way it felt to have her pouty lips wrapped around my dick. How I would spear my fingers through her blond hair, holding her head while she blew me.

I miss that.

So.

Fucking.

Much.

Her eyes widen as I push my thumb between her parted lips. "I want you, Skye." My cock stiffens painfully as her tongue teases my digit.

When she shakes her head in denial, my lips quirk and my fingers tighten on her chin to still her movements.

"Oh, but I do. Want to feel how much?"

Again she tries to shake her head.

Such a little liar.

I lay my hand over hers before dragging it to my lap. When she doesn't pull away, I press it to my rock-hard dick. A groan slides from my lips when her grip tightens around me. My hips thrust into her touch. It wouldn't take much to make me come.

Skye is the only girl capable of undoing me.

She whimpers as I loosen my grip on her chin and pull my thumb from her mouth. My breathing is harsh and choppy. I'm way too close to losing it.

Her fingers tighten around my cock, squeezing the tip. "You don't actually want *me*," she says thickly. "You want to *fuck* me. There's a difference."

Damn right there is.

I want to fuck her until she hurts as much as I do.

I groan as she continues to stroke my dick. "Does it really matter if that's all I want?"

Pain flashes across her face as the firm pressure of her touch disappears. My cock is practically throbbing. Skye twists away from me and stares silently out the windshield.

A handful of moments more and I would have come in my shorts.

I force my gaze to the white-capped waves as they roll toward the shoreline. They climb up the beach like fingers grasping at the sand before being pulled out again. I could sit here and watch the rhythmic motion of the water all day. I have a love-hate relationship with the ocean. There's beauty and grace in it but also death and devastation.

I know that better than most.

When my emotions have been locked down tight, I refocus my attention on the girl sitting beside me. No matter what I have to do to wear her down, I'll do it.

"Why do you insist on denying what we both want?" I graze my fingertips over the bare skin of her arm. Goose flesh breaks out in the wake of my touch. God, but I love the feel of her beneath my hands. I want to tangle my fingers in her wheat-colored hair and pull her close. I want to lash her mouth with my tongue until she's been reduced to a quivering mass of nerve endings. Until she understands and accepts that I'll do whatever the hell I want with her. "Don't you want to spread those pretty thighs nice and wide so I can fuck you hard?"

Those words are like a bucket of ice water being dumped over her head. She straightens on the seat and gasps at my crudeness.

Satisfaction pounds through me that I'm capable of wielding such power over her.

I want Skye to understand *exactly* how I'm going to use her.

Make no mistake, I want her disgust. I welcome it. Not only with me but also with herself for craving every dirty word that comes out of my mouth. It'll make my victory even sweeter when she finally caves in. She'll never be able to say that I lied about my intentions. She'll continue to fight me, but in the end, she'll give in.

And she'll hate herself even more when I use her up and spit her out like all the other faceless jersey chasers who fuck the players. Except Skye isn't a groupie. And that's what will kill her the most. That she allowed me to treat her like one.

With an angry fist, she bats my hand away, and I let it drop to my thigh.

"That will never happen," she seethes.

One side of my mouth hitches into a lazy smile. "We'll see," I say before starting the engine and driving her back to campus.

I hear a knock on the door before Lanie pokes her head inside my room. "Please, tell me you're not still studying."

It's clear from the books and papers spread out on the bed that I'm knee-deep in homework.

My gaze stays locked on my computer screen as I finish typing the last sentence of a paragraph. "What gave it away?"

"Come on, girl!" she snaps with annoyance. "You can't study your life away. That's no fun."

"When did I ever say I was interested in fun?"

Fun. As if that's anywhere on my radar.

How can I focus on something so frivolous when Dad's treatments aren't knocking out the cancer? We keep waiting for him to turn a corner, but that has yet to happen. The chemo makes him sick, and he has a hard time keeping anything down. More importantly, the medicine hasn't lowered his numbers. I'm losing hope, and it feels like time is running out. Most days, I walk around with a sick knot at the bottom of my belly.

"Yeah, that's part of the problem. You've become a real stick-in-the-mud." She steps over the threshold and glares. "Your excuse this morning for not attending the game was homework."

I sigh.

All right, I'll admit it was a flimsy excuse. Can I really be blamed for not wanting to spend three hours in the stands, watching Hunter on the field? Drowning in memories from high school is the last thing I need.

No thanks. This is what self-preservation looks like.

"That's it," she announces. "I'm making an executive decision. You need a break." She waves a hand at my stuff. "Put your books away. You can study tomorrow."

"No, I need to stay here and finish up these assignments." What I'm trying to do is stay afloat. I can't drown in all facets of my life. My head is barely above water where school is concerned.

"Tough shit, I'm not taking no for an answer. There's a party at the beach, and your presence has been requested. You've been hiding out in the apartment for the last couple of days. The weather is gorgeous, so let's get out there and enjoy it. What's the point of living by the ocean if you don't make use of it? Come on, Skye," she pleads. "These parties are so much fun." Lanie steeples her hands together in front of her before bouncing on the tips of her toes. "Please? Don't make me go alone. You can take a break for one afternoon."

Oh, right...the beach party.

When Josh had mentioned it at the beginning of the week, I'd felt excited at the prospect of getting to know him better. But there's no way Hunter won't be there, and I have no desire to see him.

Or be anywhere near him.

Except...it feels like my ex wins if I stay locked in my room and avoid getting to know other people. And Josh is definitely someone I want to get to know. He's the first guy who's sparked my interest in a long time. He's easy to talk to and has a great personality. He makes me laugh, and I need that right now. There's too much heaviness in my life.

Am I really going to let Hunter stop me from branching out?

Ugh.

"All right, I'll go."

Lanie straightens to her full height as her expression transforms into one of surprise. I can't say that I'm not equally shocked by my surrender.

"You'll go?" she echoes as if she couldn't have heard me correctly.

Humor ignites inside me as I reluctantly smile. "I'll go with you to the beach party." Instead of mentioning Josh, I say, "You talked me into it."

"What's going on?" Her eyes narrow. "Is this some bit of sly trickery to throw me off my game? That was almost *too* easy."

"Seriously?" A gurgle of laughter bubbles up in my throat as I throw my hands in the air. "I can't win with you."

Her lips curve before she breaks out into a wide grin. "You're right. I'm going to stop while I'm ahead. I don't care why you've agreed. I'm just glad that you did." She claps her hands together in front of her and sing-songs, "We're going to have so much fun today!"

I really hope so.

Maybe I need a day in the sun to get my mind off everything weighing me down. If there's a place capable of raising my spirits, it's the beach. How can you not feel better when you're surrounded by salty air with hot sand beneath your toes?

Warming to the idea, I hop off the bed and go to the dresser before rummaging around in the top drawer, searching for my black one-piece. As I grab it, Lanie comes out of nowhere and hip checks me. I grunt and stumble to the side.

"Sorry, girly." Her expression turns to one of disgust. *"That's* not happening. Jeez, what are you? Like eighty?"

I blink at the one-piece. There's nothing wrong with it. Who cares if it's full coverage? We can't all be perky B cups. "It's not that bad," I grumble.

She stabs her finger at the offending garment. "It's not that good either. Trust me on this. You need something that says—*hey, look at me.*"

I really don't.

Doesn't she realize that I want to blend in, not stand out?

"No," I groan. "I don't need anything to say that."

Lanie ignores my protests as she rifles through my drawer before pulling out an emerald green bikini that matches my eyes. It's the reason I bought the suit in the first place. And while I love it, it doesn't exactly leave a lot to the imagination.

"Not that one." I shake my head and hold up the suit in my hand. "I'll wear—"

She rips the garment from my fingers. "Friends don't let friends wear swimsuits that make them look geriatric."

"Now you're just exaggerating."

She arches a brow. "Wanna bet?"

I frown at the suit she's waving around in front of me. "Come on, Lanie. Give it back. Isn't it enough that I agreed to go in the first place?"

"Nope. It's my way or the highway." She shoves the green bikini into my hands. It barely fills my palms. I look down at the sheeny material as it catches the sunlight pouring in from the window. The color makes me think of a mermaid's tail. It had seemed a little magical when I tried it on in the store. I think that's why I've hung onto it instead of tossing it during one of my many cleanouts.

"You need a little sass in your ass, and this suit accomplishes that."

I snort and consider my options.

You know what?

Lanie's right. I need a little something to push me out of this funk. I have no idea if this suit can accomplish that, but I'm going to give it a shot.

What's the worst that can happen?

Don't answer that. It was more of a rhetorical question.

"All right. Fine. I'll wear it."

"Now you're just freaking me out."

I shoo her from my room. "Get ready and let's get out of here before I change my mind."

Lanie doesn't need to be told twice. She flies out of my room to change.

Forty-five minutes later, Lanie pulls her lime-green VW convertible Bug onto the gravel that hugs the stretch of road along the ocean. There's already a ton of cars parked bumper-to-bumper. I grab my straw beach bag that holds our towels and sunblock from the back seat, and Lanie scoops up the small cooler that contains water, Diet Coke, and enough snacks to get us through the evening. We slip off our sandals before stuffing them in the bag.

"Ready?" she asks.

As I'll ever be.

"Yup." I hoist my smile as we step onto the weathered boardwalk that protects the sand dunes. Before we even make it to the beach, I hear the music and loud voices. After another dozen steps, the party comes into view. Sun-kissed flesh stretches as far as the eye can see. Girls are standing around in string bikinis, and guys are sporting boardshorts or Chubbies. It may be mid-September, but the temperature on the North Carolina coast is still sizzling in the high eighties. The breeze coming off the ocean cuts through some of the heat.

As I survey the beach, looking for a place where we can set down our stuff, my gaze zeros in on Hunter. Like most of the guys, he's decided to forego a shirt and is only wearing a pair of brightly colored boardshorts. Unlike them, if the NFL doesn't pan out, he could find work as an underwear model. There's not an ounce of fat on the guy. Each muscle stands out in sharp relief against the brightly shining sun that beats down on his bare chest. My mouth turns cottony, and my lower belly clenches in response.

My reaction to him is enough to have me spinning around and hightailing it to the car. This was a terrible idea. I shouldn't have let Lanie talk me into it.

Hunter jumps in the air and spikes a volleyball over the net. The other team misses the shot, and the ball lands in the sand. Skimpily clad girls standing on the sideline bounce up and down as they cheer. Hunter knocks fists with a few teammates before getting ready for the next set.

Lanie prods me from behind, and I take a hesitant step forward, forcing myself to move. Hunter's head snaps in my direction. Even though he's wearing aviators that shade his eyes from view, I'm cognizant of his gaze settling on me. It's like being struck by lightning, and I stumble to a halt.

"Skye?" Lanie questions.

Hunter jerks his head away in a clear dismissal, and everything that had become impossibly tight slowly uncoils. I shake myself out of the stupor I've fallen into.

"Sorry." I glance over my shoulder. "What did you say?"

Lanie presses her lips together before shading her eyes and surveying the thick crowd. My heartbeat settles when she points at a spot farther down the beach, about a hundred yards away from where the volleyball net has been set up. "Should we look over there?"

"Yeah, there's more room down that way." I refuse to let Hunter ruin this for me.

We trudge through the hot sand until we find a spot to set down our towels, bag, and cooler. Lanie peels off her shorts and T-shirt. I'm about to do the same when I hear my name called over the buzz of voices that surround us. I swing around and find Josh jogging toward me. He pushes a hand through his long blond hair, shoving it away from his eyes.

His face lights up as he stops by us. "Hey! Glad you made it! I was wondering if you'd show up today."

My lips lift into a smile. There's an easiness about him that calms my jangled nerves.

I tip my head toward Lanie. "You can thank my friend. She strong-armed me into it."

"Is that so?" he laughs, clearly not offended. "Had better plans, did you?"

"Hardly." My roommate snickers. "She was locked in her room, studying her little heart out."

Josh's eyes widen as he shakes his head. "Please tell me she's kidding."

"Nope," Lanie cuts in before I can respond. Then she elbows me in the side. "I'm going to forewarn you right now. This one can be kind of a buzzkill."

"Huh." Josh tilts his head as if he's reassessing his interest in me.

I wave them both away. "All right, can we stop discussing how pathetic I am?"

"But it's so much fun," Lanie says with an impish grin. "And I was really warming to the subject."

I jerk my thumb in her direction and glare. "Ignore my ex-best friend. And here I was going to introduce the two of you, but now you can forget it."

"Then it's a good thing I already know Lanie." Josh glances at her before flashing a smile. "What's up?"

"Not much," she says. "How about you?"

Josh shrugs and his chest and arm muscles ripple. "It's all good on the hood."

With those pleasantries out of the way, his eyes settle on me. "Any chance you're interested in playing a little volleyball? I'm sure we can get in on the next game if you want."

Not a chance in hell. I'm keeping a healthy distance from Hunter for the rest of the day.

I shake my head and glance longingly at the ocean, where the bright sunlight sparkles off the waves. It's a pretty sight that never fails to soothe me.

"I was thinking of cooling off in the water."

"Sounds good to me."

Feeling a bit self-conscious, I strip out of my shorts and tank top. Josh's gaze stays focused on my face, which is a refreshing change of pace and instantly puts me at ease. When my clothing has been shed, Josh reaches out and grabs my fingers before tugging me toward the ocean.

I glance at Lanie, and she grins, giving me a not so discreet thumbs-up sign, which is her stamp of approval. I'm sure she's patting herself on the back for dragging me here.

The tide is out, leaving behind twenty yards of damp sand and seashells. Once the waves can lick at my toes, everything eating away at me fades to the background. It's almost as if the problems weighing so heavily on me get sucked out to sea.

As soon as I'm deep enough, I dive headfirst into a wave, submerging my body below the surface. Most of the girls sauntering around in their tiny bikinis would never dream of getting their hair wet, but I don't give a damn. I feel so much better beneath the water. A rush of liquid fills my ears as a wave crashes over me.

Something about the ocean is so magical. The life that thrives in its dark depths and the shells that wash up on the shore. The salty air that slides over your cheeks and through your hair. The sand that clings to your body. I missed all of it more than I realized when I was away. How did I ever leave it behind?

When my lungs ache for air, I break through the surface into the sunshine and meet Josh's gaze. A contented smile curves my lips. I can't help it. This is my happy place, and it does wonders for my soul. We swim around, bobbing on the waves as they roll in. Catching one every so often and body surfing toward the shore. We volley questions back and forth. The kind you ask when you're trying to get to know someone. It's all very easy and relaxed. There's no pressure.

It's exactly what I need.

The more I learn about Josh, the more I like him. I'm not sure if this is simply friendship or if it could grow into something more meaningful. What I do know is that there's time to figure it out. I'm not in a hurry to label our relationship.

After a while, Lanie and Jaxon join us in the surf. We splash around, diving beneath the surface. Jax picks Lanie up and tosses her into a wave. She comes up sputtering, and we all laugh. After an hour or so, we decide to head back to shore and get something to drink and eat.

As I reach for a bottle of water from the cooler, I hear, "Heads-up, Hardgrove!"

My belly plummets as I recognize the voice. Josh turns in time to leap into the air and grab the football with both hands. A grin slides across his face as he tucks the ball under one arm and sprints across the sand. With his other fist, he punches the air as he lets loose a loud whoop. He falls back a few steps and launches the ball in Hunter's direction. It spirals through the air, arcing perfectly before landing in Hunter's hands.

All the light and happiness that had been flooding through me drains away as nerves skitter across my sunbaked skin. It never occurred to me that Josh and Hunter might be friends. If that turns out to be the case, it'll ruin everything.

As if reconfirming my worst fears, Josh calls out, "I'll be right back."

No! Don't go over there!

But it's too late. He's already jogging in Hunter's direction. With every long-legged stride he takes, my dread ratchets up another notch.

My gaze slides reluctantly to Hunter, only to find him staring at me. As soon as his lips curve into a wicked smile, I know he's going to destroy this budding relationship. That thought is the only one pounding through my head as Hunter throws an arm around Josh's shoulders. My ex's lips move, but I'm too far away to hear what's being said.

Why does he have to ruin everything for me?

Stupid question.

I know exactly why.

It doesn't take long for Josh to glance in my direction with a frown. All of my hopes crash back to earth with a loud thud.

Lanie sidles up to me before nodding her head toward the two guys. "What's going on over there?"

"I don't know," I mutter. That's another lie. One of the many I've been telling recently. I know exactly what's going on, but I don't want to admit it out loud.

Her voice drops, becoming hesitant. "You know Josh is on the football team, right?"

My heart sinks further. "He is?"

"Yeah," she adds softly, "he's a wide receiver."

It never occurred to me that Josh might play football, and in the few conversations we've had, he never mentioned it. Other than Jax, I've tried to keep my distance from any guy who looks like they're a part of the Cougars. Football is like a brotherhood. They stick together. I saw enough of that in high school to know better.

Reluctantly I glance at them again only to find two sets of eyes watching me. Not knowing what else to do, I turn away. Lanie hoists her smile as we both pretend that Hunter didn't take away the little bit of happiness I'd managed to find since returning home.

What am I still doing here?

I should have taken off hours ago, but I didn't want to give Hunter the satisfaction of driving me away.

A high-pitched giggle erupts from across the bonfire. I focus more intently on the label I'm trying to peel off the beer bottle in my hand. I don't have to glance over there to know that it's the same girl who attached herself to Hunter like a barnacle before crawling onto his lap.

The last time I looked in their direction, her arms were twined around his neck as if she was afraid he might try to make a run for it. Although, that doesn't seem likely. As far as I can tell, he's enjoying the fawning attention.

A thick lump of nausea has taken up residence at the bottom of my belly. It hasn't budged since Hunter called Josh over. No matter how hard I try to banish it, the tension refuses to dissipate. Whatever Hunter said to Josh was enough to scare him away.

For a few fleeting moments, I had considered marching over to Hunter and demanding why he did that, but what would be the point? It would only reinforce how much power he wields over me. It's better to pretend that I don't give a damn and hope he tires of the game he's intent on playing.

When the dark-haired girl straddling Hunter's lap begins to nibble at his neck, I rise to my feet, unable to stomach any more of the show they're putting on. I know he's slept with half the girls on campus, but that doesn't mean I want to watch him hook up with someone in front of my face.

I need to take a breather and regroup before I lose it.

Lanie's fingers snake out and grab my hand before I can take another step away from the lawn chairs we're parked on. She's perched on Jaxon's lap, and they've been making out for a while.

Don't get me wrong, I'm ecstatic for Lanie. Jax is an amazing boyfriend. But that doesn't mean I need a front row seat to their PDA. I'm tired of being the odd woman out.

"Hey, where are you going?" she slurs. Lanie has downed her fair share of drinks this afternoon, and she doesn't have much of a tolerance for alcohol.

I nod toward the water. "Just up the beach."

I need to clear my head, and I can't do that sitting across from Hunter while a groupie gives him a lap dance.

"Want me to come with you?" Her gaze is slumberous. She looks relaxed and happy wrapped up in her boyfriend's arms. I don't want to steal her away from him. I know how much they missed each other over the summer. The way they go at it, it's like they're trying to make up for lost time.

"Nah, stay here and enjoy the fire. I won't be long."

"Are you sure?" Her gaze slides to something over my shoulder. My guess is that she sees what I've been forced to endure for the last thirty minutes.

"Yup." I paste a smile on my face. "I'm good."

Her teeth sink into her lower lip, and she worries it. "Don't be gone too long, okay?"

"I won't. It'll be a quick walk up the beach."

I don't spare my ex-boyfriend another look as I move away from the group. It's frustrating to have these feelings for him. I should be over this by now. If Hunter would leave me alone instead of trying to solicit a reaction from me every chance he got, maybe I would be able to move on.

It's only when I've put some distance between myself and the mob of people on the beach that my chest loosens, and I'm finally able to breathe again. It doesn't take long before the noise of the party fades, and I become more attuned to the waves crashing on the shore. The sound reminds me of distant thunder. I close my eyes and inhale the salty air as it rushes past me. The tension that had been filling me slowly dissipates into nothingness. Now that the sun has sunk below the horizon, there's a definite chill to the air. The water lapping at my ankles feels warmer than it did this afternoon.

My fingers go to the hem of my shirt. I'm not consciously aware of what I'm doing until it's been pulled over my head and tossed to the damp sand at my feet. Then I'm shimmying out of my shorts and throwing them on top of the shirt before wading in deeper. With every step I take, it's like toxins are being released from my body.

Once the water hits my thighs, I dive headfirst into a wave before it can crash into me. Only when I'm fully submerged does everything inside me feel like it's been righted. What happened with Josh and Hunter sinks to the sandy bottom. My hair floats around me like a tangle of seaweed, and water fills my ears.

This.

This is what I live for. It's the only thing capable of soothing all of the aches that plague me. If only it was possible to always feel this free. I know all too well that it won't last, so it's best to enjoy it while I can.

And that starts by not dwelling on Hunter Price.

HUNTER

*T*wenty minutes.

That's how long Skye has been gone.

I glance impatiently at the sports watch on my wrist.

Make that twenty-one minutes.

I crane my neck, sifting through the darkness with my eyes. The chick on my lap thinks I'm trying to give her better access to my neck.

"Hunter," she whispers, "let's get out of here."

What's she babbling about? Never mind, I don't give a fuck. I'm too preoccupied with Skye.

Seriously, where the hell did that girl disappear to?

For her sake, she'd better not have left to meet up with another dude. I put the kibosh on that situation by pulling Josh aside and giving him the lowdown. I could tell he was disappointed but too damn bad.

I glance around, scouring the vicinity for my teammate. Luckily for him, he's busy chatting up a different girl.

But still…Skye is missing in action, and I don't like the idea of her wandering off alone at night.

"I'm ready to get out of here," Lucy, the girl on my lap, coos before nipping at my bottom lip to reclaim my attention. "Wanna go back to my place?"

Hell, no.

Before I realize it, I'm on my feet. Lucy squeaks and clings to me like a baby monkey. I'm sure this will come across as douchey, but I didn't mind Lucy's antics when Skye was sitting across from us. Now that my ex-girlfriend is no longer watching, this chick has lost her purpose.

Oblivious to the fact that my interest waned twenty minutes ago, Lucy brushes her mouth against my ear. "Are you as turned on as I am?" She pulls away and searches my eyes. "I want you *so* much. Anna, my roommate, is going to *die* when I tell her about this."

Actually, Anna won't be dying anytime soon because *this* isn't going to happen.

Unsure how to extract myself from the situation, I blurt out the first thing that comes to mind. "I have to take a leak."

That statement is enough to wipe the sultry smile from her lips. "Oh."

Nothing kills an intimate moment more than telling a girl that you gotta piss. All right, that's not true. Taking a shit probably tops the list.

Not waiting for a response, I pry her arms loose. For a chick who probably weighs less than a buck twenty, she's got one hell of a grip. "I'll be back."

At some point.

Maybe.

Unwilling to throw in the towel just yet, Lucy says, "Don't take too long."

I don't get more than three steps when she bleats again. "I'll be waiting for you right here! Come find me!"

I give her a quick nod before taking off in the direction I last saw Skye. As I push my way through the crowd, I scour the area but don't see her anywhere. There are pockets of people drinking and smoking pot along the beach.

I check each group, but she remains elusive.

Where the hell did she go?

My heart rate kicks into overdrive, which is fucking crazy. Skye Sinclair is no longer my responsibility. She hasn't been for a while. I shouldn't give a damn where she is or who she's with. But I do. More than I care to admit. A mixture of jealousy and concern eat me alive.

By the time I'm a quarter mile down the shore, I'm starting to freak out. Maybe I should call beach patrol.

How could she disappear without a trace?

Is it possible she caught a ride home with someone?

Doubtful. Her shoes and bag were next to the lawn chair she was sitting on. Plus, Lanie's still hanging out by the fire. Skye wouldn't have taken off without her best friend.

An uneasy feeling takes root inside me as I glance at the dark water. The ocean, for all its beauty, can be a dangerous place, especially at night. There are rip currents that can easily suck you out to sea. Hell, sharks are spotted swimming along the coast all the time.

You know what? This is ridiculous. I'm calling beach patrol. I plow a hand roughly through my hair and continue searching the empty stretch of shoreline. I'm about to grab my cell from my pocket when I stumble across a small pile of clothing in the sand.

What the—

With a frown, I reach down to find a pink tank top and pair of jean shorts. I'd recognize this shirt anywhere. Skye was wearing it earlier today.

Squinting, I scan the water more carefully. As I do, I catch a glimpse of a slim figure diving through a wave.

Son of a b—

I cup my hands around my mouth and shout, *"Hey!"*

Of all the boneheaded things to do.

She's too far out to hear me. Every time I catch a glimpse of her, she disappears beneath the waves. Is she struggling or goofing around? With a grimace, I wade out to my calves and bellow at the top of my lungs, *"Skye!"*

My voice carries over the water, and she snaps her head in my direction. We watch each other silently as she continues to bob in the water.

When she doesn't move toward the shoreline, I bark, "What the hell do you think you're doing?" I wave her in with my arm. "Get your ass out of there right now!" I could seriously strangle this girl. Who knows, maybe when I get my hands on her, I will. Skye grew up around the water, so she knows better.

After about thirty seconds, it becomes apparent that she's not going to budge. I'm not able to make out the expression on her face, but I'm pretty damn sure I feel the heat of her glare over the distance that separates us.

She solidifies those thoughts when she yells, "Go away, Hunter! You're not my keeper. I don't have to listen to you!"

That may be so, but I'm not leaving until her ass is out of there.

"You know it's dangerous to swim alone at night!" I shout. "Get the hell out of there, or I'll come in and drag you out myself!"

She flips me the bird before sliding beneath the water. When her head disappears, my heart seizes. I take another reluctant step in her direction.

I fucking hate the water.

Especially at night.

And Skye damn well knows it. She's one of the few people who do.

As I force myself to take another step, she breaks through the surface. Air rushes from my lungs in a painful burst.

"Goddammit, Skye! Quit fucking around and get out of there right now!"

"No! I can do whatever I want!"

I press my lips into a tight line until they feel bloodless. She's not wrong. The problem is, as much as I hate her for breaking my heart, I could never forgive myself if something happened to her. I've lost enough to the ocean. I won't lose her, too.

"Fine, stay in there," I shout, "but I'm not leaving!"

Skye shrugs and dives under another wave, disappearing from sight. She has to know that she's cutting me up inside. When it becomes obvious that she won't be vacating the water any time soon, I return to the shore before dropping to the wet sand. Sooner or later, she's going to have to come out. And when she does, I'll be waiting for her.

hy won't he go away and leave me alone?
I bob in the water, watching Hunter from twenty yards away. I knew he wouldn't wade in after me. He's hated the ocean ever since his parents died. I had assumed he would hang around for a couple of minutes before getting bored and taking off. Instead, he plunked himself down in the sand. What's worse is that he doesn't show any signs of leaving. When I dived in thirty minutes ago, the water had felt invigorating. Now my fingers are pruney, and my teeth are chattering.

I'm cold.

If Hunter hadn't shown up, my swim wouldn't have lasted more than fifteen minutes. Unfortunately, he tried ordering me around like he has the right to tell me what to do.

I don't think so.

I'll be damned if I let Hunter Price dictate anything in my life. He's been a total jackass since I've returned home.

My feet are firmly planted on the sandy bottom, and my arms are wrapped around my upper body as the water brushes against my chin with each new wave that rolls toward the shore.

He may be stubborn, but guess what?

I can be obstinate, too.

He can sit there all damn night. I'll stay here until morning if I have to, just to thwart him.

I yelp as something brushes against my thigh. I have no idea what it was, and I'm not going to wait around and find out. My arms cut through the water, and I kick my feet, moving steadily toward shore. A wave propels me forward and my belly scrapes against the sand before I reluctantly come to my feet. When I glance at the place where I'd left my clothes, I see Hunter standing with his arms folded across his wide chest.

Slowly, his gaze slides down my length. His tightly clenched jaw ticks, and my belly hollows out in response. Nerves scamper along my chilled flesh.

"What the hell do you think you're doing?" he snaps.

"Swimming," I say, attempting to calm everything that is racing inside me.

I don't owe Hunter any explanations. And I sure as hell don't have to stand here and listen to him berate me.

So, guess what?

I'm not going to. Instead, I'm going to pick up my clothes and get the—

As soon as I reach down to grab my shirt and shorts, his hands shoot out, wrapping around my upper arms. His fingers bite into my flesh, and I wince.

He jerks my body and growls, "Do you have any idea how stupid that was?"

I grit my teeth to stop them from rattling. "What I do is none of your damn—"

My words fall off when he shakes me again. "Do you think I'm going to walk away when you've put yourself in danger?"

People swim at night all the time. He needs to stop being so over-dramatic.

Should I have done it while alone?

Probably not. But nothing bad happened, and I'm fine. He has no reason to flip out. Hunter needs to get back to the girl who was all up in his business and leave me alone.

"Nothing happened." When I attempt to tug my arms free, his fingers tighten around me like iron shackles. "I went for a swim. Last I looked, it wasn't a capital offense."

"You grew up around the water, Skye. You know what the dangers are."

"Yes, and I'm a strong swimmer." Again, I try jerking away but his hold remains tight. It's through clenched teeth that I mutter, "Let me go. I'm sure you have better things to get back to."

He gives me another abrupt shake. "What if something had happened, and you needed help? There was no one around. You were all alone."

This is ridiculous!

"Why do you even care?" I twist my body, attempting to break his hold, but he refuses to budge. It's like I'm fighting with a brick wall. "Let me go, dammit!"

Hunter compresses his lips and remains silent. I pant, twisting and turning in his grip.

"What the hell is wrong with you," I grunt. "Leave me alone!" Instead of releasing his hold, he drags me closer until my wet body is pressed against his.

"I wish I could."

That's all the warning I'm given before his lips crash onto mine. The hold he has on me is harsh and punishing as if he's trying to inflict as much pain as possible. I can't help but feel the pent-up anger that brews dangerously beneath the surface of his skin. This kiss is more of an assault on my senses than anything else, but it's not an unwelcome one. It would be so much easier to deal with if it were.

Even though he's still holding me captive, the palms of my hands press against his chest. Instead of shoving him away, my fingers are tangling in the soft cotton of his T-shirt to tug him closer. My nipples pebble into hard points that ache.

His mouth roves hungrily over mine, dominating my senses before dragging me under to a place where I'm no longer able to think. Sensing my surrender, he pulls away enough to nip at my lower lip.

I yelp.

The moment I open my mouth, his tongue plunges back inside to tangle with my own. This kiss can only be described as punishing, and still, I want more. His lips slide to my chin before migrating to my earlobe. He bites the soft flesh, tugging it with his teeth, before letting go and burying his face against my wet hair.

"Why did you have to come back and ruin everything?" His breath comes out in choppy bursts. "Why couldn't you stay away until I was gone?"

Does he really think I came back willingly?

I want to laugh before bursting into tears. Nothing could be further from the truth.

His words are like poisonous darts, but that doesn't stop me from baring the delicate skin of my neck for him to feast on.

"Do you have any idea how much I fucking hate you right now?" he growls.

The web of pleasure he had woven around me dissolves in the blink of an eye. All I'm left with are sharp shafts of pain that radiate from every cell of my body until it feels like I'm going to shatter into a million jagged pieces.

He fucking hates me?

After everything we've shared, those words gut me. Tears prick the back of my eyes as he caresses my neck. No matter how much time passes or what happens between us, Hunter will always despise me. There's nothing I can do to change that.

"Yet," he continues viciously, "I can't stop wanting you."

When he releases one of my arms, I half expect him to thrust me away. Instead, his hand snakes between us before settling over the front of my bikini brief.

"*This* is the only thing I want from you." He squeezes my pussy to emphasize his words as if I could misinterpret them.

My throat swells with emotion until it becomes impossible to breathe. Unable to bear his touch, I gather my strength and push him away with a surge of adrenaline. Even though he's stronger, taller, and more muscular, he still stumbles back a step.

"Don't touch me!" I hiss.

Bitterness flashes in his eyes.

The distance I had created is swallowed up when he surges forward. "Are you really going to pretend that you don't want me? We both know that you do."

When I fail to retreat, he takes another step until the tips of my breasts are able to brush against his chest. Even though he doesn't reach out and take hold of me again, his mouth lowers, hovering dangerously close to mine. My hands tighten into fists that hang uselessly at my sides.

Push him away. Don't let him do this.

Instead, I remain frozen because this is Hunter we're talking about. The first and only boy I've ever loved. As painful as it is to acknowledge, I've never stopped loving him. Even though he's nothing like I remember. Even when I can no longer see the boy in the man standing before me.

"You melt every time I touch you." His warm breath drifts over my lips, threatening to drag me out to sea like an undertow. "You crave my touch. You crave *me.*"

"No."

Disbelief slides from his lips in the form of a chuckle. "Who are you trying to fool? *Me?*" One hand rises before trailing down the length of my arm. Goose bumps rise in its wake. "I don't think so, sweetheart." He tilts his head and gives me a considering look. "I bet if I shoved my fingers inside you right now, your pussy would be drenched." There's a pause, and his voice turns husky. "Tell me I'm wrong."

A moan bursts free from my lips.

I wish I could tell him exactly that, but I can't. It's a painful admittance. I'm soaked. Needy. Throbbing for him to make good on his threat. I've spent the past few years mourning his loss. Missing the feel of his sultry kisses, the way his fingers would glide over my body, the reverence of his touch.

Nothing about this situation feels the way it used to, but right now, that doesn't matter. I have no idea if it's possible, but I want to soothe the ache that rages inside him. The pain I caused when I walked away.

He wants closure in the form of fucking. I can't give him that. I won't allow him to use me only so he can walk away when he's finished.

"You're not wrong," I admit.

A groan slides from his lips. It's a guttural sound that vibrates in the air between us.

"But that doesn't mean I'm going to do anything about it," I add.

As difficult as it is, I take a step away from him, creating enough distance between us to cool the heat we've generated before it can burst into flame and singe us both. When he doesn't spring forward to detain me, I take another hasty step before swiping my clothes from the sand and taking off at a dead run down the beach toward the bonfire. I'm safest from Hunter—and maybe even myself—when I'm surrounded by other people.

As much as I'm tempted to give in to him, he's a mistake I can't afford to make.

"Holy cannoli, he really said all that?" Lanie stops in her tracks as we maneuver our way across campus, and the girl walking behind us plows into her.

"What the hell, dude," the emo chick grumbles, giving Lanie a nasty look as she walks around her.

"Oh, calm down," my bestie huffs, glaring at the girl. Lanie isn't afraid to make waves. "And FYI—get your eyes checked. I'm not a dude!"

The girl swings back around and flips us the bird before disappearing into the crowd of early morning traffic.

"Well, that was uncalled for," Lanie grumbles. "People need to calm the fuck down and get some manners."

I grab Lanie's hand and yank her along before anyone else can crash into us. We don't need to start our Tuesday morning off with a fight.

"Dammit, I knew you were holding out on me!" Lanie shoots me a steely look before stabbing a finger in my direction. "*I knew it!*"

"I—"

"I'm going to stop you right there," she snaps, plowing a fist into my bicep.

"Ow!" I rub the spot and glare. Doesn't she know that violence never solved anything?

"Please. I barely touched you."

Lanie has three older brothers. Not only can she take a beating but she also knows how to fight dirty. I've been on the receiving end of her ire enough times. I don't want to be there again.

"If you think I'm going to let you off the hook that easily, you're crazy." She takes a breath before there's another rapid burst of words. "I'm your best friend, and you didn't tell me any of this!"

"I'm sorry." Lanie won't move on until I admit to keeping highly classified information from her. In hindsight, I should have given her full disclosure. But how could I admit what was going on with Hunter to her when I wasn't even willing to acknowledge it?

Denial. It's not just a river in Egypt.

"I should have been up front with you from the beginning, but I didn't want to make a big deal out of it." Then I add, "Trust me, you're completely caught up to speed now."

"I better be." Lanie continues to mutter under her breath about crappy best friends and how *some* people tell *other* people everything, no matter what. Which is true. Lanie shares *way* too many details. Sometimes, more than I want to know. Definitely more than Jax would be comfortable with.

My phone dings with an incoming message, and I slide it from my back pocket before glancing at the screen. Lanie scoots closer so she can take a peek, too.

"Speak of the devil," she mutters.

I groan and scan the text. "We're supposed to meet at the library after class to work on our project."

Lanie's brows skyrocket across her forehead. "That should be interesting."

Interesting isn't the word I would use to describe it. More like frightening. I'm tempted to bail, but we really need to get moving on this project. We're in our fourth week of the semester, and we haven't even started.

"We can't be in the same room without tension exploding between us." And that's a problem. One I have no idea how to solve.

"Want to know what I think?"

"Not really." I stare straight ahead, realizing that won't stop her.

"I'm going to tell you anyway." Lanie pauses dramatically before giving me her thoughts on the matter. "At some point, the sexual energy between you two is going to explode."

That's exactly what I'm afraid of.

"We can't go back to what we once were. Too much has happened between us." I glance at her as we walk past the student union. Lanie presses her lips together as a thoughtful expression settles on her face. I can almost see the hamster racing on its wheel inside her head. That alone should scare me.

Truthfully, it's a relief that she knows what's going on with Hunter. I'm running out of ideas and need Lanie's brain power. Avoiding Hunter hasn't worked. Neither has moving on with a different guy. And Hunter isn't interested in letting bygones be bygones. I'm at my wit's end, and it's eating me up inside.

"I'm not sure if there's anything you can do," she admits.

Well, damn.

"There's a lot of history, not to mention off-the-charts chemistry, between you two and it might be better if you got it out of your systems."

Please tell me that she's not suggesting we—

No. Definitely not! That would make everything ten times worse than it already is. I need to break the invisible thread that binds me to him, not strengthen it.

"You know I can't do that."

"Actually, from everything you've described, it sounds like you melt every time he puts his hands on you."

My shoulders collapse under the weight of her words. She's got me there. It would be so much easier if he would keep his distance, but he refuses to do so. He wants to bring me to my knees, and I'm afraid it won't take much more to get me there.

"I know…" Which is why I've tried so damn hard to steer clear of him.

"You're not going to like this, but my advice is to go with it. Ride the wave for as long as it lasts. Then, when it's over, you walk away without any regrets." She smacks the palms of her hands together as if dusting them off. "Closure with a big red bow tied around it."

Ha! As if anything with Hunter could be that easy.

What he said rings unwantedly through my head, and I wince.

"He hates me so much," I whisper.

"There's a thin line between love and hate, Skye. I think that's what the two of you are straddling." Her voice softens. "You broke his heart when you left."

"I know." I hate that it had to be that way, but I couldn't do anything about it.

"Have you ever considered that buried beneath all the hurt and anger, he still loves you?"

My heart constricts at the idea before I shove it away. *No.* Hunter has been perfectly clear about his feelings for me.

As we come to the fork in the path and head our separate ways, Lanie grabs my hand. "Do you want Jaxon to talk to him? You know he has your back."

Absolutely not!

With a grimace, I shake my head. "No, that'll only make everything worse." And I don't want to put Jax in the position of going against one of his teammates.

She purses her lips and gives me a doubtful look. "Is that really possible?"

I huff out a laugh even though there's nothing funny about the situation. "I have no idea, but I'm not willing to find out."

"Jax loves you. He's not going to let Hunter keep messing with you."

My lips lift into a reluctant smile. "Jax loves *you.* As much as I appreciate him willing to stick up for me, I don't want to drag him into my problems."

"He's already involved."

Lanie is a good friend, and she's always been there for me when I've needed her. I should have told her what was going on with Hunter from the beginning instead of keeping it to myself. "Let me think about it, okay?"

She nods and releases my hand before stepping toward the path that will lead to Weylin Hall where her inorganic chem class is held. "Let me know what you decide. Jax and I will help any way we can."

"Thanks." I give her a quick hug before we part ways. "Better get going so you're not late. I'll see you back at the townhouse."

She points a finger at me. "You give Hunter Price hell when you see him today!"

I roll my eyes and wave her off. I'm not sure that's the right tactic to take. Admittedly, I'm at a loss as to what to do.

I take about five steps and groan, remembering that I have a quiz in stats.

Crap.

Instead of focusing on school, my mind has been full of Hunter.

When I decided to move back home last spring, I'd accepted the fact that I would eventually come in contact with my ex. I never imagined he would still be this angry. I have no clue what will defuse the situation, and I'm tired of dwelling on it. I have more important things to focus on.

Like Dad.

And school.

Specifically, statistics.

I can't afford to fail this quiz. And there's a good chance that's what will happen.

As I enter the room, I pause over the threshold. Almost immediately, my gaze lands on Josh's blond head. He's busy pulling out his book and notepad from his backpack. Ever since he introduced himself, we've been sitting next to one another, yet after Saturday and the way he disappeared, it's doubtful he's saving me a spot. I take a step toward the other side of the room before stopping and glancing at him again.

I didn't do anything wrong. Why should I be the one to change where I sit? Plus, I want to know what Hunter said to make him back off. With a determined stride, I head to the row Josh is parked in before sliding over a few desks and settling on the chair next to him. His gaze flickers to me, and his expression turns guarded, which is glaringly different from every other interaction we've had.

A few beats of silence slip by as I wait for some kind of acknowledgment. A—*hey, sorry about flaking on you*, but there's nothing. You can almost hear the crickets chirping in the background.

As seconds stretch into minutes, it becomes obvious that Josh isn't going to bring up what happened at the beach. Instead of being deterred by his attitude, it only makes me more determined to ferret out the truth.

I clear my throat and dive right in. "Hey."

"Hi." He shifts on his chair and fidgets with his pencil as if I now make him uncomfortable. "What's up?"

Seriously?

"I don't know." I give him a meaningful look. "Why don't you tell me?"

He rips his gaze from mine before staring at the notepad in front of him. "What do you mean?"

I huff out an exasperated breath. Why do we have to play these games? "I thought we were having a good time Saturday. What happened? You disappeared, and I never saw you again."

He jerks his shoulders as annoyance flashes in his eyes. "Yeah, Saturday was a good time."

Even though I'm tempted to rapid-fire questions, I keep my lips pressed together and wait for him to continue, but like before, he remains tight-lipped. This is what pulling teeth must feel like. We only have a couple of minutes before class gets underway. I might not get another chance to get to the bottom of this. "Are you going to tell me what changed that?"

His mouth sinks further into a frown. Instead of answering my question, he asks one of his own. "Why didn't you tell me that you were involved with Hunter Price?"

The question catches me off guard. "What?"

Josh swivels on his seat and scowls. "You heard me. Don't you think that's something I should have known?"

Why would he think—

Goddammit!

I poker up in my seat like someone shoved a two-by-four up my ass. "Is that what Hunter told you?"

"Not in so many words, but the implication was there. He said you were his. So, that makes you legit or..." His voice trails off as he shrugs.

Or one of his whores he's unwilling to share.

Heat suffuses my cheeks.

How dare Hunter imply that!

I shouldn't have to explain myself to Josh, but I find myself doing it anyway. "Hunter and I were together in high school," I grit out. "We haven't been involved for a long time."

"That's not what he made it sound like." His gaze remains cool as he leans back on his chair. "You're off-limits, Skye."

Off-limits?

What the hell does that mean?

"I don't understand."

"It means that Hunter Price made sure everyone around here knows that you belong to him. No one at Claremont is going to touch you."

My mouth falls open as I gape in shock.

Before I can clarify anything else, the professor arrives, and class gets underway. Unfortunately, I'm too busy stewing to focus on the quiz. The equations swim before my eyes, making even less sense than usual.

Who the hell does Hunter think he is?

He has no right to make me off-limits.

I tighten my fist, nearly snapping the pencil in half.

Goddamn Hunter Price.

HUNTER

As soon as Skye crests the second-floor landing of the library, my gaze locks on her. Even from this distance, it's impossible not to notice that her face is contorted with anger. Or that her green eyes are flashing with fire. Or how about the way her hands are tightened into fists.

Yup, the girl is definitely pissed off.

Well…this should be fun.

I lean back on my chair and patiently wait as she surveys the floor. When her gaze collides with mine, her eyes narrow, and her jaw locks before she stalks over to the table where I'm sitting.

Rage shimmers around her.

Skye Sinclair is a beautiful girl. But she's fucking gorgeous when she has a burr shoved up her ass. My guess is that there's a massive burr with my name on it.

My cock twitches with every step that brings her closer. I almost rub my hands together with anticipation.

An unsuspecting guy with his face buried in his phone nearly gets run over as she stomps by him. One corner of my mouth hitches when she arrives at the table I'm camped out at. The vibrancy of her anger soothes the beast buried deep inside me.

"Nice to see that you're on time. Ready to get to work?"

She looks like a rabid dog as she bares her teeth before slapping the palms of her hands against the table and lowering her face until it's level with my own.

Not that it's the time or place, but my gaze falls to her lush lips.

Fuck…she's got a beautiful mouth. It's one I've spent hours exploring. The urge to kiss her pounds through my blood.

"Stay the hell out of my business, Hunter!" she growls. "You have no right to interfere in my life!"

People working at nearby tables glance in our direction. If she continues at this decibel, one of the librarians will toss our asses out of here.

"Sorry, I don't know what you're talking about." I'm willing to bet this has everything to do with Josh.

Her eyes reignite with fire. She's so wound up. It's entirely too satisfying.

"Why are you telling people that I'm off-limits?" she snarls.

"Hmm." I stroke my shadowed jaw and give her a look meant to convey thoughtful contemplation. "Did I do that?" I lift my shoulders. "I don't remember."

A frustrated growl vibrates from her chest, making her sound like a wild beast. I don't think I've ever had the pleasure of seeing Skye this enraged. Any moment now, she's going to lose her shit. "You know damn well that you did! Why do you insist on playing these games, huh?" Her voice escalates. "Why won't you just leave me alone?"

The thin veneer of my playfulness drops away as I bolt to my feet. Skye stumbles back a step as her eyes widen.

"Leave you alone?" It's like her anger is a contagious disease, and I've been infected. "That will *never* happen. Do you hear me? *Never!*"

Before she's able to suck in a breath, my hand snakes out to shackle her wrist. She yelps as I drag her away from the table to the back of the second floor where a few small conference rooms are tucked in the shadows.

"What are you doing?" she gasps, straining against the hold I have on her.

The girl can rage all she wants. I can't help but feed off her frustration over a situation she no longer controls. Even though it's futile, Skye tries to break free. If only she realized that she has just as much hold on me as I have on her. It's a double-edged sword that cuts both ways. If I were smart, I'd set her free and stop the madness between us.

But I refuse to do that.

"I'm giving us a little privacy so I can explain matters to you." I grab the handle of the first door we come to and jerk the knob. As soon as it springs open, I drag her into the darkened room before shutting and locking the door behind us. I spin her around to face me before pinning her against the wall with my body.

All of her earlier bravado drains as fear and arousal fill the space. It won't be long before I'm drunk with it. Anchoring her in place, I press my hips against her until my erection digs into her lower abdomen.

A groan slips free from her lips.

I've barely touched her, and she's already responding.

"You like that, sweetheart?"

"No!" Her voice turns breathy, and the conviction she waltzed into the library with is nowhere to be found. The way her lower body wiggles against mine has my cock growing more insistent.

My guess is that she hates herself for wanting me as much as I hate myself for the same damn thing.

I could almost choke on the irony.

I'm so fucking tired of the need that rampages through me like a sickness. I want to be over this girl. I want the memory of her to fade away to oblivion. Until Skye Sinclair is nothing more than a distant memory that no longer throbs with painful awareness.

Is that even possible?

I have no idea.

It's a depressing thought.

"You want to stop playing games?" I lower my mouth to the side of her face and press a kiss against the delicate skin. "Then just admit that you want me." I caress the side of her face with the tip of my nose. "There's no shame in wanting to fuck me."

I pull back to gauge her reaction. The way her pupils have dilated and the shallowness of her breath as her chest rises and falls in quick succession tells me everything I need to know. I won't stop pushing until she gives in to what we both want. Maybe then I'll be able to put the feelings I've been carrying around with me to rest and move on with my life. I'm going to goddamn get over her, and she's going to help me do it.

"You're wrong. I don't want you."

"Do you really want me to prove what a liar you are?" I press my lips against the outer shell of her ear. "It would be all too easy."

She swallows but remains silent.

"Is that what you want?" I pull back until my gaze can lock on hers as I finger the waistband of her shorts. I pause, fully expecting her to slap my hand away, but she doesn't. Everything about her becomes impossibly still as I flick open the clasp and drag down the zipper before slipping my hand beneath the elastic band of her panties. I barely pause before thrusting two fingers deep inside her pussy.

Fuck!

She's so damn wet that I nearly come all over myself. I rack my brain, trying to remember the last time I was this turned on, but I can't. I've screwed my fair share of girls over the years, but none have ever made me feel like this. It takes every ounce of willpower not to yank my shorts down and bury my cock deep inside her heat.

My lips settle against her ear as she trembles beneath my touch. "Mmm, so fucking wet." I can't help but gloat as I pump my fingers in her. Skye continues to insist that she doesn't want me, yet her body is sobbing. "Go ahead and tell me again how much you don't want this. How much you don't want me to touch that sweet pussy of yours."

She whimpers and drops her forehead to my chest.

"It's okay," I croon, never letting up on the pressure of my fingers. "You can let go."

As I stroke her softness, I can't stop my mind from spinning.

How many other guys have touched her like this?

How many guys have touched what's mine?

Those thoughts piss me off more than I care to admit, and I quickly shove them from my mind. I want to enjoy this victory. But what I want most of all is for her to stop fighting me. She needs to accept that this is going to happen. For the time being, her body belongs to me. It's my property, and I'll do whatever the hell I want with it. The sooner she wraps her head around that, the better off we'll both be.

"Hunter," she moans against my shirt as her body tightens around my fingers. When the muscles of her pussy spasm, I have to lock down my base urges so that I don't go off like a shot. I barely manage to keep myself in check. Years of discipline are nothing in the face of Skye Sinclair getting off in my arms. I already know that I'll be heading straight home to rub one out.

Maybe more than one.

My body is wound impossibly tight, and it has everything to do with the girl who just fell apart in my arms.

When her body goes lax, I close my eyes and silently give myself permission to inhale the sweet scent of her hair. For a moment, I pretend we're still in high school, and she hasn't blown a hole in my heart. Once I'm back under control, I drag my fingers from her warm body.

Skye lifts her head from my chest where it's been resting as her cautious gaze seeks mine out. The pleasure that had been coursing through her is still visible, giving her eyes a drugged quality.

It's a pretty look that I'm about to shatter with one careless comment that I'll wield with the precision of a samurai sword.

With a wicked smile on my face, I trace the same fingers that had been buried in her tight heat along the perfect cupid's bow of her mouth. Her eyes widen as I continue to rim them. When she inhales a ragged breath, I swoop in and lick the shiny wetness from her lips.

"Mmm, that pretty little pussy tastes just as delicious as I remember." I flick the tip of her nose with my index finger. "Don't ever lie about wanting me." Since her shorts are still gaping open in front, I slip my fingers back inside her panties and give her a possessive squeeze. "Your body will betray you every time."

I slide my hand free and step away. My gaze rakes over her, taking in her mussed appearance. There's a freshly fucked quality to her that makes my cock throb. Her nipples are stiff little points that poke through the fabric of her shirt. Unable to resist, I reach out and give each one a little tweak. It's not hard enough to be painful, only capture her attention and bring her crashing back to earth.

It's a pleasure to watch her wake as if from a dream before the harsh reality of her situation slams over her. Her face falls as she realizes what she allowed me to do with little to no resistance. Skye blanches before slapping my hands away.

This is the response I was anticipating.

"Come on, don't go all shy on me now." I smirk and point at the desk behind us. "Why don't you bend over, and I'll finish you off?"

A sharp hiss escapes from her lips as her hand slices through the air and cracks against my cheek. I welcome the bite of pain that goes along with it.

"Go to hell, Hunter!" Her voice quivers with unspent emotion.

Doesn't she realize I'm already there?

My cheek feels like it's on fire as I finger the spot where she hit me. The sting takes the sharp edge off my arousal. "I take it that your answer to a quickie is a firm *no*?"

A growl of disbelief rumbles up from her throat as she thrusts her hands against my chest and shoves me back a step.

"Stay the hell away from me!"

"That's not going to happen. And let's be honest, you don't really want me to."

I hear the sob rising in her voice before it breaks free. "Yes, I do. You're not the boy I fell in love with."

"Damn right I'm not," I snap. "You made sure of that."

"You have no idea what you're talking about."

"Really? Then enlighten me, please."

Her eyes dart away, and her shoulders collapse. All of the fight rushes out of her. Where it goes, I have no idea.

"There was a time when I loved you, but that's no longer the case."

Her harshly spoken words cause my heart to crack wide open. I'm surprised by the pain that floods through me.

"All good things must come to an end," I mock.

She remains silent, but emotion shimmers in her eyes.

My heart wavers. I need to get out of here before I say or do something I'll regret, like beg for her forgiveness. She's already made a fool out of me once. I won't give her a chance to do it again.

"See you around, Skye."

I give her a wink before strolling out of the room. Leaving her behind shouldn't be one of the hardest things I've ever had to do, but it is.

SKYE

*L*anie pushes her way through the crowd as we walk up the stairs, looking for empty seats in the student section of the football stadium. Not only is it game day but it's also against one of Claremont's biggest rivals, Clemson University. The energy in the stadium is electric. There are easily ten thousand rowdy fans filling the stands. Camera crews are busy setting up their equipment on the field. Reporters are making projections about who will come out victorious. It's been a long time since I've attended a CU game. I almost forgot what a big deal they were. Half the state will turn up for them, and the other half will be glued to their big screens.

I glance across the bright green football field at the opponents cheering section. It's packed full of Clemson fans wearing orange and purple. I'm decked out in orange and black. Both Lanie and I have cougar decals on our cheeks.

Up until this point, I've been successful at avoiding anything that has to do with football. Either I've been mired in homework or I've taken off to spend the day with Dad. But this morning, Lanie barged into my room and told me that we were going to the game and she wouldn't be accepting any of my bullshit excuses.

As we move through the student section, Lanie spots a group of friends. Introductions are made, and I realize one of the girls looks familiar. Anna and I strike up a conversation about our classes and discover that we're both in the same sociology section.

The marching band begins to play, and the cougars come out of the tunnel with their helmets in place. Hunter leads the pack, and the other players fall in line behind him as they jog onto the field. They're a formidable group.

A reluctant thrill shoots through me when I catch sight of Hunter in his uniform. It's been so long since I've seen him on the field for a game. My belly does a little flip when I realize he's wearing the same number he did in high school.

We had so many good times under the bright Friday night lights. I loved sitting in the stands and cheering for him. It was always the best part of my week. Once he took his place on the field, Hunter would search me out in the stands. All the noise and excitement would fade to the background, and for one moment, it was just the two of us. No matter how many times we did this, once our gazes locked, my heart would flip over in my chest. My friends would swoon and gush about how perfect we were together.

Afterward, there was always a party to celebrate, and we would be surrounded by people who wanted to bask in the glow of Hunter's celebrity. Even in high school, everyone knew he was talented and would end up turning professional.

It didn't matter how many girls threw themselves at him. Hunter never gave them the time of day. He only had eyes for me. After a few hours, we would take off and find a place to be alone. Most of the time, we'd end up at the beach and make out until we couldn't bear another moment of it. Then Hunter would drive me home. I'd go through the front door, and he'd sneak around back to my window. We would make love, and afterward, he'd hold me against him until I fell asleep. Sometime before dawn, he'd climb out the window so Dad and Brandi were never the wiser.

I can't think about high school without a wave of grief washing over me. Life was far from perfect, especially after Hunter's parents died, but we had each other, and somehow, that made everything okay. We were stronger together, and it felt as if we had the power to overcome anything. Those days were idyllic, and nothing has ever compared to them. Sometimes I doubt anything ever will.

I blink out of my thoughts as Clemson kicks off. It takes effort to tamp down all of the old feelings fighting their way to the surface. This is exactly why I've dragged my feet about attending a game. I didn't want to get wrapped up in the memories of what life used to be like.

The student section is so loud and boisterous that it doesn't take long for me to lose myself in the exuberance. When the Cougars make a seventy-yard drive, a cheerleader on the sideline yells through a megaphone, "Roller coaster!"

Everyone goes nuts as they throw their arms in the air and mimic the movements of our mascot. We lean to the right, then to the left, before our arms go straight up again. By the time it ends, we're all laughing and cheering. How could I have forgotten how enjoyable these games were?

When the second quarter comes to an end, Lanie bumps my shoulder with her own. "I'm glad you came, girl. This is fun."

"Me, too." I'm glad she talked me into this.

The players jog off the field to the locker room, and the Claremont marching band takes the field in perfect formation. Now that I'm no longer shouting at the top of my lungs, I notice how sore my throat feels. Lanie and I take this opportunity to make our way to the concession stand inside the concourse to grab a few snacks. From the looks of it, everyone else has the same idea. The line for concessions stretches around the corner. Lanie decides to hit the bathroom while I stand in line for the food and drinks. Every couple of minutes, I glance at my phone and hope the line will start moving. I don't want to miss the start of the third quarter.

When I finally make it to the counter, I order a giant soft pretzel along with two bottles of water. With my snack and drinks tucked into a cardboard holder, I glance around for Lanie, but she's still MIA.

Maybe I should head to the restroom and see if she's there. As I jostle my way through the crowd, my arm hits someone and I turn to apologize.

"Sor—"

The last syllable never makes it out of my mouth as my gaze collides with dark blue eyes. It feels like I've been kicked in the gut as the air empties from my lungs. I can only stand in the middle of the crowded walkway and stare as people funnel around us. A few grumble under their breaths before moving on.

"Hello, Skye."

When I'd made the decision to return home, I knew I'd eventually run into Hunter.

But Mason Price?

He's the one person I'd hoped to avoid indefinitely.

When Hunter and I started dating at the beginning of ninth grade, Mason had already been out of the house and attending Claremont. Even though he lived on campus, Mason would stop home frequently. He was a happy-go-lucky kind of guy who cracked jokes and had an infectious laugh. It was obvious from the beginning that he and Hunter shared a special bond.

Hunter wasn't the only Price who played football. Mason was a tight end in both high school and then at Claremont. The only difference was that there had never been any talk about Mason turning pro. Instead of being jealous of his younger brother's success, Mason did everything he could to help develop Hunter's talent.

It was only after their parents died in a freak boating accident that everything changed. Both brothers were hit hard by the loss, but the responsibility of raising Hunter and taking care of all the financial details fell on Mason's shoulders. My heart went out to both of them, but it bled for Mason. My dad offered to take Hunter in so Mason could finish school, but the older brother didn't want to sell their family home or be separated from Hunter. After such a devastating loss, I could understand how he wouldn't want to lose anything more.

As the months turned into years, Mason's personality changed. He busted his ass six days a week, trying to make enough for them to live on. If he wasn't working at the garage, things around the house needed to be fixed. Mason became hyper focused on Hunter reaching the NFL. He no longer wanted me hanging around the house or distracting Hunter from his academics.

In hindsight, I shouldn't have believed Mason when he said that I was smothering Hunter. He convinced me that I was the one standing in the way of his brother's goals. I didn't want Hunter to lose anything more, and I certainly didn't want to be the reason he lost out on scholarship opportunities that would be necessary for him to attend college.

I loved Hunter more than life itself and only wanted the best for him. If I wasn't the best, then I wanted to give him the chance to find it.

So I let him go.

The memories disintegrate when Mason steps toward me, closing the distance between us. His proximity has my heart slamming painfully against my ribcage.

Unlike Hunter, his brother's physical appearance hasn't changed. There are now lines bracketing his eyes, and his hair is longer than it once was, but other than that, he's still recognizable.

My brain is screaming for me to retreat, but paralysis has set in, and my feet refuse to move. I remind myself that this man can't hurt me.

I jerk my head into a tight nod and try to keep the nerves from vibrating in my voice. "Mason."

He advances another step, closing some of the distance between us. I'm tempted to move backward but hold my ground instead. As I sift through the emotions in his eyes, one thing is for certain—he's not happy that I've returned. I'm sure he wishes that I'd kept my ass firmly planted in Wisconsin.

"So, you decided to move home, huh?" he asks.

My muscles tense at the accusation that fills his voice. Where I choose to live is none of Mason Price's damn business. At eighteen years old, I'd allowed myself to be cowed by him. I'll be damned if it happens again.

"Yup." I keep my lips tightly pressed together, refusing to give him any more information.

He tilts his head as his eyes sharpen. "Weren't enjoying Madison? It seemed like you were doing so well there."

A shiver slithers down my spine. It's disconcerting to realize that he'd been keeping tabs on me. Maybe I shouldn't be surprised by that knowledge, but I am.

"It didn't work out in the end."

"That's too bad."

His gaze slides down my body before coming back to settle on my face. There's nothing sexual about it. It's more assessing in nature than anything else. I'm sure he's wondering if he has anything to be worried about where his brother is concerned.

"You look good, Skye," he says begrudgingly. "All grown up."

I shrug and will my muscles to uncoil. "Three years will do that."

"Yes, they will." There's a pause as he shifts his weight. Mason is as tall and broad as his younger brother. I don't want to feel intimidated, but I do. "Are you here to watch the game?"

It's a thinly veiled question that I see through. Mason is trying to figure out if I'm here to watch my ex-boyfriend.

My hands tighten around the cardboard container I'm holding. "Yes." I arch a brow. "Is there another reason I'd be here?"

"Nope." His gaze burns into mine. "Can't think of one."

"Me, neither."

"Well, I should probably let you get back to it." His lips quirk into a fleeting smile that doesn't reach his eyes. "Take care."

"You do the same."

With that, he turns away, taking one step and then another. The pressure in my chest loosens until I'm able to breathe again.

"Oh, and Skye?" He swings back around, and the iciness in his gaze freezes me in place. "Stay the hell away from Hunter. The last thing he needs is you fucking anything up for him." He pauses. "Got it?"

His ugly words are like razor blades slicing expertly through my delicate flesh. I open my mouth to tell him to go to hell, but nothing comes out.

Instead of waiting for a response, Mason pivots and disappears through the thick crowd. My heart pounds a painful tattoo against my ribcage as I stare at the space he'd been occupying.

"Skye?"

A hand settles on my shoulder, and I shriek before spinning around with wide eyes. For a moment, I bobble the container in my hands. Lanie quickly grabs it and raises her brows in question.

"Sorry, I didn't mean to scare you. Are you all right?" Her gaze darts from my face to the spot I'd been staring at. "What happened?"

A shaky breath leaves my lips before I whisper, "I ran into Mason."

"Here? Just now?" She cranes her neck, looking down the wide corridor, but Mason is gone. It's almost like he was never here, except my heart is jackhammering in my chest, and my palms are a slippery, sweaty mess.

"Yeah."

It never occurred to me that I would see him at the stadium. It should have. When Hunter was in high school, Mason never missed a game.

Lanie squeezes my shoulder. "You look upset. What did he say to you?"

My throat swells with emotion until I feel like I can't breathe. "He told me to stay away from his brother."

"What you do is none of Mason's fucking business," she huffs.

She's right, but still…

"He's nothing more than a bully," she continues. "If Hunter ever found out what he did, there'd be hell to pay."

"That's exactly why he can't find out," I say softly.

This isn't the first time Lanie and I have had this conversation.

Lanie's voice drops to an angry whisper. "Hunter has a right to know what his brother did. It would change everything. He holds you responsible for taking off, and it wasn't your fault."

I shake my head before closing my eyes and gently massaging my temples. After our breakup, Hunter reached out, begging me to reconsider my decision. It was so difficult to keep the truth locked inside. I ended up blocking him so I wouldn't be tempted to come clean.

"No. It would ruin everything between Hunter and his brother, and I can't allow that to happen. My relationship with Hunter is part of the past. It's over and done with. I've moved on—"

"Liar," she accuses.

My shoulders collapse. "Hunter has moved on."

This time, she snorts out her disbelief. "We both know *that's* not true."

"It is, Lanie. Hunter's on the verge of making all his dreams a reality. If there's anyone who deserves for that to happen, it's him. The past needs to stay where it belongs." I pause for a beat before adding, "And that's in the past."

Lanie shakes her head and grumbles under her breath, "You should tell him."

"There's no point. All I want to do is move on. Please, you need to let me do that." I loop my arm through hers and hoist my smile. "Now, let's get back to our seats. The game is about to start."

It's a relief when Lanie doesn't say anything more on the topic. She may not realize it, but the truth would only cause more damage, and I'm not willing to do that. Hunter has endured enough pain. We both have.

HUNTER

Normally after a football game—especially one where we pull off a W against our biggest rival—there's a party at the beach. Since it looked like rain, the festivities have been moved to a house off-campus. Claremont has a massive football following, and everyone will come out to help celebrate.

I glance at the chaos unfolding around me.

All right…so maybe these people like to party and will use any excuse to do so.

It's not even ten o'clock, and this place is already packed and getting rowdy. Music blasts from outside where a live band is busy rocking it out. They're a group of guys from campus who play at a few of the local bars on the weekends. I've heard them before, and they're pretty decent. It's a mix of covers and their own music.

Someone slaps me on the back as I shoulder my way through the crowd. "Awesome game, Price!"

Thanks, pal.

I have no idea who the guy is, but I give him a chin lift in acknowledgment.

"That was one hell of a spiral you threw at the end of the third quarter! You singlehandedly won the game against Clemson!"

Hardly.

"It was a team effort, but thanks."

Hands continue to reach out, patting my shoulder or grabbing my arm. Usually, I'd stop and shoot the shit for a couple of minutes before moving on, but I'm not in the mood to listen to a bunch of randoms rehash the game. I know what happened. I was out there on the field when it went down.

After a win, I'm always in a fan-fucking-tastic mood. All the tension ratcheting up during the week in anticipation of the game gets released. But that's not the case tonight. A restlessness brews inside me that I can't shake. Deep down, I know who's to blame.

Skye.

No matter how much I try to fight it, I'm irresistibly drawn to her. As much as she's messing with my head, I refuse to let her screw with my game. Yeah, we still won, but I made a few mistakes. Little errors that wouldn't have happened if I was one-hundred-percent focused on what I was doing.

Mason and I have a tradition. He'll call after each game, and we break it down, rehashing it one play at a time. I can't say that his assessments aren't spot-on. The guy knows his shit. He could coach high school if he wanted. Hell, he could probably coach college ball. He's good. Today, as I sat waiting for his call, I was fully prepared for him to be up my ass about the miscalculations I'd made.

You can imagine my surprise when he didn't even mention the game. Instead, he'd been foaming at the mouth about Skye. He went off on a tangent for fifteen minutes straight about how I needed to stay away from her. It was the same old refrain—she was bad news and would end up fucking me over again if I let her. I'm not saying my brother is wrong, but he's the last person I want to hear it from.

I plow a hand through my hair and glance around the party. It doesn't matter how much shit I have going on, Skye always manages to push her way to the forefront of my mind. It's frustrating as hell.

Maybe Mason is right. Maybe I need to stay as far away from her as I can get. She's only been back in town for a month, and already she's wreaking havoc in my life. There are a ton of girls on campus who are dying to sleep with me. I need to find one of them—maybe more than one—and forget about my ex-girlfriend.

An hour later, I'm nursing a bottle of water and brooding in the corner. This is fucking ridiculous. When did I become this pathetic?

"Hi, Hunter," a flirty female voice purrs before her hands graze my chest.

I blink back to the present and lift the water to my lips as my gaze settles on unusual violet-hued ones.

"Hey." I can't remember what this chick's name is, but I've seen her around campus. She's gorgeous with long auburn hair and a tight body.

She couldn't look more different than—

Nope, not even going there.

"Great game today," she murmurs.

"Were you there?"

Her red slicked lips tilt upward at the corners. "Of course. I haven't missed a single home game since I stepped foot on campus."

"Is that so?" I tilt my head and cock a brow. "Does that make you a fan of the game or the players?"

A flash of white teeth cuts through the darkness as she chuckles and presses closer. "Can't have one without the other, right?"

"Got me there." More often than not, these girls are all about the players. They couldn't give two shits about the game. Skye was always different. During our first football season together, I taught her every-thing there was to know about the sport. We'd watch college games on Saturday afternoons. By the end of the season, she was the one pointing out plays to me and yelling at the refs.

Goddammit.

I shove those memories away. This needs to stop. She's screwing with my life just like I knew she would. There has to be a way for me to evict her from my head. Even if it's for one fucking night. And maybe the chick in front of me can help do that.

It can't hurt, right?

Exactly.

SKYE

"You look seriously hot," Lanie says, dragging me by the hand as we head up the walkway to the house where a massive party is spilling out. "Doesn't she look hot, babe?"

Lanie stares at Jaxon expectantly. His gaze slides reluctantly to me before he shakes his head and shrugs. "This feels like a trick question. Why don't you tell me what you want me to say, babe, and I'll say it. Wouldn't that be easier?"

"For Christ's sake, it's not a trick question." Lanie rolls her eyes and huffs out an exasperated breath. "Just tell her that she looks smoking hot!"

Jax glances at me from the corner of his eye before muttering, "You look good, Skye."

My lips tremble upward. "Thank you."

As we reach the porch, Lanie stops and gives me a thorough once-over. I was subjected to several rounds of intense scrutiny before we left the townhouse twenty minutes ago. Without warning, she reaches out and yanks the top of my shirt down until an obscene amount of cleavage has been bared.

"Lanie!" I yelp. "What are you doing?" When I attempt to grab the material and tug it up, she slaps my hands away. "Ow!"

"I'm trying to help you by showing off the girls to their best advantage." Then she grabs my breasts and rearranges them. A groan slips free as I'm groped in front of a dozen or so people. Jaxon perks up considerably and looks way more interested in staring at me now that his girlfriend is manhandling my boobs.

"Jeez, Lanie," I grumble. "Is this really necessary?" Heat floods my face as I peek at the people strolling past. Most aren't paying us any attention.

Jaxon clears his throat. "Now *that's* smoking hot."

Lanie smirks. "Just realize this is the closest you're ever going to come to a threesome."

He shrugs. "I can live with that."

Once Lanie is done making adjustments, Jaxon fist bumps the guy manning the door and we're granted access inside. With Jax taking the lead, it's much easier to navigate the crowd. Most people—even the drunk ones—scramble out of his way. It only takes a second for us to reach the kitchen where the keg is set up. We each grab a beer and head out the back door and into the yard. A live band is playing, and everyone is drinking and dancing.

Lanie grabs my hand and pulls me toward the smash of people. "Come on. Let's go shake our asses!"

We guzzle down our drinks and hand the empty glasses to Jaxon. Lanie blows him a kiss, and then we're pushing our way through the mass of writhing bodies until we're able to carve out a small space of our own. We know all of the songs and are belting out the lyrics in each other's faces.

After half an hour, Jaxon joins us. He may be amazing on the football field, but he's a total disaster on the dance floor. The guy has no rhythm whatsoever. The fact that he's out here, giving it all he's got for Lanie, only makes him more of a catch. I can't stop laughing as Jax twirls us around in the grass.

All of the problems that had been buzzing around in my brain fade to the background. It's not something that happens very often, but when it does, I need to embrace the feeling and hold on to it for as long as possible. Closing my eyes, I stretch my arms overhead and allow the music to wash over me. I feel like a balloon floating in the atmosphere. The heaviness that has been weighing me down, tethering me to the earth, disappears. It's a relief not to think about my dad and the disease that is slowly killing him from the inside out.

The only other time I'm able to forget is when I'm with Hunter. I tell myself that I need to be strong, but the moment he lays his hands on me, I go up in flames. Pleasure takes over and swallows me whole.

How is it possible to love someone and hate them at the same time?

Unwilling to allow those thoughts to take root, I shake my head and focus on the beat of the music. There's been enough heaviness in my life. Tonight is about lighthearted fun.

The band takes a short break, and I realize that I'm a sweaty mess. But it feels good. My heart is pounding, and endorphins are pumping through my blood.

The crowd around us disburses. "Should we head inside and grab a drink?" I ask.

"You read my mind," Lanie agrees, huffing and puffing. "I was just thinking that we needed liquid refreshment."

Once we've made our way to the kitchen, Jax grabs another round of beer. We clink our cups together before draining them in one thirsty gulp. A few friends join our group, and we end up talking until the music starts up again. I glance around for Lanie, wondering if she's ready to hit the dance floor again, and realize she's MIA.

Further investigation reveals that Jax has disappeared as well.

Great. I can't believe they ditched me. How much do you want to bet they're upstairs having a quickie? Those two are ridiculous. They can't keep their hands off each other for five freaking minutes.

I grab a bottle of water and head to the living room. There's a crush of people. This party is raging. Everyone is out celebrating the win today. I run into a few people from my classes and wave, but there's no sign of Lanie or Jax. I stop and chat with Anna, the girl I met at the game, but she hasn't seen Lanie either.

After about ten minutes, I decide to call off the search party and head back outside. Lanie and Jax will turn up eventually. Before I do that, I need to hit the bathroom. There's a hallway to the left with a bunch of girls standing outside a closed door. I get in line and wait my turn. It takes about ten minutes for me to make it to the front. As the door opens and I step over the threshold, two girls shove their way past me.

"Hey!" Talk about rude! Lanie's right, people have no manners. "What the—"

I don't get the rest out before one of the girls leans over the toilet and vomits all over the place. Holy shit, that's disgusting. The toilet and floor surrounding the white porcelain are now covered in what I'm guessing was tonight's dinner.

I slap a hand over my mouth as I gag.

Look away!

But I can't. It's like a horrific traffic accident playing out before my eyes.

The second girl gathers up the other one's long hair so puke doesn't get in the brown strands, but it's too late for that. She gives me an apologetic look. "Sorry. She's not feeling good."

Clearly.

"No problem." I wave off her apology. "It was obviously an emergency." Looks like I won't be using the facilities after all. I'd rather find a bush outside.

"Just go use my bathroom," she says. "It's right down the hall. You'll have to go through the bedroom to get there."

I shake my head. "No, that's okay. I don't really need—"

"Don't worry about it. It's not a big deal." She grimaces when her friend hurls again. At least this time, the contents make it into the toilet. "I didn't want her puking in my bathroom."

Can't really say I blame her for that.

I shuffle from one foot to another as I realize how bad I have to go. "Are you sure you don't mind me using it?"

"Not at all. Just make sure you close the door on the way out of the bedroom. I don't want anyone else in there."

"Thanks." I give her a wave and take off.

Once I'm in the hallway, my stomach settles, and I glance at the closed doors. I can't remember if she said her bedroom was the one on the left or right. Or maybe she didn't tell me. Who the hell can remember with all that puke? It was psychologically damaging.

I grab the handle of the first door I come to and push it open. After a moment, my eyes adjust to the darkness, and I spot two doors. My guess is that one of them is the bathroom. I'm a few steps over the threshold when a noise from the other side of the room catches my attention, and my head snaps in that direction. I had assumed the room was empty, but apparently, that's not the case.

Great.

Like I need to interrupt someone getting it on.

With my luck, it'll be Lanie and Jax.

Mid-coitus.

Ugh.

You know what?

I can hold it. I'm just going to back right out of here and—

Another noise breaks the silence, and I squint as a couple takes form. Moonlight streams through the unadorned window, and I catch a strip of hard male flesh as the girl shoves his T-shirt up before kissing her way down his chest.

Neither of them is aware of my presence, which makes it the perfect time to sneak out. If this continues in the direction it's going, then I'm moments away from witnessing some guy get a blowie. But something holds me transfixed. The guy is tall and muscular, but I can't tell much more than that. His features are shrouded by shadows.

When the girl drops to her knees, he tangles his fingers through her long mane of hair. There's the snap of a button before it's followed by the scrape of metal teeth as a zipper is dragged down. A rustle of clothing breaks the silence before he groans.

The sound is like a lightning strike down to the tips of my toes.

I know the sound of that voice.

When I gasp, Hunter stills, and his head jerks upright. Maybe I can't see his eyes, but I feel the penetrating stare down to my soul.

Pain blooms in my chest like a gunshot wound. How will I ever be able to look at him again and not see this girl on her knees? The image has been seared into my mind for eternity.

With his gaze locked on mine, he pulls her closer. My chest tightens until the anguish is crippling. I can't breathe, and I'm powerless to look away. I'm trapped in a nightmare of my own making. My legs refuse to obey the commands of my brain.

When he tips his head back, the connection between us is severed, and I'm able to blink out of the stupor that has fallen over me. I clamp my lips together so the agony building inside can't break loose before racing out of the room and down the hall. Wetness blurs my vision as I burst into the living room, where the noise of the party rages around me. Everything is too loud, too boisterous. It echoes off the walls of my skull. There are too many bodies pressing in on me.

Blindly, I force my way through the thick crowd, moving steadily toward the front door. The moment I step onto the front porch, fresh air slams against my cheeks. I stop and suck in a deep breath before expelling it from my lungs. Even though people are pushing past me, I repeat the process over and over again until my insides loosen, and I no longer feel like I'm going to throw up.

"Skye—"

I spin around at the sound of Hunter's voice. We watch each other warily as the party fades to the background. When he moves toward me, I scramble back a step, not wanting him to come any closer. There's safety in distance, and I need that.

"Stay away from me!" I throw up a hand to ward him off. His presence riddles me with heartache. I have no right to feel that way, but it doesn't make it any less true.

How is it possible that I still love him when all he's done is hurt me?

I want to laugh at the absurdity of it, but I'm afraid I'll only end up crying.

He ignores my protests and stalks closer.

"Go back inside and leave me alone." Nausea churns in my belly at the thought of him with that girl.

"No, we need to talk."

"We have *nothing* to talk about!"

I back up another step, but there's nowhere for me to go. My arms pinwheel as Hunter leaps forward and grabs them before jerking me to him. I stumble forward and crash into his chest. With his arms banded around me, he shifts our bodies so that his back is to the staircase and I'm no longer in danger of falling.

I find myself pressed against his hard strength and inundated by his masculine scent. It's one I've spent years dreaming about. If I close my eyes, I can almost pretend we're still in high school, and Hunter worships the ground I walk on.

I shove those thoughts from my mind and focus on the here and now. From the moment I stepped foot on campus, his sole objective has been to cause me pain. The hold he has on my heart is unrelenting. He needs to let me go so that we can both move on with our lives.

With a burst of strength, I press my palms against his chest and push. Instead of releasing me, his grip tightens.

"You're such an asshole," I whisper, continuing to struggle against him.

Hunter yanks me closer as laughter falls from lips that are twisted in bitterness. "And why is that? Because you saw me with another girl? *You're* the one who broke up with *me*. Not the other way around, sweetheart. I can fuck whoever I want, and there's not a damn thing you can do about it."

The way he sneers out the endearment sends hot licks of rage bubbling up inside me. I twist out of his grip and pummel my fists against his chest with all of the fury and grief he's ignited in me. "*I hate you!*"

"That's hilarious! Why the hell would you hate me? All I ever did was love you."

His words are just another dagger through my heart. What he doesn't understand is that everything I did was for him. The sacrifices I made were so he would have the best chance of achieving his dream.

I open my mouth to fire off a scathing response before quickly slamming it shut. It's on the tip of my tongue to blurt out that he broke my heart—that he breaks it every damn day in his quest to hurt me—but my lips refuse to give voice to the words. Instead, I shake my head and keep the truth buried deep inside where it belongs.

I can't do this with him anymore.

It's too painful.

Confusion and anger churn in his eyes, and I realize nothing will salvage the situation. The secret is mine to keep no matter what the circumstances.

"You're right, Hunter. You can do whatever you want." Hopelessness fills my entire being. The weight of it threatens to bring me to my knees. "Just stay away from me while you do it."

Before he's able to hurtle any more questions or accusations at me, I rush down the stairs and into the darkness.

What I need right now is to be alone and lick my wounds. Maybe then, I'll be able to leave him in the past where he belongs and move on.

HUNTER

I watch Skye as she shoves her way through the throng of
drunk students before rushing down the sidewalk.

What the fuck just happened?

Is she seriously pissed at me?

At me?

For what?

Screwing around with a random chick?

Un-fucking-believable. I don't owe Skye anything. She's the one
who walked away from our relationship. She doesn't get to be angry. I
can mess around with whoever I want. I shift my weight as she disappears from sight.

But if that's true, then why do I feel like I got caught cheating on
the one woman I love more than anything?

What I meant to say was *loved.*

Past tense.

I *loved* her.

That's no longer the case.

I drag a hand through my hair and try to decide how to handle the
situation. Here's what I know—I can't let her walk away.

Not like this.

I don't get more than a step before a beefy hand wraps around my bicep and holds me in place.

What the fuck?

I'm in no mood to deal with cleat sniffers. I swing around, ready to bite some jackass's head off only to find Jaxon.

My gaze drops to the point of contact before it flicks to his face. "What are you doing?"

"Saving you from making a big fucking mistake."

What the hell does that mean?

I poker up to my full height and cock my head. "Excuse me?"

"You heard me, bro. You need to leave Skye alone and stop playing these games with her."

Is this guy for real?

When I yank my arm, he relinquishes his grip. "Fuck off, Jax. You don't know what you're talking about." I'm not looking to have a problem with him, but if he doesn't mind his own damn business, that's exactly what's going to happen.

"I know more than you think I do." He pauses for a beat. "You've been toying nonstop with her since she returned, and it needs to stop." He jerks his chin toward the sidewalk. "She dumped your ass a while ago. Get over it and move on." Jaxon folds his arms across his thickly corded chest. "Skye's a nice girl, and she has enough going on in her life without having to deal with your unresolved bullshit."

"What the hell are you talking about?"

Guilt flashes across his face before it disappears. "Nothing," he mutters.

I can't help but laugh at the absurdity of the situation.

Is he seriously this whipped?

Sure, I get that Jax is dating Skye's best friend, but we're teammates. He's supposed to have my back. Not be stabbing me in it. The guy needs to get his priorities straight.

I shift my weight and glare. "Are you really going to side with a chick you just met over me?"

His shoulders fall as his expression turns to one of regret. "I don't want to, but yeah, I am. You need to back off. This is your first and last warning. If you continue to screw with her, you'll answer to me. Got it, Price?"

When I remain silent, Jaxon slaps me none too gently on the shoulder. "Good talk, man."

Then he disappears inside the house. It's pretty damn bad when your own teammates turn on you.

You know what?

Fuck Jaxon.

I'll deal with his ass later. Right now, I need to find Skye. If she thinks she can walk away from me, she's got another thing coming. As much as we both want this to be over with, it's not.

I'm beginning to wonder if it ever will be.

SKYE

It takes about fifteen minutes to make it home from the party. Should I have walked by myself? Probably not, but I was too upset to stop and make other arrangements. Once home, I jump in the shower and try to wash away everything that happened this evening with Hunter. For a night that started out full of promise, it turned to shit by the end. After my shower, I wrap up in my comfy white robe and brew a mug of hot tea. There's something about a warm drink that helps settle everything inside you.

And if there was ever a time I could use that, it's now.

As I sit on the couch, I try not to dwell on Hunter and the pain that continues to pound through me. But it's all I can think about. How can I love someone so desperately when all he wants to do is lash out at me? It doesn't make sense.

I lift the mug to my lips and take another sip when there's a knock on the door.

My belly hollows as I set the cup down on the coffee table. Even before I rise to my feet, I know who will be on the other side of the threshold. My body trembles as I force myself to the entryway.

I hesitate at the door, unsure if I should answer it. I can't do this anymore. The constant back and forth is tearing me apart.

He knocks again, and my pulse picks up speed as I wring my hands together.

"I know you're in there, Skye," he says softly, confirming my fears.

If I allow him inside, I know *exactly* what will happen. Lanie's right. The sexual tension has been simmering between us since I crashed into him at the field party. And it ratchets up every time we're together. Sooner or later, it's going to explode.

I flatten my palm against the wood as if I can feel his presence on the other side. When he raps his fist against the barrier that separates us, I startle and fall back a step.

"Open the door so we can talk."

Ha!

Talking is the last thing he has on his mind.

Yet, I'm tempted to give in to what we both want. But how can I do that when I know how disastrously it will end?

Air leaks from my lungs when everything goes silent. I stand on my tiptoes and peek through the peephole. As I press my eye to the small circle, my phone breaks the silence with a loud ring. I shriek and swing around, searching frantically for my cell.

"Got you," he says.

My shoulders slump as I grab the knob and twist. Hunter stands on the other side with his phone in hand. He presses the red end button, and a few seconds later, my cell stops ringing.

"Cheater," I accuse.

He pops a shoulder into a shrug. "Maybe."

When I don't budge from in front of the door, he clears his throat, "Aren't you going to let me in?"

"No. If you have something to say, you can do it from there. I was about to go to bed."

His gaze drops from my face, taking in the fuzzy robe I'm wrapped in. I glance down to make sure everything is covered.

"You still have that?" he asks softly.

"Why wouldn't I? It's my favorite." That's when I remember it was Hunter who surprised me with it for Christmas during our senior year of high school.

Our eyes lock and hold as we fall into silence. Once again, I'm left wishing that everything could be different between us. Even though we've spent the past few years apart, it still feels as though our lives are entwined, and nothing will ever separate them.

"I can't do it," he murmurs, interrupting my thoughts.

I rack my brain for meaning. It feels as if I've missed part of the conversation. "Can't do *what?*"

"I can't stay away from you." A weary acceptance fills his voice. "God knows I've tried."

He takes a step forward, and my heartbeat hitches. When he takes another, I scramble backward, trying to keep distance between us. But how much is enough? How much will stop this from happening? Fire leaps in his eyes as he tracks my movements farther into the townhouse.

"I've tried everything to get you out of my head." His voice drops as he stalks closer. "I don't know what else to do."

"We can't."

When my thighs hit the back of the couch, I realize there's nowhere else for me to go. Hunter is so close. Body heat radiates from him in heavy waves. He lifts his hand before gently tracing the curve of my jaw with his fingers. "I've told you from the beginning that it's what we both need."

His wide palm cups the side of my face, and I'm so tempted to close my eyes and sink into his touch.

"You want this as much as I do. Do us both a favor and admit it."

My shoulders collapse because he's right.

I want *this*.

I want *him*.

But I'm also aware it won't end well. Up until this point, that knowledge has kept me from giving in to the deep-seated need I have for him.

"We need closure in order to move on with our lives."

When his lips brush the other side of my face, I melt.

Sensing my surrender, Hunter presses delicate kisses along my throat before nipping me with sharp teeth. I groan and bare more of my flesh to him. This is exactly what I was afraid of when I opened the door. The moment Hunter lays his hands on me, I come undone.

"I need you, Skye," he whispers.

My heart soars.

"I need to fuck you out of my system once and for all."

And just like that, it crashes. The silky web of seduction he had been weaving around me disintegrates. A pile of ash sits at the bottom of my belly. That's all this will ever be for him.

Fucking.

So he can move on.

From me.

This is in no way a seduction. Perhaps his touch is gentle and his kisses soft, but his intentions are clear. If I give in to his demands, what happens between us will be screwing, plain and simple. I'll mean nothing more to him than the girl who was on her knees at the party. That thought sickens me enough to rekindle my anger. I press my palms against his chest and shove with all my might. He doesn't go far, but it's enough for me to evade his hold.

Undeterred, Hunter swings around to face me.

"If you're looking for someone to suck your dick, I suggest you find the girl from the party. She seemed eager to please." The memory flashes painfully through my head. The way his hands had tangled in her hair right before he pulled her toward him makes me sick.

A slow smile curves his lips. "Jealous much?"

"Hardly." I shake my head, refusing to admit the truth, even to myself. "More like disgusted."

"Really?" He tilts his head. "And why is that?"

I press my lips together, refusing to answer. Whatever I say will only end up incriminating me, and I won't give him any more leverage.

Hunter's muscles bunch and flex as he prowls closer. "We've been through this. We're not together. It shouldn't matter what I do."

I tip my head in acknowledgment. "You're right. It doesn't."

"Then it shouldn't matter how many girls I fuck, right?"

"Nope, not at all." But the sad truth is that it does. Every girl he's slept with is a score across my heart. When I was living halfway across the country, it was easier to pretend that Hunter wasn't involved with other people. Now that I'm at Claremont, it's in my face.

"If it makes any difference," he says softly. "When I closed my eyes, it was you I was imagining. It's *you* that I want."

Lies.

He doesn't *want* me. Not really. Not in a way that matters.

I force myself to say, "You want to fuck me so you can move on."

"You're right." He shrugs unapologetically and steps closer. "That's exactly what I want." With gentle fingers, he caresses the line of my jaw. "Aren't you ready to let go of the past and move on? We need this, Skye. We need to say goodbye."

If only it were that simple.

What I'm afraid of is that it will only make things worse. But I can't continue to do this with him. Something has to give.

"Okay."

It's almost comical the way his dark brows shoot across his forehead. He looks as startled as I feel.

"Okay?"

I jerk my head into a tight nod. If I think about it too hard or for too long, I'll chicken out and change my mind. The two of us having sex is a disastrous idea.

Hunter doesn't ask any further questions. Instead, one hand whips out and tugs me to him. I stifle a yelp of surprise when his mouth slants over mine, dragging me beneath the surface to a place where thinking becomes an impossibility. It's enough to quiet the clamoring voices inside my head.

His hard body presses close to mine until all I feel is his unrelenting heat. It's like the sun beating down upon my flesh. All I want is to bask in the warm glow of it.

With one hand, he tugs the belt around my waist until the knot unravels, allowing the robe to gape open. He pushes the plush material away from my shoulders until it puddles in a thick pile around my feet.

Hunter pulls away enough so that his gaze can slide down the length of my naked body. It's been years since he's seen me without clothing, and I've changed during that time. My breasts are heavier, and my hips fuller.

A groan breaks free from his lips as his eyes ignite with heat. That response is enough to silence the insecurities raging through my head.

"How is it possible that you're more gorgeous than I remember?"

When my mouth opens under the firm pressure, his tongue slips inside to tangle with my own. He drags me closer until all of my soft curves are aligned with his hard ones. I moan at the feel of his thick erection jutting against my belly. Barely has he touched me, and I'm soaked.

His mouth lifts from mine long enough to mutter, "Tell me that you want this."

Only now do I understand that I've been fooling myself from the very beginning. I thought it was possible for us to peacefully coexist at the same school, but it's not. There's too much history. Too many hurt feelings that simmer beneath the surface. Maybe neither of us wants to feel them, but they continue to lurk in the darkness. It's like a monster that needs to be fed.

Will this be enough to satisfy the beast?

I have no idea.

I only know that it has to be this way.

"I want this." I draw him closer so that my fingers can slide from his shoulders to his neck before tunneling through his thick hair. "I want *you*."

His lips are bruising in their intensity. It's as if he doesn't want to hesitate for a single moment or I'll change my mind.

But that's not going to happen.

His hands drop from my back to my ass before he lifts me so my legs can wrap around his waist as he walks us into the hallway.

"Which room?" he mutters against my lips.

"The one on the left."

With our mouths fused, he carries me through the doorway before placing me in the middle of the queen-sized bed. His gaze doesn't leave mine as he grabs the back of his T-shirt and yanks it over his head before tossing it to the floor. Then he's back, his mouth roving hungrily over mine as his hands palm my breasts. His mouth slides over my chin before traveling south to my collarbone as he works his way lower.

"Do you have any idea how much I've missed these?" he murmurs against my warm flesh.

There have been too many times to count when I laid awake in my dorm bed, longing for his touch. Sometimes, I would squeeze my eyes closed and caress myself, imagining that it was Hunter, but it never felt the same.

When he tweaks my nipple between his thumb and forefinger, a shaft of pleasure spears through me, and a moan escapes. He captures one turgid peak with his lips before drawing the bud deep into his mouth. My fingers spear through his hair so I can pull him closer. It doesn't take long for me to grow restless beneath him. When I can't stand another moment, he releases the bud with a pop before sliding to the other side and repeating the process. After a few moments, his mouth drifts from my breasts to my ribcage. When he arrives at my navel, he swirls the velvety softness of his tongue around it before sinking lower. My breath catches as I await his touch.

Hunter peers at me from between my thighs. His warm breath feathers over my throbbing center. I arch my back, needing to feel his mouth sliding over my heat.

"How much do you want me?" His tongue swipes over my clit.

A whimper falls from my lips as the ache intensifies. It's not possible for me to want Hunter any more than I already do.

"You need to tell me." There's a pause. "Tell me how much you want to be fucked." He presses a soft kiss against the top of my slit before his tongue slips inside me.

I groan and widen my legs, needing more.

"Say the words, Skye," he cajoles. His warm breath ghosts over my heated flesh, driving me to the brink of insanity. "I want to hear just how much you missed my dick buried inside your pussy."

"I missed it more than you'll ever know," I whisper. Whatever he wants me to say, I'll do it. I need him more than I need air to breathe.

"I bet you did." His hands slide to the inside of my thighs before he gently presses them apart, widening my legs until I'm completely exposed. His gaze settles on the most intimate part of me. The longer he stares, the more moisture gathers. Reaching out, he traces the lips of my pussy, circling around the outer edges before slowly moving toward the center.

"So fucking pretty."

I lift my hips, wanting him to drive his fingers deep inside me, but he doesn't. He takes his time, relearning my flesh, tormenting me until it feels like I'm going to come right out of my skin. When he finally slides one thick finger inside my sheath, my body squeezes the digit, and a long moan breaks free. His expression turns to one of intense concentration as he slowly pumps his finger in me.

My eyelashes flutter shut, and pleasure radiates from my center in hot, suffocating waves. I don't remember the last time I felt like this. Maybe never. Thin wisps of an orgasm curl like smoke deep in the pit of my belly.

"You're so damn wet. You need this, don't you?"

"Yes," I gasp, unable to focus on anything other than the ecstasy unfurling in me.

"Good, I'm going to give you everything you need." His gaze flicks to mine. "For the rest of your life, you'll mourn the loss of my dick."

If he wasn't playing with my body, stroking me into submission, those words would have the power to wound me, but the only thing I'm capable of focusing on is the pleasure that continues to pummel my senses.

My hips gyrate in perfect rhythm with his thrusts. All of my muscles lock as I hurtle toward the edge. I'm one pump away from fulfillment when he withdraws from my body. A whimper of protest leaves my lips. He slaps my throbbing clit with the tips of his fingers, and I yelp.

"Be patient."

It's not hard enough to hurt, just sting before exploding with more pleasure than I thought possible. Now that he's no longer stroking me, all that mounting ecstasy has nowhere to go. My harsh pants fill the room as everything in me pulses with newfound awareness before slowly disintegrating into nothingness.

I want to claw my way out of my skin as a scream builds in my lungs.

Hunter comes to his feet, sliding both his shorts and black boxer briefs over his trim hips. I prop myself up on my elbows so I can watch. When he's completely naked, he pauses, giving me time to look my fill.

Good Lord but he's gorgeous. His body was made to be appreciated. All that sharply honed muscle and athletic grace.

Hunter's expression remains inscrutable as he moves to the side of the bed. There was a time when I knew his thoughts, but that was years ago. No longer do I know the man before me.

He hooks his hands under my arms and drags me to the edge of the bed until my head hangs off the mattress. My heart pounds a painful staccato as adrenaline rushes through my blood. It's silently that I watch as he takes his place before me. His muscular thighs flank each side of my head as he wraps a hand around his shaft and brings the bulbous tip to my lips.

"Open."

A thrill shoots through me as I quickly comply with his command. The crown of his cock slides between my lips and over my tongue. I close my eyes and enjoy the feel of his girth filling me. Already I can taste the salty moisture that has beaded at the tip.

Hunter groans as he starts off with slow strokes. With each thrust of his hips, he slips farther inside my mouth until he can nudge the back of my throat. I widen my jaw and focus on breathing through my nose, drawing in deep breaths as he fucks my mouth. My hands drift from his thighs to his ass until my fingers are able to bite into his muscular cheeks with every gyration.

It's music to my ears when his breathing grows ragged. I slide one hand from his backside to his cock before knocking his hand away and wrapping mine around the thick length. Then I pull him closer until he's able to sink all the way inside me. Every time I swallow, the muscles of my throat contract around him.

"Fuck, that feels amazing," he groans.

His fingers go to my breasts to play with my nipples. He tugs and pinches them. It's a heady cocktail of pain mixed with pleasure, but it's the pleasure that overwhelms my senses. With my mouth full of cock, I moan out my enjoyment. When I can't stand another moment, he strokes his way over my ribs, hips, and thighs until each hand can wrap around an ankle. He pulls my legs wide, shackling them against the mattress so I'm completely exposed. The length of his body presses against mine, pinning me in place as his mouth fastens onto my clit, drawing the tiny bud into his mouth.

That's all it takes for him to drive me over the edge and explode. Not once does he let up on the pressure of his lips and tongue. His hips continue to gyrate as he sinks so far down my throat that I feel the root of his cock against my mouth with every stroke. My orgasm doesn't have a chance to fully dissipate when he lifts his mouth and releases the pulsating bundle of nerves. He straightens before slipping his dick from my mouth, and I gasp.

Hunter grabs my hips and flips me over before dragging me to the edge of the bed. I pant as he spreads my thighs wide. His hand slides from my ass to the middle of my back before pushing me down and pinning me to the mattress.

Only when I'm in position with my ass in the air does he ask, "Are you on the pill?"

"Yes."

"Good. I don't want anything between us when we fuck, not even a condom. I want you bare."

Before I can fully grasp his intent, he thrusts deep inside my soaked pussy until he's buried to the hilt. My muscles stretch around him, adjusting to his size. It feels so damn good that I almost see stars.

"Fuck," he groans as if reading my thoughts.

His hands settle on my hips as his fingertips bite into my flesh to hold me still. It takes less than a dozen strokes for him to come. His body becomes impossibly tight as he growls out his release. I close my eyes, feeling the hot jets of his orgasm paint my womb. He's the only boy I've ever allowed inside me without protection. We were each other's firsts. As soon as we decided to have sex, I went to the doctor and got a prescription for the pill. In all the years we were together, we never used a condom. In retrospect, it was pretty stupid considering that the pill can fail. I guess we were lucky.

There's a fragile moment of connection that binds us together as Hunter collapses on top of me. With his chin resting against my shoulder, his choppy breath fills my ear. A sigh of contentment falls from my lips, and I wonder if it's possible for this encounter to be more than a way for him to evict me from both his head and heart. My thoughts are cautiously optimistic. I'm almost afraid to acknowledge them.

When I walked away, I caused irreparable damage.

But still…

This feels as if it could mean so much more.

As soon as the tension drains from his muscles, Hunter stretches to his full height and pulls out of me. I blink, bewildered by the loss of his heat and his heavy weight pinning me to the mattress. The haze surrounding our encounter begins to clear, and reality threatens to crash down upon us.

I rack my brain for something to say, something that will send our relationship careening in a different direction. Is that even possible? Or has too much harm been inflicted for that to happen?

My teeth sink into my lower lip as I search his face for clues as to what he's thinking, but his expression remains unreadable as he grabs his boxers and yanks them up his legs in one swift movement.

A chill sweeps over me. "You're leaving?"

I wince as he tosses a cold look my way. It's as if he can't be bothered with anything more. Any tentative emotional bond that had been forged between us is quickly severed.

"Yeah." He glances around for his shorts and shirt before gathering them up and tugging them on. In less than sixty seconds, he's fully dressed and ready to bolt.

He takes a step toward the bedroom door before glancing at me. I have yet to move. It's as if I've been stunned into a strange paralysis.

It's only when his gaze drifts over my naked body that embarrassment scorches my cheeks, and I realize how truly meaningless this has been.

I've had sex with half a dozen guys since Hunter. Two of them were one-night stands, but none have ever made me feel as dirty and used as I do now. With shaking fingers, I grab the edge of the comforter and flip it over me in an attempt to shield my nudity.

Our gazes lock, and he shifts his weight. I'm waiting for that damnable smirk to appear on his face, but it remains elusive.

It's as if neither of us knows how to wrap up this encounter.

Hunter's shoulders slump as regret flashes in his eyes. "Guess I'll see you around, Skye."

I press my lips together, unwilling to say anything. If I do, the tears I'm holding at bay will flood my eyes, and I don't want him to see how much his behavior has wounded me. I won't give him the satisfaction.

When it becomes apparent that I'm not going to return the farewell, Hunter jerks his head into a tight nod before walking out of the room.

Once the apartment door closes with a soft click, I fall back against the bed and stare sightlessly at the ceiling. It takes effort to blink back the wetness, but I refuse to shed another tear for Hunter Price.

He wanted closure, and he got it. Then I toss the covers from my body and head to the bathroom for another shower. There was a time when I loved the scent of Hunter on my skin. That's no longer the case.

SKYE

I peer through one of the long thin windows that flank the front door, but don't see any movement inside. After thirty seconds, I rap my fist again and wait. Dad's silver Volvo is parked in the drive while Brandi's white Mercedes is conspicuously absent. It's not like I'm keeping track of my stepmother's daily itinerary, but I know enough to realize that she's usually at the gym around this time, which is why I swing by. The less contact I have with Brandi, the better off we all are.

The lunch I was forced into attending a couple of weeks ago is something I won't be repeating any time soon. Dad is going to have to accept that wife number three and I will never be besties.

If I can live with that, so can he.

My forehead scrunches with concern as I peer through the glass. If someone doesn't answer the door soon, I'll be forced to walk in, and I *really* don't want to do that. Even though I lived with Dad and Brandi after Mom moved to Wisconsin in eighth grade, this place no longer feels like home.

I nibble my lower lip as concern blooms in the pit of my belly. Did he have a doctor's appointment? I try to keep track of those as well as the test results, so I know what's going on.

When I spoke to Dad on the phone yesterday, there had been a deep weariness filling his voice. This chemo has been taking more of a toll on him, and I don't like it. His appetite has plummeted, and in a matter of weeks, he's lost a noticeable amount of weight. When he looks and feels good, it's easier to pretend that the doctors are wrong, and he'll beat the prognosis. When he's tired and unable to keep food down, it's more difficult to do that. It makes the cancer seem like an unrelenting, unstoppable force.

Worry will eat away at me, and I find myself zoning out in class, dwelling on what the future will bring. School has never been a challenge before, but it is now. Sometimes, it feels like I'm drowning. And we're only a month in! I've been kicking around the idea of withdrawing for the semester, but I'm conflicted. A part of me wants to push through the rest of this year so Dad can watch me walk across the stage and graduate from CU. If his disease progresses the way his doctors expect it to, he won't be around for any other milestones, and that thought makes me sick to my stomach.

With my hand on the knob, I tentatively turn the handle and push the door open. "Hello?" I call out, pausing over the threshold as silence settles around me. I force myself to step inside and close the door. "Dad," I holler, "are you home?"

As I stand in the foyer, an avalanche of *what-ifs* bury me alive.

What if something happened to him during the night?

What if there was an emergency?

What if he's at the hospital?

My heart beats into overdrive, thudding painfully against my ribcage.

"Dad?" I yell urgently, panic threading its way through my voice. With shaking fingers, I slide the phone from my back pocket, ready to call Brandi.

"Skye?"

All of the emotion that had been whirling through me collapses at the sound of my father's voice.

I glance up at the second-floor landing and find him leaning against the railing. Both hands are wrapped tightly around the black iron. I take quick stock of his appearance. His hair is mussed, and he's wearing his flannel robe.

"Were you in bed?" It's almost eleven. Not that it's unheard of, but still...

It's not like him. And right now, any behavior out of the ordinary sets me on edge.

"Yeah, I had a hard time sleeping last night." He jerks his shoulders into a shrug. "This medicine really upsets my stomach."

"Did you tell the doctor? Is there anything they can give you to help with the nausea?"

He drags a hand over his face. "I have an appointment tomorrow, and we'll talk about it then. I wanted to give this drug enough time to work."

It's disturbing how drastically his appearance has changed in just a few days. There's a haggardness to him that wasn't there before. How is he supposed to fight cancer if he isn't able to nourish his body?

"Do you want me to run out and get you something? A protein shake or maybe a smoothie? A sandwich from the deli?"

He grimaces and shakes his head as if he can't abide the thought. "I don't have much of an appetite." When I stare silently, he tacks on, "Maybe later."

A feeling of helplessness fills me. "Where's Brandi?" Should Dad really be left alone if he doesn't feel good?

"She's out running a few errands. She'll be back soon."

"I have some time, Dad. Do you want to come downstairs, and we can watch something on TV?"

"You know what, kiddo, I think I'm going to lie down for a while. My eyes are burning."

"Okay." I nod and try to hold back the flood of tears that prick my eyes. "Should I hang around until Brandi returns?"

"Nah, you can head back to school. I'm sure you have a lot of work to do."

He's right. I do. Homework and reading assignments have been piling up. But I'd much rather spend time with him than worry about school. By comparison, everything else in my life feels so much less important. Half the time, I don't even want to bother with it.

"You know," I blurt out, "it's not too late for me to withdraw for the semester. I have until next Friday to get a full refund."

Then I could help out more. After all, someone needs to prepare nutritious meals, and it isn't going to be Brandi. I don't think she knows how to operate the stove. I've done my research, and there are a lot of cookbooks out there for people who are battling cancer. If I had more time, I could prepare him healthy dishes to help fight this disease from the inside. That's what he needs.

School can wait.

Dad can't.

"Skye?"

I blink and realize that he's at the bottom of the stairs. "Yeah?"

Sorrow fills his eyes, and it nearly breaks my heart. "We've talked about this before. I don't want you to take the semester off."

"I know but..." I shrug helplessly as my gaze skitters away. "There's a lot going on. I could stay here at the house and help out." At this point, I'll do whatever it takes to make his life easier. Even if that means putting up with Brandi.

"You know what I want?"

I perk up. "What?" All he has to do is say the word, and it'll be done.

Dad reaches out and takes hold of my hand before giving it a squeeze. His fingers feel cool and clammy against mine. "For you to keep living your life."

Everything in me seizes, making it impossible to suck in a full breath. "But, Dad—"

"That's what I want," he says, cutting me off. "Just like I want Brandi to keep living hers. We can't let cancer stop everything. If it does, then this disease wins, and I'm not about to let that happen." He searches my eyes. "Got it?"

I press my lips together and jerk my head into a nod. If I try to open my mouth, I'll burst into tears, and I don't want to do that. He has enough to worry about without dealing with all of my emotions.

He holds out his arms. "Come here, kiddo."

I fly into his embrace and bury my face against his chest. My arms band around him, and I can't help but feel there's less of him to hold on to. It's as if he's slowly slipping away from me a few pounds at a time. And I have no idea how to stop it from happening. I want to hold him tight and never let go, but I'm afraid it will hurt him. His body seems so fragile.

He presses a kiss to the top of my head. "I love you, Skye. And I'm proud of the woman you've become. I want you to keep working toward your dreams. That's the best gift you can give me."

"I will." It takes all of my self-control to keep my voice from wobbling with the thick emotion that is welling up inside me. "And I love you too, Dad."

After a few minutes, he clears his throat. "Maybe I'll have you run out for a smoothie after all. Do you mind?"

I shake my head. "Not at all. Peanut butter banana?"

His lips stretch into a thin smile. "Yeah, that sounds good."

"Okay. I'll be back in a few."

"I'll be waiting."

For today, but what about tomorrow? Or a week from now? How about six months down the road? Will he still be here waiting?

At some point, Dad won't be.

And that thought terrifies me.

SKYE

"You were right, this was a great idea." Lanie kicks off her sandals and stretches out beside me on the rolling green lawn in the middle of campus.

I smile and pull our sandwiches from the brown paper bag. Lanie ordered ham and swiss minus the mayo. Believe it or not, she doesn't like mayonnaise. She's lucky I still consider her a friend. I have an Italian loaded down with salami, prosciutto, and provolone. The deli at the Union has the best subs. It only takes a few moments before the wrappers are off and we're digging into our lunch.

Lanie keeps up a steady stream of conversation as we plow our way through the hoagies. There's a gentle October breeze that wafts over us. Everyone seems to have the same idea this afternoon. People are tossing around Frisbees and footballs. Some are lying in the grass and studying. Or, like us, they've opted to bring lunch outside and are sitting in small groups.

Maybe after my last class this afternoon, I'll come back and study here instead of at the library or townhouse. There's something about feeling the warm sunshine stroking over your bare skin.

I'm doing my best to stay on top of my classes, but no matter how

169

hard I try, it feels like I'm constantly falling behind. As soon as I make a bit of headway, there's an avalanche of assignments and reading that leaves me buried beneath it.

Hunter and I settled on the topic of vaccinations for our health project. I'm in the beginning stages of gathering information on diseases, along with the statistics and occurrences in different populations. It's definitely interesting, and I'm glad we chose it. The problem is that I'm constantly playing catch-up with my other classes, so I haven't been working on it as much as I should. If I don't carve out time soon, I'll be up shit creek when it's due at the end of the semester.

Statistics has gone from bad to worse. The concepts are challenging, and I usually end up in the math tutor lab a few times a week. Even if I wanted to ask Josh for help—which I don't—he's keeping me at arm's length. It doesn't matter how many times I've insisted that Hunter and I aren't involved.

Except...that's no longer true.

Ugh.

I shake my head, trying to loosen thoughts of him from my mind. Instead of enjoying my lunch with Lanie, I'm dwelling on my ex. I force my gaze to coast over the crowd. Almost immediately, it lands on his dark head. It's as if my thoughts have conjured him up. And just like that, my appetite disappears.

With a sigh, I lay the sub on its red-and-white-checkered wrapper before wiping my hands on a napkin. As much as watching him hurts, looking away is impossible. It's like I'm trying to inflict as much damage onto myself as I can.

This is going to sound terrible, but Hunter is the only thing that distracts me from Dad's situation. When we fuck, I'm able to forget about what cancer will eventually steal from me. As painful as those encounters end up being and the self-loathing I feel afterward, I need that mental break.

Trust me, I'm aware of how messed up the situation is.

Most of Hunter's fan club is comprised of girls who hang on his every word. It's like he's preaching the gospel over there. He flashes a smile at a tall blonde with big boobs. In response, she trails her finger-tips over his bicep and gives him a flirty look.

It's enough to have the bile rising in my throat.

Look away! Don't do this to yourself.

Instead of listening to my inner voice, my gaze stays locked on him. If I force myself to watch long enough, will the feelings I have for Hunter shrivel up and die?

So far, that has yet to happen.

"Skye?"

Lanie's voice cuts through my thoughts, and it's what finally yanks my distracted attention away from Hunter. A strange concoction of regret and relief fills me. "Hmm?"

Concern is etched across her face as she points at my half-eaten sandwich. "I thought you were starving?"

I shrug, refusing to acknowledge what killed my appetite. "Guess I wasn't as hungry as I thought."

Lanie glances over her shoulder. Her expression darkens when she spots Hunter and his harem of dedicated fangirls. She grumbles something under her breath in Greek before softening her tone and turning back to me. "Maybe we should pack up and go somewhere else."

That probably would be for the best, but I'm not going to do it.

Instead, I smooth out my features and paste a smile on my face. I have bigger issues to worry about than Hunter Price. "No, it's fine. Let's finish up our lunch and enjoy the sunshine."

Her gaze falls to her lap before she skewers me with it. My guess is that I'm about to get a dose of tough love.

"You need to stop sleeping with him, Skye."

And there it is, the unvarnished truth, no-holds-barred.

"I know," I mumble. The pseudo-relationship I've gotten myself tangled up in isn't a healthy one.

Also…full disclosure sucks.

Of course I shouldn't be sleeping with him. I don't need Lanie to tell me that.

The first time we had sex, I'd assumed it wouldn't be happening again. Especially after the way he left without barely any acknowledgment at all. The only thing that would have made that episode worse is if he'd Venmo-ed me money afterward.

But that hasn't turned out to be the case. We've had sex half a dozen times. After the deed is done, it's always the same. Hunter rolls from the bed without a word and leaves. Each time we hook up, a tiny part of me wonders if maybe we'll break down the barrier that stands between us, but that has yet to occur.

Maybe I've been a little slow on the uptake, but I've finally come to the realization that it isn't going to happen.

I've become the one thing I never thought I would be.

A booty call.

And Hunter has more than enough of those. That thought is almost enough to gut me. Not that I've asked, but my guess is that I'm not the only girl he's sleeping with. The sub I'd been eating threatens to make an unexpected reappearance.

"I'd like to march over there and chew his ass out for hurting you," Lanie growls from where she lounges across from me. "He's such a dumbass."

Hunter is many things, but a dumbass isn't one of them. This is all on me. *I* did this.

I shake my head and glance away. "He's not forcing me to do anything I don't want to." And that's the sad truth of it.

She gives me a hard look that says—*bitch, please...*

Then she hits me where it counts. "I know you still love him, but can't you see he's using that against you? He deserves a good dick punch. One that will leave him singing soprano for the rest of his life."

Even though nothing about this situation is amusing, the corners of my lips tremble at the image. Maybe Hunter deserves that, but someone needs to slap some sense into me as well for continuing to allow him inside my body.

"You can't keep doing this," she says.

Lanie's right. I can't.

But am I strong enough to walk away?

To finally say goodbye?
I don't know, but I'm going to have to find out.

HUNTER

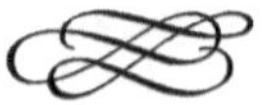

"Catch you on the field, Price," Sam says, giving me a fist bump as we part ways.

I quickly jog up the wide stone steps of Hastings Hall before finding the room for health. My body goes on high alert the moment I stroll through the door. Without glancing around, I already know Skye has beaten me here. The tiny hairs at the back of my neck rise.

It sucks to be so attuned to her presence.

As I slide onto my seat, I resist the temptation to turn around and look her way. Instead, I pull out my book and notepad. Then I sit back and tap my fingers on my desk and wonder when Bennet is going to begin class. I glance at the clock on the wall, and the chick next to me smiles. I should be all over that, but the truth of the matter is that I have zero interest. Skye is the only girl I want.

One hundred and sixty-two seconds is exactly how long I'm able to resist the urge before swiveling in her direction. I can't *not* look at her. She's like a fucking drug pumping through my system. How the hell do you evict someone from your head when you weren't even aware they'd been hiding out there for years?

If I knew the answer to that, I wouldn't be in this damn mess.

Here's what I do know—fucking her hasn't helped one damn bit. If anything, that plan has backfired spectacularly. Instead of getting my fill of that girl and losing interest, I want her more than ever.

How's that for a kick in the balls?

The moment she fills my line of sight, everything in me loosens, and I sit back and drink in everything about her. Her blond hair has been swept up into a messy bun at the top of her head. My fingers itch to tunnel through her long strands. God, but I love her hair. It's sexy as hell. Her gaze stays focused on the desk in front of her. If it weren't for the slight trembling of her hands, I'd assume my presence had no effect on her.

There's something intensely gratifying about that.

My gaze roves carefully over her face. Sorrow lurks in her green eyes. I'll admit there have been times when I've been tempted to ask what's going on, but I don't.

Are you kidding me?

Of course I don't.

As soon as the urge strikes, I force myself to leave. For my own self-preservation, I can't afford to get emotionally entangled with Skye again. Hell, I shouldn't be sleeping with her. All I've done is jack myself up inside. Instead of being focused on football, I have Skye on the brain.

My eyes shift to Jaxon. The strain between us has bled onto the field. As soon as our gazes collide, his expression turns stony. It really chafes my balls that he's taken Skye's side in all this. It goes to show you just how pussy whipped the guy is. We're teammates. He should have my back, no questions asked.

The guy needs to mind his own fucking business and stay out of mine.

With one final glance at Skye, I turn on my seat as Dr. Bennet gets class underway. This is one course I'm not concerned about. Even with a twenty-page paper, it's more of a blow-off. I can crank that shit out in my sleep. When Bennet starts to drone, I tune her out, and my mind gravitates to Skye. I daydream about the last time we were together and how good it felt to slide into her tight heat. Just one thought of her pussy has my cock straining against my shorts.

Fuck.

Without realizing it, I've fallen into the trap of our past. I've never had anyone consume me the way she does. The time I spent with Skye was Mason's biggest gripe when we were together. He wanted me one-hundred-percent focused on football and my future, not some damn girl. My brother and I have always been close. Even before Mom and Dad died, we were best friends. But their passing has only made us tighter.

Without Mason and all of the sacrifices he's made for me, it's doubtful I would be poised for the NFL. I owe him everything. He's pushed me when I didn't think I had anything else left to give. And it was him who picked me up after Skye dumped my ass.

Which is precisely why I've kept my trap shut where she's concerned. I can't even imagine his reaction if I told him that we were hooking up. Actually, that's not true. He'd go ballistic. I don't need my older brother to tell me when I'm screwing up. I'm fully aware of the situation. If I were smart, I'd end things with Skye. It's not like this is a real relationship. It's fucking, pure and simple. Emotions aren't involved.

Or so I tell myself.

The remaining thirty minutes of class drags by. It's a relief when Bennet dismisses us for the day with a reminder to continue working on our project. Already a month and a half have flown by, which seems crazy.

As I leave the classroom and head into the already crowded hallway, someone touches my arm. A zip of electricity shoots through me and I know it's Skye. The moment my gaze falls on her, she releases her hold. Even though her fingers were only there for seconds, it feels like the print of them has been inked onto my flesh like a tattoo.

"Do you have a minute?" Nerves dance in her voice as her gaze darts away before coming back to rest on mine.

I'm tempted to grab her and—

"Should I wait?"

My gaze jerks to Jaxon, who hovers over her like he's her full-time bodyguard. A mixture of jealousy and frustration flares to life inside me. If I didn't know better, I'd suspect Jax had a thing for her, but I realize that's not true. He's totally into Lanie. I've seen them together enough times to recognize when a guy is head over heels in love with a chick. Jax is so whipped, he can barely see straight. I hope for his sake that Lanie is worth the trouble because let's face it, relationships go south.

"No," she says quietly.

I refocus my attention on Skye as her gaze bounces between the two of us before finally settling on me again. "We need a few minutes to discuss our project. I'll see you at the townhouse later."

Clearly unhappy with the dismissal, Jaxon's lips flatten as he gives me the stink eye. "Fine, I'll catch you later."

With one last glare aimed in my direction, Jax reluctantly takes off. At some point, I'm going to have to fix things with him. We can't have this strife between us. It's not good for the team.

When Skye remains silent, I raise a brow. "You wanted to talk?"

Even though my curiosity has been piqued, I don't want her to know that. When we hook up, it's always me who initiates it. It's not like she's ever denied me, but it would be nice to know she wants me with the same intensity I crave her.

What the hell am I thinking?

Why does it even matter?

Her tongue darts out to moisten her lips, and I have to clamp my mouth shut in order to stifle a groan as a shot of lust arrows straight to my dick. The crazy thing is that I had her a few days ago, so I should be good, but obviously, that's not the case. No matter how much time I spend inside her, it's never enough.

This situation is more fucked-up than I'd allowed myself to believe.

"Yeah, do you have a few minutes?"

"A couple, but it needs to be quick."

When Skye pauses, glancing away as if uncertain what to do next, I take matters into my own hands and grab her fingers, towing her through the hallway. By now, all of the classrooms have emptied, and there's less of a crowd, making the passage easier to navigate. I pull her into the first darkened room we come to before closing the door and locking it.

She wrings her hands together as her gaze drops to my mouth.

Is that what she wants?

A fuck?

Fine by me. I'm more than happy to oblige.

When I stalk closer, her eyes widen, and she takes a hasty step in retreat as if to keep the same amount of distance between us. I corral her toward the far wall until there's nowhere left to go. Her back hits the drywall with a thump, and her hands flatten against it. The tiny pulse in her throat flutters like the wings of a hummingbird.

"Hunter—"

"Did you really want to discuss our project?" I press my body against hers until she can feel the thickness of my erection jutting into her belly. She groans as I shackle her wrists with my hands before sliding them up the wall and above her head.

"No."

My lips curve into a smile. "Good, because I'm not interested in talking about it either."

Before she can say anything else, my mouth slants over hers, swallowing up the thoughts she has yet to voice. Even though I'm the aggressor, she's like an assault on my senses. Without any prodding, Skye opens under the firm pressure of my lips, and our tongues tangle.

With one hand, I hold both of her wrists captive before the other streaks down to my athletic shorts. Once my dick is free, I bunch the material of her skirt in my hand before tucking the hem into the waistband. I pull her panties to the side, and in one clean stroke, thrust into her tight sheath.

Fuuuuuck.

The moment I'm buried deep inside her warmth, I close my eyes and revel in the euphoria that fills me. No matter how often we screw, it's like this every time. Pure nirvana.

Just when I think it can't get better, her muscles contract around me, and it's the best damn feeling in the world. It's like her pussy is trying to choke the life out of my cock. I come with a groan, my hips pumping against her as I hold one of her legs around my waist so I can drive deeper.

How am I ever going to get enough of her?

Of this?

Stars cloud my vision as I lower my forehead, resting it against her shoulder until I can catch my breath. As much as I want to stay buried in her and enjoy the bliss washing over me, I know it won't last. As soon as the haze of our frenzied fucking clears, the reality of our situation will crash down around our heads. Reluctantly, I pull out of her heat and tuck my dick back into my shorts.

Skye bites her lip and refuses to meet my gaze. Her fingers shake as she pulls her panties in place and smooths out her skirt. Sadness fills her eyes until they are overflowing with it. For the first time since I grabbed her fingers and pulled her through the door, I wonder if I made a mistake. Maybe this wasn't what she wanted. Maybe she sought me out for a different reason altogether.

I open my mouth to say something. Anything that will change the trajectory of this relationship...if that's even possible. But nothing comes out.

A heavy swath of silence blankets us, becoming almost suffocating. Instead of clearing the air, I pick up my backpack and make a beeline for the exit. As I twist the lock and open the door, I hesitate, forcing myself to swing around and face her.

How can I leave when there is so much that needs to be hashed out?

I lick my lips as a sliver of uncertainty scuttles down my spine. Fuck, this is so much harder than I thought it would be.

"Skye—"

"I can't do this anymore," she blurts. Her voice grows stronger as the words spill from her lips. "I've given you all the closure you're going to get from me."

Stunned by her outburst, I snap my mouth shut. Thank fuck she beat me to the punch, and I didn't have the chance to pour my heart out. Can you imagine how much of a dumbass I would have felt like then?

Exactly how many times do I need to get burned by the same chick before I learn my lesson?

Want to know what that was?

A narrowly averted disaster.

I jerk my head into a tight nod before sauntering out of the room with my dignity intact.

This is for the best, I tell myself. *It needed to happen.*

But if that's true, why do I feel so fucking empty?

HUNTER

I rush through the doors of the emergency entrance at Claremont Medical before skidding to a halt at the front desk. An intimidating woman who looks more ripped than I am is manning the operation. It's entirely possible she's not a nurse at all, but security. My money is on her to take someone down to the ground if it becomes necessary.

"Excuse me," I say, capturing her attention from the computer screen she's staring at. "My brother was brought in about an hour ago."

When she glances up, her entire expression transforms as she goes all fangirl on me.

"Hunter Price!" Her hand flies to her nonexistent chest. "You're even more handsome in person than you are on TV."

I shift from one foot to the other. "Oh…well, thank you."

Before I can ask about my brother, she says, "My husband, Roger, is a huge fan! He's not going to believe it when I tell him that you were here tonight."

"Umm, right." I glance around for someone else who can help me, but the place is empty. "About that…my brother was in a car accident before being brought here. I'd really like to know how he's doing."

"You got it, sugar. I'll look it up right now." She peers at the computer screen and then at me. "Who's your brother?"

"Mason Price."

She taps away on the keyboard and clicks through a couple of screens. "Yup, he's here. They brought him in an ambulance, and he was admitted about an hour ago. Would you like me to take you back there?"

"Yes!" A tidal wave of relief washes over me. "That would be awesome." Mason can't be too banged up if I can go back and see him, right?

She pops to her feet with an impressive amount of grace. "Would you mind if I snap a picture? I'll be quick, and then we'll hustle you back there."

I plow a hand through my hair and paste a smile on my face. I'm used to this kind of behavior, but still...Mason was brought to the hospital by an ambulance. And while I know his condition isn't dire, I'd rather see for myself that my brother is okay.

When the hospital couldn't get a hold of me, they called the university, who relayed the information to the coaching staff, and they told me during the middle of practice. To hear that Mason was hurt was like a punch to the gut. All I could imagine was the one person I have in this world being ripped away from me.

Just like my parents.

What I need right now is to see Mason's face with my own eyes.

That's it.

But apparently, that's not going to happen until this woman gets her photo op.

"Sure, that's fine."

"I'm Donna, by the way." She snaps a few pictures of me alone before throwing an arm around my shoulder and taking a dozen more. Five minutes later, I'm gritting my teeth as she takes her sweet damn time scrolling through the snapshots and inspecting them. "The camera really loves you, doesn't it?" she muses.

Yup, aware of it. "So...about my brother?"

Her head jerks up as if she's forgotten the reason I'm standing here in the first place.

Seriously, lady?

"Right! Let's get you back there."

I follow Donna over to a set of double doors where she swipes the key card hanging on a lanyard around her neck. The doors swing open, and voilà, we're allowed entrance to the emergency department. She keeps up a steady chatter about the season and my prospects of going into the draft. I make a few noises, and that's enough to keep her yapping my damn ear off.

Donna is beginning to grate on my nerves.

Who knew the woman was going to be so chatty?

The hallway opens up into an expansive space with a desk in the middle of it. Small, curtained rooms surround the perimeter.

She makes a beeline for the room closest to us and yanks back the curtain without any preliminaries. The moment my gaze lands on the hospital bed my brother is stretched out on, all of the sickness and nerves churning at the bottom of my gut dissolve. I'm not much for religion, but I send up a quick prayer of thanks that Mason wasn't taken from me.

With a small flourish, Donna waves her hand in my brother's direction as if she's pulled off the David Copperfield magic trick of the century. "Well, here he is."

Instead of taking off, she shuffles her feet as if reluctant to part ways.

I force a smile. "Thanks again."

"No problem. Anything for you, Hunter Price. Make sure you stop by the front desk on your way out and say goodbye." She gives me a wink before leaving.

Sheesh.

Mason's lips lift into a smile. "Looks like someone has a fan club."

I roll my eyes.

My brother attempts to chuckle before wincing and clutching his ribs. "Damn that hurts."

I grab a chair and drag it over to the bed before dropping down on it. "What the hell happened?"

He huffs out a sigh and settles against the sterile white pillows that prop him up. "Got T-boned through the intersection. Some dumbass kid who was texting and driving. He didn't see the red light and blew right through it."

I drag a hand over my face. "Fuck."

"Yeah. Believe it or not, he walked away without a scratch. He's one lucky son of a bitch. Me? Not so much. I have two broken ribs."

My gaze skims over the length of him again. This could have turned out so much worse. Other than cracked ribs and a few stitches on his forehead, Mason appears all right.

A nurse bustles in and examines the clipboard at the end of the bed before checking his vitals.

I rise from the chair and stretch. "I'm going to grab something to eat. I'll be back in a few. You want anything?"

"Nah, I'm fine. I've got kind of a headache right now."

I glance at the nurse to see if this raises any red flags. When her expression remains neutral, I duck out of the room. After a couple of steps, I realize that I have no idea where the cafeteria or gift shop are located. All I want is something to drink and maybe a protein bar. I'm famished. My stomach is starting to eat away at its own lining.

Two employees later, I find a small coffee shop that sells actual food. Fuck a protein bar, I'm getting a sandwich. I have no idea how long Mason is going to be stuck here. It could be thirty minutes or a couple of hours.

Maybe I should pick up a few of them just to be safe.

I grab two ham and cheeses and a bottle of water before paying for everything at the cash register. Once the food has been bagged up, I swing around, ready to head back. Let's hope that finding my way to triage isn't nearly as confusing as getting here was. Had I been smart, I would have left behind a trail of breadcrumbs. It's entirely possible Mason will get released and his ribs will have healed up by the time I return.

Fuck...I still can't believe this happened. I'm grateful the damage wasn't more extensive. What the hell would I do without Mason? He's all I've got. Without him, I'd be alone in the world. My heart lurches at the idea. I blow out a steady breath and remind myself that he's fine. In a few months, his ribs will have healed up, the stitches on his forehead will have faded into a scar, and life as we know it will have gone on.

That's what I need to focus on.

With my bag in hand, I take a step and grind to a halt.

Dean Sinclair is standing in the hallway outside of the coffee shop, staring down at the phone in his hand. It's been years since we've seen each other. He looks thinner than I remember.

Uncertain if I should say hello, I hesitate. Brandi was friendly enough when I saw her a month ago, but I'm not sure if I would get the same warm reception from Dean. Although, he has no reason to be pissed off at me. His daughter is the one who walked away.

Now…if Skye happened to mention our recent involvement, that would make it an altogether different scenario. Dean would definitely kick my ass, and I can't say I'd blame him for it. In hindsight, I'm not proud of my behavior.

Maybe it would be better if I got the hell out of here and saved us both from an awkward conversation. A wave of sadness washes over me. After my parents died, Dean took me under his wing and made sure I was all right. That's one of the reasons it hurt so much when Skye broke up with me. I didn't just lose a girlfriend, but her family as well.

Decision made, I head into the hallway, ready to sidestep him.

"Hunter?"

Well, damn.

I stop as my gaze coasts over him. With his head tipped down, I'd noticed the weight loss, but it's more pronounced now that I've gotten a good look at his face. He was always so robust and larger than life. A prickle of unease flares to life in my gut.

"Hey, Mr. Sinclair." I step forward and shake his hand. "How are you doing?"

His lips curve into a ghost of a smile that doesn't quite reach his eyes. "Can't complain. How's football going?"

"The season is off to a good start. We're five and one." I notice the gauze-covered tape on his arm and wonder what he's doing at the hospital. Is it a simple blood draw or more than that?

"Yeah, I've been watching." He glances at my leg. "How's the knee feeling? I heard about the ACL injury last season. That was a tough break."

I shrug and gloss over the gory details. "It's as good as new. The surgeon was one of the best in the country, so I'm confident there won't be issues down the road."

"That's great news. I was concerned when I heard about the injury. I thought about reaching out." He shrugs. We both know why he didn't. "You must be excited about the draft after missing out last year."

"I am. I'm focused on getting through the next couple of months and keeping my knee healthy."

He nods. "Looks like you've got everything lined up, Hunter. I always knew you'd get there. We're all real proud of you."

"Thanks." My chest expands and I get a little choked up. The past six years have been a tough road. "I've always appreciated your support."

Silence settles over us as I shift my weight and point to the bandage. "Are you here getting your blood drawn?"

Dean glances at his arm. "Yup. I started a new chemo treatment about a month ago, and they're checking the numbers."

"Chemo?" I echo with disbelief.

Dean has cancer?

When the hell did that happen?

"Yeah, I was diagnosed with colon cancer last year."

"Oh." My mind spins, and I try to grasp on to a coherent thought. But it's impossible. *Dean has cancer.* "I'm sorry to hear that, Mr. Sinclair."

He shrugs as if there's nothing more to say on the topic.

It hits me like a ton of bricks that this is the reason Skye transferred to CU. She never said a damn word about it, and I didn't bother to dig deeper and ask questions. I was too busy being pissed off that she'd turned up again when I had so much on the line. It never occurred to me there might be a legit reason for her to relocate.

I scrub a hand over my face. "Do you mind me asking what stage the cancer is in?"

"Four."

"Shit." The word is out of my mouth before I can stop it.

A humorless chuckle escapes from Dean's lips. "That pretty much sums it up, but we're fighting it the best we can. If this drug doesn't give us the results we're looking for, there's a new trial opening up in a month or so, and that one might be a possibility. It's all a waiting game."

Dean has cancer.

"How is Skye taking it?"

He looks away as emotion swims in his eyes. He's always had a real soft spot for his daughter. "She's handling it about as well as can be expected. She mentioned withdrawing for the semester, but I don't want her to put her life on hold." His gaze hardens as it settles on mine. "She's had a rough couple of years."

I straighten to my full height as my heart skips a beat. "What do you mean by that?"

What the hell has been so hard? Dumping my ass and moving away?

He presses his lips together before muttering, "You know what? Never mind."

His behavior…it's odd. I'm not quite sure what to make of it.

"What's going on with Skye?" The hair at the back of my neck prickles, and I lift my hand to rub it. He's keeping information from me, and I need to know what it is.

"I'm sorry. It's not my place to get involved."

"I don't understand what you're talking about—involved in what?" My voice escalates, and a few people glance our way.

Instead of answering the question, Dean claps me on the shoulder. "It was great running into you, Hunter. I hope everything turns out the way you want it to." Then he steps around me and heads for the exit.

I swing around and stare after him in shock.

He can't leave me hanging like this.

What the hell was he talking about?

I take a few strides in his direction before reaching out to grab his arm. As my fingers sink into bone, I loosen my grip, not wanting to cause him any pain.

"Mr. Sinclair, what's going on?"

"Look, I shouldn't have said anything." His voice grows agitated. "It's not my place."

"What does that even mean? *Not your place?* If something is going on with Skye, I want to know about it." Neither of us mentions that I'm no longer her boyfriend, and when it comes down to it, I have no right to any information regarding her welfare.

He pauses as his gaze searches mine. "You need to have a conversation with your brother."

Mason?

I jerk back. "What does Mason have to do with this?"

"Just ask him."

"What exactly am I supposed to ask?" I shake my head as frustration gathers inside me.

Ignoring my question, he says, "I'm sorry, Hunter. I really have to go. Brandi's waiting in the car for me. Take care and good luck." With that, he slips out of my fingers.

Even after he disappears through the door and into the fresh air, I stare after him in bewilderment. It was like he was talking in riddles. What the hell does any of it mean?

I'm shaken from those thoughts by a tap on my arm.

"You're Hunter Price, right?"

I force myself out of those thoughts and hoist a smile. "Yup." Everything is about image these days. I already have one strike against me with my injury; I don't need another.

"Can I get a quick photo with you?" the woman asks.

"Sure. No problem." I keep my expression cemented in place as she snaps a few pictures, but my mind continues to spiral. Is it possible the medication was messing with Dean's head? I mean...that can happen, right? Some of those drugs are really powerful and have a lot of side effects.

As I walk through the corridors, the conversation plays over in my head as if it's on a constant loop. I'm tempted to chalk it up to mental confusion, but Skye's father hadn't seemed out of it. He'd looked thinner, tired, but his mind had been sharp. There was nothing about our interaction that made me feel like he was losing it.

By the time I make it back to the emergency room, I'm no closer to finding an answer than I was before. Why would he drag Mason into this? Nothing about our conversation had made sense. Instead of continuing to dwell on it, I decide to put the whole thing out of my head. I have enough to worry about without looking for problems where none exist.

"Hey, good news," Mason says as I draw back the curtain. "They're going to release me in about an hour. They want to hold on to me for a bit longer and make sure I don't have a concussion, but it all looks good."

"That's awesome." I set the paper bag from the coffee shop on the small table next to the bed.

"Damn right it is." He closes his eyes and settles against the pillow. "I want to get the hell out of here."

"I know. Did they give you anything for the headache?"

"Yup. Two Tylenol that will end up costing me a couple of hundred bucks."

I snort. He's right about that.

"You were gone for a while. Everything good?"

"Yeah, it's fine." I lift my shoulder into a shrug. "It took a while to find the coffee shop. This place is like a maze." The conversation with Dean flashes through my head. What's the point of mentioning it? It was all a bunch of nonsense. Yet the words are out of my mouth before I can stop them. "I ran into Dean Sinclair."

Mason cracks open his eyes and rolls his head toward me. "Oh? What was he doing here?"

I drag a hand through my hair as another wave of disbelief washes over me. "He was diagnosed with cancer last year."

My brother's expression softens. "That sucks."

"It really does." I'm still blown away that Skye didn't mention anything about it. I know things have been rocky between us, but still…

I would have liked to know what was going on with her father. Maybe if she'd told me, I wouldn't have been such a dick.

"Is it bad?" my brother asks, interrupting my thoughts.

"Stage four."

He blows out a breath. "Fuck."

I drop onto the chair and lace my fingers together in front of me before staring at them. "That was my reaction, too."

"Guess that would be the reason Skye transferred to Claremont."

I remain silent as Mason shifts against the pillow, trying to get comfortable. "I'm sorry about her father, but I'm glad she didn't come back for you."

Bewildered by the comment, my head jerks up. "Jeez, Mase, that's a shitty thing to say."

He shrugs as his gaze skitters away. "Yeah, but it's the truth."

"You know, there was a time when you actually liked her, and we all had fun together. What changed?"

"Life," he snaps before closing his eyes and huffing out a breath. "That's what. Do we really have to talk about this now? My head is fucking killing me. Skye Sinclair is the last person I want to think about. That girl is part of your past. Leave her where she belongs."

"And what if she's not?" It's the one question that has been plaguing me since she returned. No matter how hard I've tried, I haven't been able to stop thinking about her.

Mason's eyes spring wide before narrowing. "What the hell does that mean?"

"There's a lot of history between us. Leaving her in the past isn't as easy as you seem to think it is. And you know what?" I straighten my shoulders before admitting, "Maybe I don't want to."

"It's been three years, bro. You've both moved on." He sits up and winces before falling against the pillows. "Are you forgetting about the way she dumped your ass? You were together for almost four years, and she left you behind without a second thought."

I press my lips into a tight line. He's not wrong. That's *exactly* how it went down. The pain of it still radiates beneath the surface. I've been trying to tell myself for years that it didn't matter anymore. I was over it. *Over her.* Only now am I able to admit that it's not the truth. Wanting to be over someone doesn't necessarily mean that you are.

I drag a hand over my face and stew in the chair I'm sitting on. Dean's words continue to reverberate throughout my brain. Mason's hatred for Skye churns there as well. None of it makes sense.

"The best thing that girl ever did for you was leave," Mason grumbles.

Unable to sit still, I spring to my feet. "You know that's not true. I loved her." I pause before pushing out the rest. "And she loved me." No matter how it ended between us, Skye loved me. I refuse to believe any differently. What we had was real.

"Yeah, well…apparently not. Get over it and move the fuck on. I'm tired of talking about her."

Agitation pounds through me, and I find myself pacing the tight space. It only takes a few strides, and I'm spinning around, moving in the opposite direction. "She did. I know she did."

Why is he doing this? It's as if he's deliberately trying to drive the knife deeper.

I spin toward him and stop. "Why do you have such a problem with Skye?"

"As long as she stays away from you, I don't have any problems with her."

The fury brewing in his eyes bewilders me. I've never understood it.

"She was nothing more than a distraction," he mutters.

"That's not true." Skye was my everything, and he damn well knows it.

After our parents died, Mason's attitude about her did a complete one-eighty. He bitched about the amount of time we spent together. He couldn't understand why I wanted to be tied down to one girl.

He'd make sly little comments that were meant to stir up trouble. For the most part, I blew off his grumblings, but maybe there was more to them than I'd assumed.

Dean's words force themselves to the forefront of my brain.

Ask your brother.

"Did you have something to do with Skye breaking up with me?"

Guilt flickers across Mason's face before it disappears, and he laughs off the question. "Give me a damn break. I really hope you're not being serious."

Why else would Dean tell me to ask Mason?

What other explanation could there be?

"Just tell me that you had nothing to do with her leaving." Maybe this isn't the time or place for this conversation, but I need to hear him confirm it.

"Bro, are you sure you're not the one who cracked your head? You're not making a damn bit of sense."

Maybe I'm not, but it doesn't escape me that he hasn't denied the accusation.

Say the fucking words. That's all he needs to do. Then we can move on.

My gaze stays pinned to his as I step closer to the bed. "We've always promised each other that we would never lie. Do you remember that?"

Mason presses his lips together and remains silent. It's enough to jack with my nerves.

"Tell me the truth, Mase," I plead. My tongue darts out to moisten my lips. "Tell me that you had nothing to do with Skye taking off after graduation."

His gaze slides away from mine as he mumbles, "I'm fucking exhausted, Hunt. Can we do this another time?"

"No."

Storm clouds gather in his eyes. "What does it matter? It happened years ago. It's over and done with. You need to move on."

He's not denying it.

"Why would you do that?" I shake my head in disbelief. It can't be true. Yet...all he's done is dance around the question. "You knew how much I loved her." My voice continues to escalate. "I wanted to marry that girl!"

His upper lip curls with disdain. "You were too damn young to be making that kind of decision. She was holding you back from reaching your full potential. Who knows if you would be where you are today if she hadn't left town!"

"Dammit!" I plow my hands through my hair. "You had no right to interfere in my life!"

Mason pokers up on the bed and winces before stabbing a finger in my direction. "I had every fucking right! Mom and Dad died, and I was the one left in charge! I was the one who had to make all the decisions! Your head was buried so far up that girl's ass. It was ridiculous, and she needed to go." He spreads his arms wide and grunts as pain flashes across his face. "You should be thanking me right now, not giving me shit about some chick from high school."

This can't be happening.

It's not possible.

I open my mouth to blast him, but nothing comes out. There are no words for the betrayal I feel. The sight of Mason makes me sick to my stomach. There's no way I can stay here. If I do, I'll end up saying something I might regret.

When I pull back the curtain, he says, "Hey! Where are you going?" For the first time since we started this conversation, fear creeps into his voice.

I don't bother to answer.

"Hunt!" he calls out desperately. "They're going to release me soon, and I need a ride home."

"Figure it out on your own," I call over my shoulder, leaving the room behind.

It's like my whole goddamn world has caved in around me, and I'm trapped beneath the rubble.

How could Mason betray me like this?

How could he go behind my back and get rid of the one person who meant the most to me?

HUNTER

I push my legs harder until the burn consumes me. Slowly it spreads from my legs, to my torso, to my chest before infecting my entire body like a virus. It drowns out the loud buzzing in my head. The only problem is that it's not a long-term solution. The moment I stop, it all comes rushing back at me, threatening to suck me under.

It's been days since I discovered the truth, and I'm still as pissed off as I was at the hospital. It never occurred to me that Mason could be behind our breakup.

Why the hell would I suspect that was a possibility?

He knew how much I loved her. It took months for me to get over the loss. That summer sucked ass. I moped around the entire time, locking myself in my room. How ironic that it was Mason who consoled me. He sat beside me, saw the pain that was eating me alive, and said nothing.

How could he do that?

How could he be so fucking coldhearted?

He's been calling and texting nonstop, but I can't bring myself to pick up the phone. I have nothing to say to him. There is no forgiveness in my heart.

And then there's Skye. Why didn't she tell me what was going on? Why did she go along with it and leave?

That's the part that doesn't make sense.

How much could she have loved me if she was willing to walk away without a fight?

By the time I race around the corner and the ocean comes into view, I know exactly where I've been headed this entire time. It's the place where Skye and I made so many memories in high school. The sun peeks over the horizon as I draw closer to the water. Reds and pinks have been splashed across the eastern sky.

Normally, these morning runs calm me from the inside out. I'm able to center myself and get my Zen on. The traffic is light, and there aren't a lot of people out and about. I'll cross paths with a few other joggers or early risers out walking their dogs. That's the extent of it. But none of that matters today because there is no peace to be found. My head continues to swim, and my gut churns.

Even before my gaze sweeps across the beach, I know she'll be there. A solitary figure staring out at the rolling waves as they crash against the shore.

The last thing I should do is stop. I'm a fucking mess inside. There are too many emotions festering beneath the surface. It's all raw and ugly.

My pace slows, and I find myself changing course.

For the past couple of days, I've been able to keep my brain occupied with school, practice, and working out. I'm so mentally and physically exhausted by the end of the night that I fall into bed and crash. But Skye is never far from my mind.

At this point, I'm not even sure if it's possible for us to move forward in any kind of tangible way. It feels as if too much time has slipped by. Too much has happened between us. I've lashed out and hurt her when she was at her most vulnerable.

Skye's huddled body tenses as I drop down onto the sand beside her. Instead of acknowledging my presence, she ignores me. Her gaze stays fixated on some point in the distance.

Our last interaction crashes unexpectedly through my head, and I wince, feeling like an asshole. There hadn't been many words between us, just sex. A frenzied coupling that left me unfulfilled and empty. Every interaction between us had been like that. As much as I'd wanted her, I had needed to keep my distance more. It had been about protecting myself so that I wouldn't get hurt again.

If I'm being completely honest, I had wanted to punish her for walking away. Not once had it occurred to me that she might have been in pain as well.

What a fucking mess.

"I can't do this with you, Hunter," Skye says wearily. "Not right now."

She angles her head just enough for her gaze to settle on mine. So much heartbreak swims in her green depths that she is practically drowning in it. Her pain is like a punch to my gut. Only now, when it's too late, am I able to fit the pieces together and make sense of the puzzle I've been staring at for the past two months.

When I remain silent, she adds, "There's too much going on."

Thick emotion swells in my chest and threatens to swallow me whole. At that moment, all I want to do is wrap her up in my arms and tell her that everything will be all right. Except I don't know if that's true, and there's no way she would welcome my comfort. Not after the way I've treated her.

"I ran into your dad." I pause as her eyes become shuttered. "I know about the cancer."

Emotion moves across her face in a wave. Surprise, then sadness. "He told you?"

"Yeah. I would have preferred to hear it from you instead."

Her mouth drops open as she swings toward me. We stare for a painful heartbeat before laughter falls from her lips. Great big belly guffaws that leave me confused. "Are you kidding me? Why the hell would I tell you anything?" As unexpectedly as it started, it abruptly dies away, and her green gaze spits fire. "Since when does being fuck buddies make us friends?" Slowly, she shakes her head. "News flash— it doesn't."

My shoulders slump under the weight of her words. "Fine, you're right," I mutter, scooping up a handful of sand. Tiny grains fall through the cracks between my fingers. "No matter what's happened between us, I still care about you and your family."

She snorts. "I'd really hate to see how you treat people you don't care about."

Ouch. Direct hit. But it's one that I deserve.

"Look, I—"

"I don't need your sympathy," she snaps. "I came here to be alone. So, if you wouldn't mind," she makes a shooing gesture with her hand, "go."

There has to be a way for me to rectify the situation. "Skye—"

"*No!* I'm serious." She waggles a finger between us. "There's no need for any of this. We're not friends. As far as I'm concerned, we're *nothing.* Ever since I returned, all you've wanted to do is hurt me, and you know what?" Her voice falters as she pushes on. "You've accomplished your goal. You should feel really proud of yourself. Now it's time to move on and leave me be."

The accusation in her voice leaves me flinching. "I'm sorry."

She drags her fingers through the sand and jerks her shoulders into a shrug. "It doesn't matter anymore."

"Yes, it does." Desperation fills me. I'm not sure what kind of reaction I was expecting from her, but it wasn't this ambivalence. It's as though she's too exhausted to even give a damn.

"Why?" she asks. "Why does it matter?"

"Because I know Mason was behind our breakup."

That statement is met with silence. Long moments tick by as my nerves stretch taut. For the second time in a matter of minutes, I've managed to surprise her.

"Your brother told you what he did?" she asks carefully.

"Not in so many words, but he sure as hell didn't deny it. But the real question is—why did you go along with it? Why didn't *you* tell me what was going on?"

With a puff of breath, she draws her knees to her chest before resting her chin on them. Waves crash against the shore, and the breeze blows through our hair. A response doesn't seem forthcoming.

As I turn restless, she says, "I didn't want to stand in your way." Her voice fills with emotion. "You'd already lost so much."

"Do you realize that when you left, you took away everything that mattered to me? You had no right to make that decision on your own. You walked away without giving me a choice in the matter."

She blinks back the wetness as it fills her eyes. "At the time, I did what I thought was best. It wasn't an easy decision." She turns her head until our gazes are able to fasten. "And now look, you're so close to having everything you've ever wanted."

"What I wanted," I snap, "was *you!*" How does she not understand that?

Her body deflates, and her voice drops. "It's over with, Hunter. There's no way for us to go back and rewrite the chapters of our story, no matter how much we might want to."

"You're right, but we can give ourselves a different ending."

"I'm not sure that's possible." She rises and dusts off her shorts.

How can she leave when so much needs to be said?

I scramble to my feet as well. "Skye—"

"You know what?" A little bit of her weariness falls away. "It's a relief that you finally know the truth. Leaving you was the hardest thing I ever had to do, but I did it. I loved you enough to let you go. As far as moving forward," she shakes her head, "I can't do that with you. There's too much going on in my life for me to deal with anything more. I'm barely holding on as it is." When her voice thickens, she pauses. Only after she's gotten her emotions under control does she continue. "Can you understand that?"

My shoulders collapse as the fight in me drains away. What else is there for me to do? Instead of arguing and trying to wear her down, I jerk my head into a nod.

I've hurt Skye enough. The last thing I want to do is cause further damage.

SKYE

Even though I tell myself that Dad is getting better—or at the very least, staying the same—deep down, I know the disease is getting progressively worse. The chemo makes him sick and he continues to shed weight. It's painful to watch. There's nothing I can do to make it better. I've never felt this powerless in my life. It seems like we're always waiting for the next test results and what it will tell us. We're always hopeful that it will be positive and let down when it turns out to be more bad news. The numbers continue to steadily creep up. The doctors want to give it more time in hopes that the medicine will finally do what it's supposed to. But that hasn't happened. And there's no guarantee it will.

Not a day goes by when I don't pop over for a visit. I try to bring a smoothie or a new protein cookie for him to try. Anything with nutritional value I can get in him feels like a small victory in this battle being waged against cancer.

Today I've brought chicken noodle soup. Instead of knocking on the front door like I usually do, I walk in. If I'm lucky, I can time my visits when Brandi is out doing whatever the hell it is that Brandi does. Plus, I enjoy having Dad to myself. Sometimes, we talk about my grandparents and what his childhood was like growing up in Chicago.

I've started to jot down names and dates so I can remember these family stories later on.

I close the door and yelp in surprise when I find Brandi standing silently in the foyer. She's wearing yoga pants and a gray T-shirt, which is odd. I've noticed wife number three likes to glam it up, even when she's hanging out at home.

"Brandi!" My hand flies to my chest. "You scared me!"

"Sorry." Her lips barely lift. "I heard the door open and wasn't sure who it was."

It's only after I hold up the container of chicken noodle soup that I get a good look at my stepmother. She's not wearing a drop of makeup, and her face is splotchy as if she's been crying.

The soup is instantly forgotten as panic takes hold. "What's going on?"

Brandi compresses her lips into a thin line and gives me a quick head shake as tears flood her eyes. She attempts to blink back the wetness before glancing away as a shuddering breath escapes from her lips.

"Where's Dad?" Dread snakes through me like adrenalin. It's enough to weaken my knees.

She points toward the family room before turning away and climbing the stairs to the second floor. I watch as she disappears from sight. The soft sound of their bedroom door closing resonates through the eerily silent house.

Unsure what to do, I stand rooted in the entryway. My heart thumps painfully against my breast, and I raise my hand, rubbing gently at the spot that now aches. The room shrinks until the walls feel as though they are pressing in on me. My chest tightens, and sucking in full breaths becomes impossible. I'm tempted to sink to the floor and close my eyes to get my bearings.

Is this what a panic attack feels like?

The voice inside my head urges me to leave. To walk out the door so I don't have to hear any more bad news. But I can't do that. I have to pull it together. Dad needs me.

I suck in a shaky breath before slowly exhaling it. Then I force one foot in front of the other. Silently, I count the steps as I go. It takes exactly sixty steps for me to reach the family room, where I find Dad parked in his favorite recliner. It's a dark brown corduroy and ugly as sin, but he loves it. It's the one piece of furniture Brandi was unable to purge from his former life. It's the only thing that foils her perfect decorating scheme. For obvious reasons, I love it.

My footsteps stutter as I take him in. Even though I was here yesterday, he seems both thinner and paler. How can someone's physical appearance deteriorate so rapidly? It doesn't make sense.

I blink back the tears, unwilling to let them fall. I'm afraid that once they start sliding down my face, it'll be impossible to stop them.

"It's a line drive to left field!"

The baseball announcer's voice from the TV cuts through my thoughts. It takes a moment for me to realize that he's watching the game from last night on the DVR. Dad has been a die-hard Cubs fan since he was a kid. He's ecstatic that his favorite team has made it to the playoffs this year. He's been waiting a long time for this.

I clear the emotion from my throat, and Dad's gaze cuts to mine.

A small smile tilts the edges of his lips. "Hey, kiddo." He glances at the paper bag in my hand. "What do you got there?"

I look down in surprise, having forgotten about it. "Oh, um, soup. Do you want some?"

With a grimace, he shakes his head. "Not right now. Brandi forced me to drink a protein shake, and it's not sitting well. But thanks."

"No problem." I point toward the kitchen before heading in that direction. "I'll put it on the counter. Maybe later, you'll want to give it a try." With robotic steps, I walk to the next room and set the bag on the marble island next to Dad's pill bottles. There must be a dozen of them. He has a medication box that can hold enough pills for seven days, and he keeps the container next to his recliner for easy access. I've seen him take a small handful at one time. No wonder his stomach is always upset. Maybe the chemo destroys the cancer, but it kills everything else, too, including his appetite.

Dad clicks off the television as I settle on the couch across from him.

Unsure where to start, I say carefully, "I saw Brandi when I came in. She seemed upset." I search his face. As much as I'm afraid to ask, I need to know. "What's going on?"

A puff of air slides from his lips as he glances away. The silence that stretches between us makes my nerves dance more frantically.

"The doctor is taking me off this medicine." He stares out the window before his gaze returns to mine. "The numbers aren't getting better."

I swallow past the lump of nausea that has wedged itself in my throat. That's a good thing, right? Now they can try something else. Something that won't make him so sick all the time. "Okay. What's next?"

One beat passes.

Then another.

I shift on the couch as unease fills me.

"There isn't anything else left, kiddo. At this point, we've exhausted all of the viable studies. The one Dr. Waterman thought I might qualify for isn't taking new patients."

I shake my head. No, that can't be right. "But—"

"The numbers are too high, and nothing has helped to lower them."

Tears sting my eyes. "But you said there were other treatments you could try. New drugs get approved by the FDA every day. Maybe there are other experimental studies you can participate in. You can't give up, Dad!" My voice rises, turning panicky. "You can't do that!"

His shoulders fall as wetness shines in his eyes. "I'm sorry, Skye. I know this is difficult to hear, but I've been fighting this disease for the past year, and I'm tired. The doctors have done everything they can."

"I don't understand…" I shake my head. "You're not going to take anything? You're just going to let it get worse?"

"That's what's happening anyway. The chemo isn't knocking out the cancer the way it did in the beginning, and it's continued to spread. I'm riddled with it."

"But Dad—"

"I have two to six months left. I don't want to spend the rest of my time sleeping and feeling sick to my stomach. I want to make every day count, and I can't do that on chemo." He waves a hand, his face filling with disgust. "There's no quality of life on this shit. Haven't you seen that for yourself?"

Unable to hold his gaze, I stare sightlessly out the family room window overlooking the wooded backyard. The sky is a deep cornflower blue, and the sun peeks out from behind a few clouds. How can it look picture perfect outside when my world has been blown to bits?

"I don't want you to *die*," I whisper. My voice catches on the last word, and I burst into noisy tears. I've been preparing myself for this moment, but I don't feel anywhere near ready to accept it.

I curl up on the couch in a tight ball as all of the anxiety, grief, and sadness I've kept bottled up inside is released in a wild torrent of emotion. When I finally manage to pry open my eyes, Dad is beside me, brushing the hair away from my face with gentle fingers. I can't remember the last time he did that.

Wetness fills his eyes, and his voice becomes thick with unspent emotion. This is the closest I've seen him come to crying, and it breaks my heart. "I don't want to die either, but there's not a choice in the matter. I had a feeling this was the way things were headed, and I've tried to make peace with it. You need to do the same."

Is that a joke?

"How am I supposed to do that? How can you even ask that of me?"

He strokes his hand rhythmically over my hair, and I focus on that instead of this harsh new reality. "You have to know that if there were anything else I could do to change the outcome, I would." He releases a shaky breath. "The prognosis was never good. We knew this wasn't a battle I was going to win. I wanted more time, and that's what I was given, but we've come to the point when the treatment is doing more damage than good. I can't live like this anymore."

"I really thought we'd find something that would send you into remission."

"Everyone dies, kiddo," he says quietly. "It's just a matter of when."

"That doesn't make me feel better!" I wail as tears course down my cheeks.

"I know, but it's the truth."

"Well, the truth sucks."

"I'm not saying that it doesn't, but it is what it is. And fighting it, refusing to accept it, won't change the result. As difficult as the situation is, I need you to be strong." He searches my eyes. "Can you do that for me?"

"No." I shake my head frantically. "I can't be strong. Not about this. Not when I'm going to lose you." I want to sob out my pain until all the tears inside me run dry, and even then, I don't know how anything will ever be all right again.

He kisses the top of my head and whispers, "You're the strongest person I know, Skye. You're going to get through this. Please, kiddo, let's enjoy the time I have left, okay?"

I press my lips together and swipe at my eyes.

He's asking for the impossible, but what choice do I have?

I want to be as strong as he believes I am, but I'm not sure I have that kind of strength in me.

I thought saying goodbye to Hunter was the hardest thing I'd ever have to do, but I was wrong. Saying goodbye to my father will be.

HUNTER

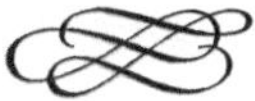

I slide onto my seat for health and throw a quick glance over my shoulder only to find Skye's desk vacant. This is the second time this week she's been absent.

Where the hell is she?

In the pit of my gut, I know something is wrong. It's not like her to blow off class for any reason. Even when we were in high school, and I'd try to persuade her to skip class, she would refuse.

I've shot her a few texts, but it's been stereo silence from her end. And yeah, I get it. Skye wants me to leave her alone, but how can I do that when I'm being eaten up by concern? She might not want me to care, but I still do. I've just done a shit job of showing her that.

Midway through class, I catch Jaxon's gaze and jerk my head toward the unoccupied seat next to him. He shrugs and looks away, purposely avoiding my eyes. Jax knows exactly what's going on, but he isn't going to tell me. I've been a douche, and we both know it.

Bennet drones on, and I find myself clock-watching, which makes this class feel like it's never going to end. Once Dr. B dismisses us for the day, I pack up my shit and join the flow of students fleeing the classroom. Even though I'm quick, Jax is faster. I have to jog to catch up to him, weaving my way through the herd in the hallway.

"Hey," I say, pulling up alongside him.

He gives me a sidelong look but doesn't stop walking. "What's up, Price?"

The tension simmering beneath the surface of our friendship ratchets up a couple of notches. There's no longer any easy camaraderie between us.

Instead of prolonging the moment, I do us both a favor and cut to the chase. It's obvious neither one of us wants to have this conversation. "What's going on with Skye?" When he remains silent, I grow impatient. "Is she sick or something?"

"Dunno." He tosses a glance my way. "And if something *were* going on, it wouldn't be any of your damn business. So just stay out of it."

It pisses me off that Jax is playing games. I lay a hand on his shoulder and jerk his body toward mine. We skid to a halt in the middle of the hall. People grumble and funnel around us.

"Just tell me where she is." I pause before admitting, "I'm worried about her."

"Seriously?" Jax snorts. "You've been a complete dick since she came back. And now you're concerned?" He shakes his head before knocking my hand off his shoulder. "Sorry, bro, I'm not buying it. I've already warned you to leave Skye alone. You're the last person she needs to deal with."

"Not that it's any of your business, but everything's different now. She didn't breakup with me because she wanted to. She dumped me because of Mason."

Jaxon steps closer, invading my personal space before driving a finger into my chest. "You know what? I don't give a shit why she broke up with you. That was Skye's choice to make. Whether Mason forced her hand or not, at the end of the day, she chose to walk away. Instead of respecting that decision and leaving her alone, you made her life hell the first opportunity you got. The way you acted was complete bullshit, and we both know it." Disgust fills his face. "I'm disappointed in you, Price. I really thought you were better than that."

Well, fuck me.

I swallow down the thick lump of embarrassment that has lodged itself in the middle of my throat and admit, "You're right." That's the thing about clarity. It can be a real bitch. It's painful to take a hard look at your own behavior and realize that you've fucked it up good. "I shouldn't have messed with Skye. I should have let our past go and moved on."

Jax watches me silently as if he's not quite sure he can believe me.

If I'm going to be honest, I might as well bare my whole fucking soul. What do I have to lose at this point? "I love her, Jax. I always have. There are no excuses for my behavior, and you're right to call me out on it, but I'm concerned. I just want to know that she's all right. That's it."

Silence settles around us, and I wonder if he'll say anything more.

"I swear to God, Price," he grumbles, watching me through narrowed eyes, "you better not make me regret this. I give zero fucks if you're my QB." Jax huffs out a breath before admitting, "She's at the townhouse. Her dad isn't doing well. You don't need to worry about her falling behind in class. She already emailed Bennet to let her know what was going on, and I've been taking notes for her."

Dean had looked pretty bad when I ran into him at the hospital. If it's gotten worse…

"I know about the cancer," I say.

Jax's shoulders fall, and sorrow fills his voice. "I guess the chemo isn't working, and they've decided to stop treatment."

I drag a hand over my face. Skye must feel as if her legs have been knocked out from underneath her. Even though she doesn't have any love loss for Brandi, that hasn't stopped her from having a close relationship with Dean.

I almost forget about Jax until his heavy hand lands on my shoulder. "I'm serious, dude. You mess with her, and I'll come for you."

"I know you will." My lips quirk at the corners. "Thanks for telling me."

He jerks his head into a nod and takes off, leaving me alone in the crowded hallway.

Two months ago, I let all the hurt and anger that had been festering beneath the surface get in the way of my better judgment. For all I know, it's too late to reverse the damage I've inflicted. But none of that matters anymore. What Skye needs now is my friendship and support. She's the one who helped me through one of the most brutal times in my life, and I need to return the favor. Once an idea takes root, I head to my house and pick up my car. Then I drive over to Skye's townhouse and rap my knuckles against the door.

One minute slowly ticks into two without an answer. So I knock again and don't stop. My knuckles hit the wood over and over again until they feel bruised and tender.

When I don't think I can stand another moment, the door flies open, and Skye stands before me in a yellow tank top and navy sleep shorts. Her hair is a wild tangle around her head, and her eyes are red and puffy from crying. She's an absolute mess, but she's the most beautiful girl I've ever laid eyes on.

"Hunter, what are you doing here?" She looks less than thrilled by my presence.

"I wanted to make sure that you were all right." My voice drops. "Jax told me about your dad. I'm sorry."

Fresh tears gather in her eyes, and my heart cracks wide open. This girl has always been my weakness. All I want to do is pull her into my arms and comfort her, but before I can do that, she slams the door in my face. I wedge my foot between the wood and the frame, and it bounces off my athletic shoe.

Skye stumbles back a step as I push the door open. "I don't know what you think you're doing, but you need to leave!"

I shake my head and hold my ground. "I'm not going anywhere."

With a grunt of anger, she flies forward and throws all her weight against the door, but her strength is no match for mine. It doesn't take much to overpower her.

Even though Skye must know this battle is futile, it doesn't stop her from trying with all her might. "Go away and leave me alone," she growls.

"I'm sorry, I can't do that." She may not want me, but she needs me. Somehow, I have to do the impossible and prove that I won't hurt her again.

When her strength wanes, she lets go with a soft cry, and the door flies open, bouncing off the rubber stopper.

Skye screws her eyes shut as if it's possible to block out the world. Or maybe just me. "Please, Hunter, I can't do this with you right now." A pathetic sob breaks free. "*I just can't.*"

"I know." I step inside the townhouse and quietly close the door behind me. "I'm sorry for what you're going through. All I want to do is help." I pause for a beat. "Can you let me do that?"

She shakes her head furiously as tears leak from the corners of her eyes before rolling down her face. "I want to be alone."

All it takes is one long-legged stride for me to swallow up the distance that separates us. I reach out and cup her cheeks in the palm of my hands before tipping her face upward. Teardrops hang off her lashes as she glares. "Get dressed. We're going out."

Renewed fire flashes in her eyes as she shakes her head. "I'm not going anywhere with you. I'm tired. I want to sleep." She points at the entryway. "Leave."

"Sorry, can't do that." I turn my wrist and glance at my sports watch. "You've got two minutes to change. Otherwise, I'll carry you out the way you are." I shrug. "Either way, you're coming with me."

Skye bristles with irritation before batting my hands away. "I told you already, I'm not going anywhere but back to bed."

I look at my watch again before flicking my gaze to hers. "You've already pissed away one minute. Do you want to waste any more?"

"You need to go!" When I don't leave, she stomps her bare foot. "I'm serious! You can't come in here and order me—"

"Time's up."

"What? No!"

Ignoring her protests, I drop my shoulder and wrap my arms around her waist. She lands against my body with a soft grunt. I'm trying to be as gentle as I can, but she's fighting me every step of the way. Skye is in so much pain that she can't see straight. Her fists pound against my lower back as she calls me every dirty word she's ever heard. I'm almost impressed with the foul language that rolls off her tongue.

When she's secured over my shoulder, I swing around and head for the door.

"This is kidnapping!" she screeches at the top of her lungs. "I'm going to call the police and then you're going to get it! They arrest people for shit like this!"

"How are you going to do that without a phone?"

"You're a real bastard, you know that?" she yells, battering me with her fists.

"Yup, totally aware of the character flaw. But I'm going to make it up to you."

"By kidnapping me? Are you out of your mind?"

I mull over the question. "I don't think so, but anything's possible."

"I hate you, Hunter. I really do."

Her words are like poisonous darts against my skin. As much as they hurt, I deserve them and so much more. Sorrow fills me until it's almost too much to bear.

"No, you don't," I say softly. "Your heart is breaking. Your dad is sick, and he isn't going to get better." I pause. "Let me help you through this, Skye."

The fight drains from her body, and she goes slack. Quiet sobs fill the air. All I want is to pull her into my arms and console her, but I need to get her out of here first. Once we reach my car, I lean down and yank open the door handle before carefully lowering her onto the passenger seat. Skye avoids my gaze as I click the belt into place. After she's locked inside the vehicle, I jog around to the other side and slide in beside her. I shove the key in the ignition and turn it. A second later, the Mustang purrs to life.

As we pull out of the parking lot, she asks through stiff lips, "Why are you doing this?"

I chance a look in her direction, but her gaze stays trained on the windshield. "You need me."

A bitter laugh falls from her lips. "You're the *last* person I need. All you've done is hurt me."

My shoulders sink under the heavy weight of her words. "I know."

Her head falls back against the headrest before she turns away from me. There are no more questions. It pains me to see Skye so broken.

I take her to the only place I imagine will help.

The water.

The ten-minute drive to the beach is made in silence. As I pull along the side of the road, Skye lifts her head and glances at the ocean. Bright sunlight glints off the waves as they roll toward the shore.

With quick fingers, I peel off my shoes and socks before hopping out of the car. I keep my eye on her as I move around to the passenger side. I'm half-afraid she'll take her chances and make a run for it, but she remains seated. I toss the keys in the glove compartment and unclip her belt before scooping her into my arms.

This time, she doesn't put up a fight.

With her body cradled against me, I slam the door shut and head to the boardwalk that leads to the beach. Skye slips her arms around my neck and burrows her face against my chest. Her warm breath feathers over my throat. I tighten my arms around her, wishing it was possible to steal her pain and make it my own.

Once I hit the sand, I don't stop. The tide is out, leaving behind a vast expanse of damp beach in its wake. Shells decorate the sand and crack beneath my feet. It takes a minute for the water to lap at my toes and swirl around my ankles before being dragged out again. As much as I hate the ocean, I keep moving at a steady pace. I walk until the cool liquid rushes around my calves. My heart explodes in my chest, beating harder. Faster. The pounding fills my ears as the waves brush against my thighs before gradually climbing to my hips.

A gasp slides from Skye's lips when the water touches her. I don't remember the last time I was out this far. It must have been before the accident. A part of me wants to turn around and get the hell out of here, but I continue until the waves lap at my chest. Skye's grip tightens as the water surrounds us. When she bursts into tears, I reposition her until her legs can wrap around my waist and her head can rest against my shoulder.

One gut-wrenching sob is all it takes for the floodgates to open. I hold her close as she releases her heartbreak. Grief slides down her face before getting swept away by the ocean. We stay in the water until her tears run dry, until she has nothing more to give.

SKYE

e lie stretched out on oversized towels that Hunter grabbed from the trunk of his car. Other than a few people strolling past us, we have the beach to ourselves. I close my eyes and listen to the sound of the water lapping against the shore and the seagulls crying overhead. The wind slides over my face as the sun's warmth strokes my cheeks. Things that would normally bring me peace aren't enough to mend the tattered fragments of my heart.

I will never be whole again.

Exhaustion overtakes me, making it difficult to pick up my head or even suck in a breath. I want nothing more than to dissolve into the sand and become nothing. Maybe then everything won't feel quite so painful. The thought of not being able to see Dad or pick up the phone and call him leaves me feeling lost. As if I'm no longer tethered to the earth.

I'm not ready for this.

I will never be ready to say goodbye.

That thought breaks my heart all over again.

Hunter shifts next to me and the heat radiating from his body is a reminder that I'm not alone. Our towels are arranged side-by-side, and his head rests near mine. There's something about his steady inhalations that I find comforting.

"Do you feel any better?" he asks softly.

I crack my eyes open, and the bright sunlight blinds me. My eyelids flutter against the harshness of it before my pupils adjust. My world has been painted in an ugly shade of gray, and all this vibrancy feels excruciating.

Hunter turns his face toward mine, and I feel the heavy weight of his stare pinning me to the towel. I shrug and remain silent. There are no words for the way I feel.

"You know," he says quietly, "I didn't get a chance to say goodbye to Mom and Dad. They were here one day and gone the next."

I swallow past the thick lump that has wedged itself in my throat. I know exactly how painful the death of Hunter's parents was for him. The suddenness of it left a catastrophic impact that reverberated for years. It was almost impossible for him to find closure and move on.

"As fucked-up as the diagnosis is," he says, "I'm glad that you get this time to spend with your dad. Every day that he's here is a gift. You have the chance to tell him everything that's important, everything you want him to know. And when it's finally time to say goodbye, you get to do that, too."

The air rushes from my lungs in an agonizing burst that leaves me gasping.

"Maybe you'll get more time than the doctors think, or maybe it'll be less, but the point is that you get *time*. You have no idea how precious that is. Don't squander it, Skye. I know everything feels like shit right now but be grateful for the time you've been given because once it's gone, there's no getting it back."

My voice is barely a croak when I whisper, "I can't think about it like that." Tears leak from the corners of my eyes as I turn away from him and curl into a tight ball. "It hurts too much. I'm barely able to get through each day as it is."

In the time it takes for me to suck in a shuddering breath, Hunter curls his body around mine, cocooning me in his strength. I don't want to find comfort in his presence, but I do. The way he holds me is achingly familiar. When the sobs turn into more of a torrent, his grip tightens. It keeps me grounded in the here and now, so I don't blow away in the breeze.

"I know, baby, I know. Let me help you through this."

He brushes the hair away from my neck before pressing a kiss against the delicate flesh.

I roll onto my back and stare into his eyes. There were times when I thought I would drown in the utter blueness of them. Even though nothing is the same between us, they still hold the same power over me. He strokes my face tenderly before kissing the teardrops from my cheeks.

"If I could take away your pain, I would."

I shake my head, knowing that's not possible. The grief that fills me is so consuming, I'm not sure if I will ever find my way out of it.

"Tell me what you need," he pleads.

There's no way for me to answer that question because it doesn't feel like anything can save me from the darkness pressing in on me.

When I remain silent, he says, "I'm here for you. I will *always* be here for you."

I lift my hands and trace the sharp angles of his face. He presses into my touch as if he needs the contact as much as I do.

"Just hold me," I whisper. "Please."

Hunter scoops me into his arms and presses me tightly against his chest. Only then am I able to block out everything but the steady thumping of his heart. My world shrinks until that's all I'm conscious of. And in that sound, I finally find comfort.

HUNTER

As soon as I step foot in the small lecture hall, I scour the area for Skye, but she remains conspicuously absent. I drop onto my usual seat before slipping my phone from my backpack and firing off a text to Lanie. Since Skye has gone back to avoiding me, I've been getting all my intel from her best friend. Lanie and I are now texting buddies.

I set the phone down and drum my fingers on the desk while waiting for a response. It doesn't take long for her to get back to me.

Chill out, stalker-boy. She's on her way.

She adds an eye-roll emoji. Then a second message rolls in.

Good luck.

Yeah, I'm going to need it.

A few moments after the texts pop up on my screen, Skye rushes through the door before sliding onto her seat next to Jaxon.

Now that she's here, I can calm down and focus for the next fifty minutes. Well, that's the plan. Dr. Bennet isn't exactly the most scintillating of public speakers. Throughout the class, my attention wanders, and I find myself glancing over my shoulder to see what Skye is up to. Not once does her gaze drift my way. She studiously avoids me the entire time. It's like I'm not even there.

If it weren't for Lanie, I wouldn't know what the hell was going on. I'm trying to respect Skye's wishes by giving her time and space. I realize that's what she needs from me right now, but it's difficult when all I want is to be near her.

From what I've been able to get out of Lanie, Skye is still having a rough time of it. If she's not attending classes or visiting her dad, she's locked in her room. She's closed herself off from the people who care most about her.

I'd thought we'd made a small breakthrough at the beach, but that turned out not to be the case. It's been two weeks since we've talked.

Lanie's new nickname for me is stalker-boy. Unfortunately, it fits. That's exactly what I've become. For the time being, all I can do is hover on the periphery of her life.

Once Bennet dismisses us for the day, I pack up my stuff and head for the door. I'm surprised to find that Skye has already disappeared from the room when I wasn't looking.

Damn, that girl is fast.

I hurry into the hall and search for her blond head before shoving my way through the crowd. All of my muscles tighten as I pull alongside her. I have no idea what kind of reception my presence is going to be met with.

"Hey," I greet in an overly cheerful manner that sounds nothing like me.

"Oh, hi." She shoots me a shuttered glance I'm unable to decipher.

Yup, this was a bad idea. I should abort the mission. Already I can tell this won't end well for me. But now that I'm at her side, I find myself reluctant to part ways.

When she says nothing more, I clear my throat. "It's been a while. I wanted to check in and see how you're doing."

My gaze slides carefully over her, cataloging all the subtle changes most people wouldn't notice. There's a hollowness in her eyes that kills me, and it's obvious that she's lost weight. Her clothing hangs a little looser from her frame. Lanie mentioned that she hasn't been eating much lately.

Protectiveness surges through me. All I want to do is wrap her up in my arms and make everything better, but I know she won't welcome the gesture. Skye has been keeping me at arm's length. Any effort on my part to get closer to her is quickly shut down.

She shrugs and keeps her gaze focused straight ahead. "It's fine."

That's so far from the truth, it's not even in the same realm. I wish she would be honest with me, but I've lost that privilege. And I have no idea if I'll ever earn her friendship back again. Right now, we're nothing more than acquaintances.

"Is it?" I probe gently.

Skye presses her lips together as we push out of the building before heading down the stairs. The brisk November air hits us, and she sucks in a deep breath before exhaling it.

Once we're out of the flow of traffic, I hike my backpack onto my shoulder. "I don't know if you have plans right now, but I was wondering if I could take you somewhere."

Caution fills her gaze as she shifts her weight. Her hand tightens on the strap of her backpack. "I don't know if that's a good idea."

Carefully, I close the distance between us until I can reach out and slip her fingers into my hand. That simple touch is enough to settle my jangled nerves. I have no idea if the contact has the same effect on her.

"I want to help you, Skye. That's it. Will you let me do that?"

She stares down at our clasped hands. "I don't know," she mumbles.

I rack my brain for a way to convince her to come with me. "Just give me an hour of your time, and I won't bother you again. What we're going to do...it's important."

She gnaws her lower lip as indecision flickers across her face.

"Please?" I squeeze her fingers. "It's just for an hour."

"All right," she says quietly.

Unwilling to waste another moment—or give her time to change her mind—I drag her through the heavy traffic on the pathway as we trek across campus. Instead of firing off a bunch of questions, Skye remains silent. Once we arrive at Middleton Hall, I slow my pace.

Color stains her cheeks from our rushed hike. "You know that your legs are much longer than mine, right?"

I run a hand through my hair as the corners of my lips lift. She's right, they are. I was so afraid she would change her mind that I wanted to get here as quickly as I could. "Sorry about that. I didn't want to be late."

Wariness enters her eyes as she glances around. "Late for what?"

Now that I've dragged her here, uncertainty fills me. It's entirely possible that I've overstepped my boundaries. Maybe this was a terrible idea, and I'll only end up pushing Skye further away from me. But I'm more frightened that she won't get the help she needs. It's my concern for her that overrides all other thoughts and feelings.

"Come on." I grab her fingers and tow her through the glass door to the front desk. Once there, I give the receptionist a polite smile. "Hi, Skye Sinclair is here for a ten o'clock appointment."

Skye's mouth goes slack with shock. My guess is that she just figured out why we're here. Well…why *she's* here.

"Wonderful. I'll let Dr. Mestoff know right away." The older woman extends a hand toward the grouping of chairs near the window. "Have a seat. It won't be long."

This time, it's Skye who seizes my hand and drags me to the waiting area. Her nails dig into my skin. Already I can tell that I'll be sporting crescent-shaped indentations for the rest of the day.

Skye whispers furiously through stiff lips, "Oh my God, you made an appointment for me at the counseling center?"

It might be asked in the form of a question, but it's not one.

She doesn't give me a chance to open my mouth before snapping, "And you didn't even bother to ask if that was something I wanted? Who the hell do you think you are?"

I shift my weight and lower my voice, hoping she'll do the same. The last thing we need is campus security getting called. "I thought it might be helpful for you to talk with someone about what you're feeling."

Her hands tighten into fists at her sides as she growls, "Why the hell would you think that?"

"Because you're going through a really tough time." I gesture with my hand toward the offices. "Maybe they can give you better ways to cope."

She presses her lips together so tightly they lose their color.

"I was trying to help," I add.

"Maybe you should try to *help* a little less. Or, hey—here's an idea," her eyes ignite with anger, "why don't you mind your own business instead of butting into—"

"Skye?"

We both swing toward the receptionist. There's a serene smile pasted across the older woman's face as if Skye hasn't been chewing my ass out in front of her.

A look of dread washes over Skye's features. "Um, yeah?"

"Dr. Mestoff is ready to see you now."

"Oh." Skye's gaze darts to the door as if she's contemplating an escape.

It's obvious from the look on her face that she's reluctant to meet with the counselor. I didn't do this to make her uncomfortable or piss her off any more than she already is. I'm at a loss as to how to help her. And I'm not the only one who's worried. Jax and Lanie are, too. She's become a shadow of her former self.

"Give it a try," I encourage. "What's the worst that can happen?"

"Fine," she grumbles before taking a few steps toward the receptionist.

"Do you want me to wait for you? I don't mind."

The icy look she tosses over her shoulder is enough to freeze me on the spot. "What do *you* think?"

"Umm…yes?"

She grits her teeth as a low growl vibrates from her chest before she disappears down the narrow hallway. I get the feeling she would have been all too happy to rip me a new one if there hadn't been a witness. A moment later, the receptionist returns and takes her seat behind the desk. I stuff my hands into my pockets and pace the waiting area. Sure, I could take off and avoid the wrath of Skye when she's done with her appointment, but I'm not going to do that.

If she's pissed at me for taking matters into my own hands and trying to get her the help she needs, then so be it. I'll take her anger over silence any day of the week.

SKYE

$\mathcal{A}$t the end of our appointment, Dr. Mestoff grabs a card from the coffee table before scribbling something on the back and handing it to me. The front has her name and contact information.

"We run several groups on campus for students who are dealing with grief. I wrote down where they meet and the times." She gestures toward the card. "You're welcome to join us and try it out. It's an open group, meaning that people drop in when they're in need of support. Sometimes they share, and other times, they simply listen. It's whatever you're comfortable with."

I glance up and meet her soft brown eyes. "You really think this could help?"

"I do. Feelings of grief can be difficult to deal with, especially alone. Many people find comfort in talking about it with others who are in similar situations. I also understand that not everyone is comfortable meeting and talking in a group setting, which is why one-on-one counseling is available. What's important to know is that Claremont has services to help you. Any time you need to talk, all you have to do is make an appointment at the center. Most of the time, we can squeeze you in the same day."

"Thank you." Rising to my feet, I slip the card into the front pocket of my jeans.

Dr. Mestoff walks me to the door. "I hope this was helpful, Skye."

I'm surprised to realize that I actually feel better. Nothing has changed in regard to my dad, but maybe there are better ways for me to deal with my emotions. "It was. Thank you."

"Good." She nods and holds the door to her office open for me.

With a quick wave, I exit the room and head down the hall before finding the front entrance of the building. My mind rehashes everything we discussed. It was, at times, emotional, but what helped was knowing that the feelings I'm experiencing are normal, and there are professionals on campus who can equip me with tools to better deal with what's happening.

As I pass the front desk, I give a quick wave to the receptionist. Out of nowhere, Hunter pops to his feet, and I muffle a squeak of alarm. I wasn't expecting him to wait around for me, especially after I gave him such a hard time about the appointment.

"Everything go all right?" he asks cautiously.

"Yeah, it did." I glance away and lower my voice. "I'm sorry for the way I acted earlier. I was caught off guard when you brought me here. I didn't think this was something I needed." I pause and force out the rest, "But I was wrong."

A rush of air leaves his lips, and his shoulders release their tension. "Good. I'm glad it worked out. I was kind of afraid you'd want to kick my ass after that."

The image his words conjure up makes me chuckle. "I guess you lucked out then. Don't be too disappointed. I'm sure you'll give me plenty of other reasons to kick your butt."

"You're probably right." A smile flirts across his lips as he nods toward the entrance. "Are you ready to get out of here?"

"Yeah."

As we push through the doors and leave the counseling center behind, Hunter clears his throat. "I was wondering if you wanted to grab lunch."

Thrown off by the invitation, I glance at him. A little zip of electricity skitters down my spine when I find him already watching me. He's the only guy who has ever made me feel this way, which is exactly why I *shouldn't* have lunch with him. I have enough going on in my life without adding any more complications. And Hunter Price is definitely a complication I don't need. "Do you really think that's a good idea?"

His gaze darkens, and his voice drops. "Spending time with you is always a good idea."

My heart skips a beat. I don't want to make a mistake where Hunter is concerned. Keeping my ex at a distance is so much easier than being around him. I don't have to think about the attraction that hums through my body whenever he's near or the fact that I still love him. There are times when I suspect I'll always feel this way about Hunter. He was my first and only for so many things. It's impossible for that not to hold meaning.

Before I can think better of it, I hear myself say, "Okay."

His lips curve into a full-blown smile. One that makes my pulse flutter with awareness.

Twenty minutes later, we're walking through the door of Melvin's. It's a diner we used to frequent when we were in high school. We were here so often that the staff knew us by name. It's the one place I've avoided since my return.

As soon as I step over the threshold, I'm flooded with memories. There are so many of them that I have to stop and catch my breath. I glance at Hunter, wondering if he feels the same way. Our gazes meet, and his lips tip upward as he propels me toward the back of the restaurant.

"Should we grab our usual booth?" he asks.

Probably not. Already I'm being slammed with so much nostalgia that I'm practically drowning in it.

"Sure."

We slide into the same booth we've sat in over a hundred times. A waitress bustles over and hands us menus. Even though I know what I want, I bury my face in the plastic to avoid looking at Hunter. I need a break from the intensity of his gaze and the feelings coursing through me.

"Can I start you two off with something to drink?" she asks.

"Sure, we'll both have Cokes." There's a pause. "And I think we're ready to order."

I lower the menu and chance a peek at Hunter. I'm about to tell the waitress what I want when he beats me to the punch.

"We'll have two cheeseburgers with the works and a large chili cheese fry to share."

It's exactly what we used to order whenever we stopped by.

The waitress scribbles on her notepad before glancing at us. "Anything else?"

One side of Hunter's mouth hitches as he pops a brow. He knows what I want to add.

"A chocolate milkshake," I say.

The older woman flashes me a grin. "You got it, honey."

She disappears, once again leaving us alone together. My gaze travels over the restaurant, looking for any subtle changes that would mark the passage of time, but there aren't any. Everything is exactly as it was when we were in high school. The décor, the menus, the smell of greasy food being fried in the kitchen. Like Hunter, it's all so familiar, and it tugs at something deep inside me.

Our drinks are delivered, and I take a sip before asking, "Do you come here often?"

Melvin's is a fifteen-minute drive from campus. There are a lot of restaurants closer to the university. This place has always been more of a hangout for locals than the college crowd. That's part of its charm.

"Nope." Hunter shakes his head. "I haven't been back since high school."

"Oh. I thought…" My voice trails off as confusion fills me.

"After you left, I didn't want to come back. It was difficult to be around anything that reminded me of you."

"I'm sorry," I mumble as my gaze drops from his. "Maybe this was a mistake, and we should have stopped somewhere else."

Hunter reaches across the table and snags my fingers. "Don't be sorry. You didn't do anything wrong, and coming here after all this time feels right. I'm glad you agreed to have lunch with me. I haven't given you any reason to trust me, but I really hope we can be friends." His grip on my hand tightens. "I've missed having you in my life."

I suck in a breath as the intensity grows between us. A change in conversation seems to be in order. "Thanks again for making an appointment at the counseling center. It's not something I would have done on my own."

"You're welcome. I'm glad it was helpful."

His thumb rubs delicate circles against my palm. The caress is distracting, and I feel myself getting lost in his touch. When I realize what's going on, I have to jerk myself out of the haze.

I clear my throat and refocus my attention on our conversation instead of the attraction humming below the surface of my skin. "Dr. Mestoff mentioned a grief group they run on campus."

"That sounds interesting. Are you going to check it out?"

"I think so. And I'm going to make another appointment to see her next week." What she helped me realize today is that I can't handle this on my own. Dr. Mestoff has thrown me a lifeline, and I need to grab it with both hands.

It's almost a relief when the waitress arrives with our burgers, milkshake, and an order of chili cheese fries for us to share. Another punch of nostalgia hits me. It's difficult not to be wistful for what Hunter and I once shared.

"Enjoy!" she says before taking off.

"This looks so good!" My belly rumbles, and I realize how hungry I am. Lately, it doesn't seem like I have much of an appetite. I can't remember the last time I sat down and had a full meal.

"Eat up." He grins before we dig into our burgers and fries. Every once in a while, I take a sip from my shake. How is it possible that it tastes even better than I remember?

I point at the ice cream drink. "Do you want some?"

We used to share them all the time.

"Sure."

I slide the tall glass toward Hunter. His gaze stays pinned to mine the entire time he sips from the straw. It's the silliest thing, but butterflies wing their way to life in the pit of my belly.

When he's done, he gives it back. "It's better than I remember."

My lips curve into a smile. "That's funny. I was thinking the same thing."

After that, we fall into an easy conversation as we finish our lunch. Hunter tells me about his ACL injury and how worried he was that he'd never get the chance to play football again. A pang of regret fills me. I wish I could have been there to help him through that tough time. Football has always been Hunter's drive and purpose in life. I tell him about UW-Madison and what it was like to live in the Midwest.

Once we've finished every last bite and the check has been paid, I rise to my feet. "Give me a minute to use the restroom."

"No problem." He flashes me a smile. "I'll be here waiting."

Five minutes later, I'm headed to our booth when I spot someone talking to Hunter. My footsteps stutter when I realize that it's Mason.

What's he doing here?

My heart thumps a painful staccato against my ribcage. As I take a hasty step in retreat, fully prepared to hide out in the bathroom, Hunter glances up, and our gazes catch. Even from this distance, it's easy to see that he's pissed off. His jaw is tightly clenched, and his mouth is an angry slash across his face.

I gulp and freeze.

He immediately moves from the booth before coming to his feet. Mason turns, and his gaze lands on mine. I'm almost shocked by how much his appearance has changed from when I ran into him at the game. There's a haggardness to him as if he hasn't slept in weeks.

When Hunter holds out his hand toward me, a silent command filling his gaze, I force myself to close the distance between us. When I'm no more than a few feet away, Hunter reaches out and slips an arm around my waist. Strength radiates from him, and I take comfort in that.

Mason shifts his weight, his gaze focused on his brother before it reluctantly slides to mine. Silence descends, becoming equally as stifling as the tension that fills the air between them. If it were possible to slip out of Hunter's arms and make a dash for the door, I would.

Mason pulls off his ball cap and plows a hand through his hair. He winces as he lifts his arm. That's when I notice the scar cutting across his forehead.

Even though I shouldn't feel anything other than disdain for Mason, my heart fills with sorrow. When their parents died, his life was turned upside down. He was forced to grow up overnight and shoved into a stressful situation he was ill-prepared to deal with. Not once have I ever doubted that he loved Hunter and wanted only the best for him. It's how Mason chose to go about it that was wrong. In the end, he hurt the one person he spent years trying to protect.

"Mason was just leaving," Hunter snaps. "Isn't that right?"

Misery flashes across his older brother's face as he nods. "Yeah." Mason shuffles his feet before hesitantly turning toward me. "I owe you an apology, Skye. Forcing you to leave was wrong. All I wanted was for Hunter to have the best chance of making it to the NFL. I didn't want to see something else get taken away from him." He gulps as his gaze flickers to his younger brother before coming back to settle on mine. "I realize there isn't anything I can do to make it up to either one of you, but I'm sorry for the pain I caused."

Hunter's arm tightens around me as he pulls me closer. From the stoic expression painted across his face, I realize there is no forgiveness in his heart.

Mason must recognize it as well. "Okay then," he mumbles. "I should go." Tentatively he lays a hand on Hunter's shoulder. "Maybe you can stop by the house this weekend, and we can talk."

Hunter shrugs off his brother's hand. "I don't think so. There's a lot going on."

"Oh." Mason's shoulders sink. "Maybe another time then."

"Yeah, we'll see."

Mason's gaze flits to mine. There is so much sadness filling his eyes that it's almost too much to bear. This is the reason I didn't tell Hunter the truth. I didn't want to cause a rift between them.

Hunter's muscles remain locked in place until his brother disappears from the restaurant. Only then does his grip on me loosen.

"I'm sorry about that." There is so much pain buried in those words. "If I'd known that we would run into him, I would have never brought you here."

"It's not your fault. You don't have anything to be sorry about."

He sighs as sadness fills his gaze. Maybe he won't admit it, but this conflict with Mason weighs heavily on him. How could it not? Other than his older brother, Hunter is alone in the world. Ever since their parents died, it's been just the two of them. They need each other.

"We should probably head back to campus," he says.

I hoist my smile and nod. "Yeah, that would probably be a good idea."

As much as I've enjoyed spending time with Hunter, a little distance is needed.

HUNTER

ell...that didn't go as planned. We'd been having a great time before Mason showed up and blew it all to shit.

I flick my gaze at the girl sitting quietly next to me as we head back to campus. I have no idea what's going through her head. I'm almost afraid to ask. "Are you okay?"

"Yeah, I'm fine." She shifts her body toward mine. "I didn't realize that you and Mason weren't talking."

My grip tightens around the steering wheel. Even thinking about what my brother did pisses me off. If he's under the impression that some lame-ass apology is going to fix things between us, he's got another thing coming. As far as I'm concerned, there's nothing my brother can do to repair the damage he inflicted.

"I haven't spoken to him since the car accident." My jaw clenches as I push out the rest. "Not since I found out what he did."

"Oh." With her brows furrowed, she turns and stares out the windshield.

Fury and resentment bubble up inside me, and I try to tamp it down. "I have nothing to say to him. Maybe when I've calmed down, we'll be able to hash things out. But right now?" I shake my head.

"That's not going to happen." I can't imagine a time when I'll be able to look him in the eyes and forgive him for driving Skye away.

Her hand settles on my forearm. "I'm sorry that he hurt you."

I spear a hard look in her direction and remind her gruffly, "He hurt both of us, not just me. He took away the most important person in my life." It still blows my mind that he did it. What the hell had Mason been thinking?

"I should have said something, but I didn't want to cause problems between the two of you. You and Mason have always been so close. He's the only family you have left. It seemed selfish to take that away from you."

I jerk my shoulders and keep my gaze focused on the ribbon of road stretched out in front of me. "He put you in a shit position, Skye, and I don't blame you for any of it. He's the one I hold accountable. And now he has to live with the repercussions."

"I know, but he's your brother," she says gently. "No matter how messed up what he did was, in his mind, he had your best interests at heart. He wanted to see you achieve your dreams."

"If that were true, he wouldn't have taken *you* away from me. As much as I love football, you have always been the most important thing in my life."

Not only did he steal years from the past but he also stole our future. How can I forgive him for that? I've never gotten over the loss of Skye. As much as I wanted to believe that I had moved on, it was never the truth.

"I hope, at some point, you'll consider sitting down and talking to him." Her voice fills with emotion as she looks away. "You know better than most that people can be yanked from your life without any warning. Don't waste time being angry. Let it go and move on."

Easier said than done.

Silence surrounds us as I pull into the parking lot of her townhouse. I cut the engine and angle my body toward her. There is so much I want to say, but I'm not sure if Skye is ready to hear it. There's a good possibility she may never be ready.

The moment my gaze locks on hers, it feels like I'm drowning in her green depths. Attraction sizzles in the air between us. When it becomes almost suffocating, Skye clears her throat and shifts on the leather seat. It's a struggle to hold back and not pull her into my arms.

"Thanks again for the counseling appointment," she murmurs. "And for lunch."

"There isn't anything I wouldn't do for you." Unable to help myself, I lift my hand and cradle her cheek in my palm. My thumb strokes absently over her lower lip.

She's so fucking beautiful. Not only on the outside but on the inside as well. She's the best person I know. I've never loved anyone the way I love her. I can't imagine going through the rest of my life without Skye by my side. Yet here I am, mentally preparing myself for the possibility that she may never reciprocate my feelings. I allowed my anger and resentment to fuck up everything between us. Just like Mason has to live with the consequences of his decisions, so do I.

Her breath catches, and it's the sexiest sound in the whole damn world.

"I should go," she whispers.

I nod when she remains seated next to me, her gaze locked on mine.

Slow, I tell myself. I need to take everything with her at a snail's pace. Skye has enough going on in her life without me pushing her into a relationship. What she needs from me is friendship and that, I can give her.

I close the distance between us until my mouth can ghost over hers. When her pupils dilate and her lips part, I reach around her, grab the handle, and pop open the door.

"I'm glad we could do this," I murmur. Our faces are no more than an inch apart. It wouldn't take much to press my lips against hers.

"Me, too."

"I'll see you soon?" I need to know that she isn't going to lock me out of her life again. The past couple of weeks have been brutal.

Skye nods as her teeth sink into her lower lip.

A groan rumbles up from my chest.

She leans forward until her mouth brushes against mine. As

fleeting as the kiss is, it doesn't make it any less meaningful. And then she's gone, disappearing from the inside of my car. My gaze stays fastened on her as she walks to the door. After she slides the key into the lock, she glances over her shoulder and meets my eyes. A moment of connection passes between us, and it only reaffirms everything I know to be true in my heart.

This girl is my everything.

SKYE

"Give it to me straight." Lanie drops down next to me on the couch with a massive bowl of vanilla ice cream with chocolate sauce poured over the top. It's more sauce than ice cream. "How pissed off are you about the counseling appointment? You know how much I hate it when you're angry."

"I'm not mad." If anything, I'm grateful my friends care enough about me to seek out support when I'm unable to do it for myself. "It was really helpful. In fact, I've already made another appointment for next week."

She shoves the spoon in her mouth before saying, "I'm glad you're going to talk to someone. We've all been really concerned about you."

"I'm sorry, I never meant to worry you." I glance down at my fingers. "I was trying to deal with everything the best way I knew how."

"Oh, honey." Lanie reaches out and squeezes my hand. "You know how much Jax and I love you. There's nothing we wouldn't do for you." She gives a helpless shrug. "But we weren't sure how to support you."

"You're a good friend, Lanie. You've always been there for me. And that's enough."

All of this emotional upheaval is a mess. There are times when I'd like to talk with someone and just unload, but if I do, I get upset and break down. It's both physically and mentally exhausting. It just seems easier to keep everything bottled up inside where I don't have to dwell on it, but that's not good either. I'm hoping Dr. Mestoff can help me deal with all the anger and sadness I'm experiencing in a healthier way.

I stifle a yawn before rising to my feet. "I'm tired. I think I'll go to bed."

Life, at the moment, is grueling. Most of the time, it feels like I'm simply going through the motions. I'm doing my best to keep it all together, but it's not easy. I have to remind myself to focus on one day at a time. If I start imagining what life will look like in a month or six months, I get overwhelmed, and my brain shuts down. Then all I want to do is crawl into bed and sleep. Apparently, that's not a very effective strategy for dealing with grief.

"All right. I'm going to wait up for Jax. He's staying over tonight."

I smirk. "So what you're telling me is that I should plan on using my noise-canceling headphones?"

"You know it, girl," she says with a laugh.

"I'll have them ready." As I head to the bedroom, I call over my shoulder, "See you in the morning."

"Night."

After changing into a tank top and shorts, I wash my face and brush my teeth before turning out the lights. Once between the sheets, I close my eyes, but sleep refuses to come. Everything that happened today loops through my brain.

Hunter.

The appointment with Dr. Mestoff.

Lunch at Melvin's.

And running into Mason.

No matter what I'm thinking about, my mind always circles back to Hunter. He's the one constant in all this. If I'm being honest, it's been that way since the very beginning. Hunter was such a major part of my life. After we broke up, I spent years trying to push him from my thoughts. There have been times when I was successful in my attempts, but it's impossible now that we attend the same college.

I've spent the past couple of weeks trying to avoid him. It seemed easier that way. With Dad's illness, I've pared my life down to the bare essentials. But Hunter makes that difficult. The man I spent time with this afternoon was so reminiscent of the boy I fell in love with. Earlier today when he dropped me off, it took everything I had inside to force myself from the car. Instead of leaving, I wanted to curl up in his arms and stay there forever. When we're together, it's as if my chest loosens, and I can finally breathe again.

Making a split-second decision, I roll over and swipe my phone off the nightstand. Before I can overthink it, I tap out a message and press send.

Thanks again for today.

It's short, sweet, and to the point. Almost immediately, my cell dings with an incoming message. Anticipation rushes through me as I open the text.

You don't have to thank me. I want to help.

A warm feeling grows in my heart, and a smile curves my lips.

It helped more than you could know.

For the first time in weeks, I feel like I'm going to get through this. There are resources available, and I don't have to do it all by myself.

Whatever you need, baby, I'm here.

Baby.

Pleasure shoots through me. It's what he used to call me when we were together.

Unsure how to respond, or even if I should, I set the phone down and roll onto my side. Something is so achingly familiar about being with Hunter. Now that he knows the truth, it feels like it would be all too easy to fall back into a relationship again. But is that necessarily a good idea?

I'm already drowning in my life. Anything more and I'll go under.

When my phone chimes with another message, I tell myself to ignore it. My resolve lasts for approximately thirty seconds before I roll over and snatch the phone off the table.

One text leads to another as we slip into an easy conversation and spend the next two hours rehashing the past. It feels so good to talk to him again. If there's one person who understands what I'm going through, it's Hunter. A part of me wants so badly to let him back into my life, but I need to be cautious.

By the time he finally tells me to go to bed, my eyelids are drooping, and I'm about to fall asleep. We make plans to meet up at the library in a few days to work on our project.

With everything going on, I haven't put nearly the amount of time into researching our topic as I should have. Whenever I have a free moment, I choose to spend it with Dad. Everything else in my life feels so much less important. Unfortunately, my grades reflect that decision. Unwilling to dwell on school, I push it from my head.

One day at a time, I remind myself. That's all I can do.

Remember I'm always here for you, baby.

As I drift off to sleep, his words bring me more comfort than they probably should.

HUNTER

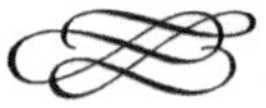

"**G**reat game last weekend, Price!"

I flash a quick smile. "Thanks, man."

"We're all looking forward to this Saturday's game against Georgia. It's going to be a tough one."

"Yup." I tip my head in acknowledgment. "I've been watching a ton of game film."

"Good luck, we'll be cheering for you."

"Appreciate the support." With that, I pull open the doors to the library and jog up the staircase to the second floor where I'm meeting Skye. There's a definite pep in my step. I can't wait to have her all to myself for a couple of hours. Maybe we're only working at the library, but it doesn't matter. It's enough to be close to her.

I'm trying my best to navigate this new relationship with Skye. She needs me to be her friend and that's exactly what I'm trying to give her. *Friendship.* Instead of being all up in her face, I've pulled back and have been giving her space to breathe. Space to work through her emotions.

It sucks. All I want to do is protect her from anything that will cause her heartache. When she hurts, I hurt. That's just the way it is. I've accepted it.

Skye still holds me at a distance, but it's not as great as it once was. Every night, I fall into bed, and we text for hours. It's like we're getting to know each other all over again. It's only through our silent messaging that she's willing to open up and tell me everything that's going on in her life. She talks about her dad and how she wants him to make a miraculous recovery but knows that's not going to happen. It breaks my heart that she has to go through this.

As soon as I reach the landing on the second floor, I glance around, immediately spotting Skye tucked into a corner with her laptop open. I take a few steps before realizing that she's not alone.

Some dude is chatting her up.

And he's got that look in his eye.

You know the one I'm talking about.

If he could gobble her up in one tasty bite, he'd do it. My natural inclination is to rush over and stake my claim, but I won't do that. At the end of the day, Skye isn't mine. She's free to see whoever she wants.

It takes a few moments to lock down the jealousy surging through me. Once I'm fairly confident I won't tear this guy limb from limb, I force myself to walk slowly toward them. Skye glances at me as soon as I sidle up to the table.

"Hey," she says with a smile curving her lips. I have no idea if that look is meant for me or the bonehead who hasn't made himself scarce. For all I know, *I'm* the bonehead who needs to leave.

"Hey, yourself." I shift and glance at the guy even though I'd much rather ignore him. His face lights up as soon as he recognizes me. He should be reserving that look for Skye, not me. Doesn't he realize how completely amazing this girl is?

Don't worry, I won't be the one who clues him in.

"Hunter Price!"

I give him a chin lift in greeting. "How's it going?"

"Awesome, man!" His head bobs manically.

"Great." I give Skye a bit of side-eye, and her smile widens. Normally, I don't mind being recognized, but right now, all I want is to enjoy a little one-on-one time with her. I've been looking forward to it all damn day.

"Hunter, this is my friend, Max. We have sociology together."

Cool. Now leave.

"Nice to meet you," I say with far more politeness than I'm feeling.

"Right back at you!" Max enthuses. "I'm a huge fan! I can't wait to see where you get drafted this spring."

"Yeah, me, too," I agree.

Skye clears her throat as Max continues to stare worshipfully. "Hunter and I are meeting up to work on a project for our health class."

"Oh." Max's face falls as he shifts his weight. "I guess I should leave you guys to it."

Yup, that's exactly what you should do.

"I'll see you in class, Max," she says.

"Yup, catch you on Tuesday." His gaze strays to mine. "Hey, Price… I was wondering if maybe you'd like to grab a beer later." He pauses before tacking on, "You know, if you're not too busy."

Ummm…

This conversation has definitely taken a turn for the awkward.

I glance at Skye, hoping she's going to throw me a much-needed lifeline. But her head is bowed, and her shoulders are shaking. Clearly, I can't count on her for any help.

"Thanks for the offer, but I think Skye and I are going to be here for a while."

A crestfallen expression flits across his face. "No problem." He jerks his thumb toward a table on the other side of the second floor. "I should probably get back to what I was doing."

When I nod, he adds, "Maybe we can grab that beer some other time."

Sheesh.

"Sure."

His smile broadens, overtaking his face. He looks like a kid on Christmas morning. "Great!"

I give him a small salute when he finally takes off.

That was seriously painful.

Once he's gone, Skye glances up at me with a smile simmering around the corners of her lips. Well, I'm glad someone found the situation amusing. It sure as hell wasn't me.

I slide onto the chair across from her and unpack my computer from my backpack.

When she remains silent, I nod toward the table her friend now occupies. "He seems nice." In a creepy stalker kind of way.

She glances at him and shrugs. "He's a good guy." A smile flashes across her lips. "He liked you a lot."

I roll my eyes. There are a ton of people like that on campus. Cleat sniffers and jersey chasers. What I've come to realize is that it's not you specifically they're interested in. It's your celebrity. The sooner you can grasp that, the sooner you can weed out those kinds of individuals. It's best to keep a tight circle of friends that you can trust.

Skye was always the most important person in my circle.

Silently, I acknowledge that Mason may have guilted her into taking off, but I'm the one who lashed out and hurt her when she returned. What I did was unforgivable.

I know it.

And so does she.

Just like Skye said at the beach—we can't alter the past, we can only change the future.

I clear those thoughts away before digging around in my backpack and grabbing my health class folder. Nerves churn in my gut as I slide it across the table toward her. "There's something I want to show you."

Her brows furrow as she picks up the folder. "What's this?"

I gesture toward the red plastic she now holds in her hands. "Open it and see."

My breath lodges in my throat as she pulls out the twenty-five-page paper I've been working on in my spare time. It's not like I have a ton of it, but it's funny how much time opens up when you stop playing video games and hanging out with the guys.

"I don't understand," she mumbles, thumbing through the pages before glancing up at me.

Even though I shrug, wanting to play it casual, my heart jackhammers painfully in my chest. It's only now that I wonder if she'll be pissed off. What if she's mad that I wrote it up myself without asking for her input? We've been emailing back and forth, so I was able to take what she sent and synthesized it into a cohesive piece about vaccinations. I also spoke with my childhood pediatrician and got his professional opinion on the matter before emailing a spokesperson from an anti-vax group, the National Vaccine Information Center, along with The World Health Organization who is a proponent for vaccines. In the end, I feel like it's a pretty damn good paper.

But…that doesn't necessarily mean Skye will appreciate me hijacking the project.

The longer she remains silent, the more jacked up I feel, which is ridiculous. I have nerves of steel. On a weekly basis, I play football in front of ten thousand screaming fans and have to make split-second decisions that could potentially cost us games. And somehow, this means more.

Skye means more.

"It's finished?" Shock reverberates throughout her voice. "You completed the entire project?"

"Um, yeah." I'm tempted to rip the paper from her fingers and stuff it in my bag. "I had some extra time. It wasn't a big deal."

"Wasn't a big deal?" she echoes, carefully looking over the pages. "You contacted the World Health Organization and," she points a finger at the third paragraph on page ten, "an anti-vax group?" Her wide gaze lifts to mine.

"Yeah, they were awesome about getting back to me and answering my questions. So was Dr. Zelman, my old pediatrician." I clear my throat. "We're going to grab lunch next week."

Skye collapses against her chair and shakes her head. "I can't believe you did this."

"Are you mad?" Honestly, I can't tell.

Her gaze falls to the paper before she blinks her eyes.

Well, shit…she's crying. No one cries over something happy. Especially schoolwork.

"Look…" My voice rises in panic as I wave my hand toward the folder. "If you don't like how I organized the information, feel free to add whatever you want, or we can start over from scratch. I don't really care."

"What?" Skye glances at me with tears swimming in her eyes. "Redo it? Why would I want to do that? It's absolutely perfect."

The air rushes from my lungs as everything in me collapses with relief. Okay. Good. She's not pissed off, but she's still upset. "Then why are you crying?"

A tear treks slowly down her face, and her voice fills with emotion. "I can't believe you did something like this."

Doesn't she get it?

I would do anything for her.

"I know you've got a lot going on, and I thought if I took care of this on my own, you wouldn't have to stress over it. Then you could spend more time with your dad."

Wetness slides down her cheeks as she glances at the paper in her hands. "This is really amazing, Hunter. Thank you."

Unable to bear Skye's tears, I pop to my feet and walk around the table before hunkering down in front of her. I slip her hands into my own. As I do, everything settles inside me.

"Whatever I can do to help you, I'll do it." Maybe this isn't the time or place, but I can't hold back anymore. I don't want her to ever doubt my feelings. "I love you, Skye. I always have. Even when I didn't want to, you were still there in my heart."

She sucks in a shaky breath before her teeth sink into her lower lip.

Yup. It was too soon. I should have kept my feelings to myself. Instead, I blew my load and ruined everything. If I know Skye, she'll probably push me away again, and I'll be back to square one.

Hastily, I add, "I get that you're not there yet, but I hope someday, you'll love me the way you used to. For now, I'll be the kind of friend you can lean on." I swallow down my disappointment. "Even if that means you need to date other people." I jerk my head toward the guy on the other side of the library and force out the rest. "Like Max. Although, as your friend, I'm going to be completely honest. You can do a lot better than—"

She slips a hand free from mine before laying it across my lips and silencing me.

"Shush."

My brows rise.

"Is it my turn to talk yet?" she asks.

I nod and wait. I've kind of made a mess of things. Usually, I'm smooth when it comes to the ladies, but not with Skye.

"You're right, I wanted time to deal with what's going on with my dad. I didn't want to think about anything else, but you've made that impossible. You've been here for me when I've needed you the most. As much as I've tried to move on, I couldn't do it."

Does that mean what I think it does?

"I love you, Hunter," she whispers.

A grin breaks out across my face as relief rushes through my body, filling me with a happiness I haven't felt since we broke up.

"I love you, too." I jump to my feet, tugging her up with me before yanking her into my arms and sealing the moment with a kiss. I pull away enough to add, "So." I smack my lips against hers. "Fucking." One more time. "Much."

Her lips curve, and when her mouth opens, my tongue slips inside.

God, I've missed this.

Someone clears their throat from behind us, and we jump apart only to find one of the librarians glaring at us with her hands planted firmly on her hips.

"Perhaps you two should take this elsewhere," she grumbles.

That's the best damn idea I've heard all day.

I grin at Skye. "What do you say? Are you ready to take this elsewhere?"

A blush fills her cheeks as she nods.

"Perfect." I shove everything into my backpack as she does the same, then I grab her hand and tug her down the steps and out the library doors.

Now…I'm sure you're thinking that I'm going to go all caveman on this girl and drag her back to my place so I can have my wicked way with her.

Well, guess what?

You couldn't be more wrong. My plan is to take this nice and slow. We're going to ease back into this relation—

"Want to go back to my place and fool around?" she asks.

"Fuck yeah! I thought you'd never ask!"

With that, I grab her hand, clenching it tightly in my own. I let her get away once. There's no way in hell I'll let it happen again.

EPILOGUE

HUNTER

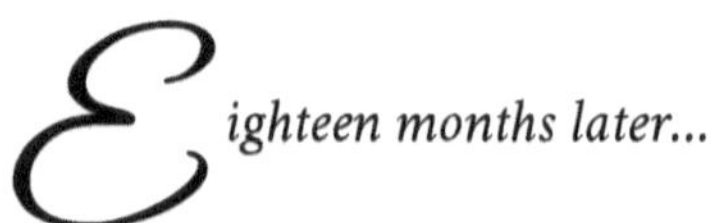 *ighteen months later...*

SKYE WADES out into the water with a small decorative box that holds her father's ashes. As much as I hate the ocean, there's no way I'd let her do this alone. Once the water swirls around her calves, she turns until the wind hits her back as it whips toward the shore. I step behind her and slip my arms around her waist before resting my chin on the top of her head.

As we stand silently, her body trembles with emotion. It's been more than a year since Dean passed away. Some days, the grief nearly eats Skye alive. The hole he left in her life has been impossible to fill, but I've been doing my best to ease the ache of his loss.

This trip to Claremont has been an emotional one. Even though Dean has been gone for a while, this is just another part of the grieving process she has to pass through.

"It's time, babe," I whisper in her ear. "Time to let him go."

Skye nods as if she knows this in her heart but is unwilling to accept the reality. "I wish he would have lived long enough to see me graduate."

"Me, too." I press a tender kiss to the top of her head. "But he did get to walk you down the aisle."

She turns until our gazes can lock. Even though her lips lift into a ghost of a smile, tears stream freely down her face. "Thank you for that. It meant so much to Dad."

I shrug. "We both know it was only a matter of time before it happened." The circumstances might have been less than ideal, but after being separated from Skye for three years, I was more than happy to make her my wife and bind her to me for the rest of our lives.

A soft sigh escapes from her lips. "Do you have any idea how much I love you?"

My heart clenches. There's no way I could ever tire of hearing her say those words. There was a time when I didn't know if she could feel that way about me again. The fact that Skye was able to forgive me makes me feel like the luckiest bastard in the world. It's the only reason I relented and allowed Mason back into my life. Our relationship isn't what it once was. At this point, I don't know if it'll ever be the same again.

We've been married for more than a year, and it's been the most amazing time of my life. Everyone has always assumed that my dream was to play professional football, and I'm not going to lie, I did want that, but it was never more than I wanted Skye. Without this woman standing by my side, all of my accomplishments would be meaningless.

After graduation, we settled into our life in Atlanta. I was drafted by the Falcons and started training camp in the summer. Skye applied to and was accepted at Georgia State for graduate school. She's working on a master's degree in educational psychology so she can become a school counselor. We've also been talking about starting a family. Once she finishes school and finds a job, we'll work on that. For the time being, we're enjoying our life together.

"It can't be more than I love you," I tell her because it's the truth.

The water continues to lap at our legs as Skye holds the tiny turquoise and silver box clenched tightly in her hands. Even though her father will always be in her heart, it's still difficult to let him go.

It's gently that I ask, "Should we do it together?"

The breath she had been holding escapes in a rush as she nods. Carefully, I place my hands over hers as we open the box and then the small bag inside that holds a portion of Dean's ashes. Together we turn it over until all of the tiny fragments scatter before getting carried away on the breeze.

I tighten my hold on Skye as she sobs quietly in my arms. "He was so proud of you, baby."

She sniffles and continues to fight back the emotion. "I miss him so much."

"I know. It's going to take time, but eventually, the pain of his loss will lessen. You'll remember all the good times you spent with him. Your dad wouldn't want you to mourn him forever. He'd want you to live your best life and find your happiness."

Her gaze latches onto mine. "I did find my happiness. *You.*"

Those words mean everything. "I'm always going to make you happy, baby. Always."

She tilts her head until I can capture her lips with my own. The sun breaks free from the clouds and beats down on us.

This woman owns me heart and soul.

And I wouldn't have it any other way.

KING OF HAWTHORNE PREP

SUMMER

My gaze wanders over the water as white-capped waves roll rhythmically toward the sandy shore. When the wind picks up, a warm breeze rustles through my hair, and I tip my face toward the sun before stretching.

Could life get any better than this?

Doubtful.

A family friend was kind enough to let us borrow their beach house in Door County for the week. Mom and Dad surprised us with the impromptu vacation a few days before we were supposed to leave.

The house we're staying at isn't like one of the newly renovated million-dollar monstrosities that flank us with their gargantuan square footage, swanky pools, and perfectly groomed lawns. But it's steps from the beach and has breathtaking views of Lake Michigan. At just fifteen hundred square feet, this house has three cramped bedrooms, an outdated kitchen, and a ton of seashell décor. Even so, there's something charming about it.

Sweat beads my forehead as I haul myself from the chair I'm sprawled on and saunter to the water's edge. It might look as inviting as the Caribbean cast in varying shades of cerulean and turquoise, but it doesn't feel like it. Especially when my skin has been crispifying for hours beneath the sweltering sun.

A breath hisses from my lips as the frigid liquid rushes past my ankles. The first couple of steps are the worst. As soon as numbness sets in, it gets better. Braving the water, I continue forward as the waves swirl around my calves. I do a little dance, bouncing up and down on my toes, trying to get used to the cold as it sinks into my bones.

I force myself to move deeper until the water reaches my hips.

It's now or never.

With that brief pep talk, I suck in a breath and dive beneath a wave as it peaks and curls. Water rushes around me, instantly chilling my overheated flesh. After a moment, I break through to the surface and expel the lungful of air from my body.

It's easier to submerge myself the second time as I dive to the bottom before trailing my fingers through the fine-grained sand in search of clamshells. When my lungs burn, I pop up again before floating on the surface so the sun can warm my skin. With my eyes closed, I stretch my hands and legs, allowing the waves to rock my body. My mind drifts as the rhythmic motion lulls me to a contented place. Every once in a while, I lift my head and search for our little blue one-story cottage to make sure I haven't drifted to far down the shore.

My plan is to make the most of our little beach vaca before returning to Chicago next weekend. There's so much that needs to be accomplished before senior year begins in the fall.

A couple of months ago, I registered for an introductory astronomy class at a local university about thirty minutes from the house. Next on the agenda are campus visits. I've scheduled tours for the University of Chicago, Northwestern, and the University of Michigan in Ann Arbor. My three dream schools have impressive astronomy programs. To round out the summer, I've snagged a volunteer position at the Adler Planetarium. I'm scheduled to start next Monday at nine o'clock sharp.

Long after my fingers turn pruney, I drag myself from the water.

As I trudge toward shore, a bleached clamshell glints in the sunlight from the bottom and catches my attention. Stilling my movements, I bend over to inspect it. A wave crashes over me, stirring up the sand and covering the shell. Once the debris settles, I turn, brushing my fingers across the bottom until they land on it again.

"Nice view."

I yelp and swing around, straightening to my full height only to come face-to-face with the most gorgeous boy I've ever seen. My breath gets lodged at the back of my throat as his mahogany-colored eyes pierce mine with unwavering intensity. Rooted in place, it's all I can do to take in the thick slashes of his eyebrows before my gaze slides to the slant of high cheekbones, and then on to a perfect cupid's bow of a mouth.

Damn.

He's seriously hot.

Like...*way out of my league* hot.

My heart riots painfully against my chest as I continue to stare. His brows rise as humor sparks to life in his eyes.

Is he waiting for a response?

Did he ask a question, and I wasn't paying attention? I hit the mental rewind button and quickly sift through our limited conversation.

Nice view.

Nice view?

Wasn't I bent over at the time with my ass in the air?

Heat slams into my cheeks with the force of a tsunami. That's *exactly* the pose I'd been striking. When he said *nice view*, he'd been commenting on my behind. The very same behind barely covered by a thin strip of fabric because the beach has been fairly empty since we arrived on Saturday. This guy is one of the few people I've seen.

"Ummm, thanks," I force myself to respond.

His lips slide into a smirk as if I've amused him.

I need to pull it together before I humiliate myself any further. Although, let's be honest, that ship has already set sail. Right now, I'm operating strictly in damage control mode.

Is it possible that he hasn't noticed my awkwardness?

Any chance of clinging to that unlikely prospect is blown out of the water when he tilts his head. "Did you just thank me for admiring your ass?"

All right, so he noticed.

The heat radiating from my face intensifies a few hundred degrees until self-combustion seems likely. Not to mention, welcome.

"Yeah," I mumble, attempting to rip my gaze from his, but that proves to be impossible. It's as if I've become ensnared by the dark depths assessing me in such a forthright manner. "Apparently I did."

The sound of his deep chuckle reverberates throughout my entire body before darting straight to my—

"I'm Kingsley." He steps forward, closing some of the distance between us. His proximity makes my heart pound faster. "And you are?"

Humiliated?

Embarrassed?

Mortified?

It's a dealer's choice.

"Summer," I mutter instead. When you daydream about talking with a really hot guy, this isn't exactly how you picture it playing out.

Relief rushes from my lungs when his gaze flicks from me to the house I'm standing in front of. There's something powerful about his stare, leaving me to feel as if he's able to pick through all my private thoughts, and it's a disconcerting sensation. I want to run and hide, but my feet refuse to move. I'm frozen in place.

He points at the house on the dunes. "Is that yours?"

"Yes." I clear my throat along with those disconcerting thoughts. "We're renting for the week."

He nods as his attention returns to me where it stays put. That same feeling of nervousness fills me. "Who knows, maybe I'll see you around, Summer."

A wave of heat wafts over me at the sound of my name sliding from his lips. I tamp down the response and shrug, trying to play it cool even though it's much too late for that.

"Yeah, maybe."

He flashes a wide grin as if not fooled by my nonchalance before taking off at a brisk pace down the beach.

Now that his attention is no longer focused on me, I'm free to look my fill as all those well-honed muscles shift and bunch as he jogs away. We're talking broad shoulders with a broad, muscular back that tapers into a trim waist. Loose black athletic shorts cover his trunk and thighs. My gaze drops, wanting to commit every detail to memory. Damn, even his calves are well-defined.

There's no way a guy built like that is in high school. He's definitely in college. I'd like to know what university he attends so I can submit an application. As his figure grows smaller in the distance, I realize I don't even care if they offer astronomy as a major.

I chuckle and shake my head at the thought of planning my future around a boy I spoke with for all of two minutes.

Never.

Going.

To.

Happen.

I have plans. Lots of them. And I would never derail a single one for a guy.

No matter how good-looking he is.

Once the boy fades from sight, I blink out of my thoughts and head back to the house. In all likelihood, I'll never see him again.

Want to read more of King of Hawthorne Prep? Buy the book here -)
https://books2read.com/u/4A7K8p

CAMPUS PLAYER

DEMI

"Morning, Demi!" Gary, one of the stadium custodians, calls out with an easy smile and wave as he saunters toward me. "Up and at 'em bright and early this morning, I see."

My heart jackhammers beneath my ribcage from the twenty-minute run as I flash him a grin. "Always!"

"You have a good one! I'll see you tomorrow!"

Since I've already moved past him, I holler over my shoulder, "Same place, same time!"

Even with *The Killers* pumping through my earbuds, I almost hear the deep chuckle that slides from his lips. Our morning greetings are a ritual three years in the making. I've been running through the wide corridor that leads to the stadium football field since I stepped foot on campus freshman year. This will be something I miss when I graduate in the spring. Five days a week, I'm up at six, logging in a four-mile run before returning home, jumping in the shower, and heading off to class.

At this time of the day, the stadium is still relatively quiet, with only a few people wandering the hallways. There's something both serene and eerie about it. I've been here on game days when there are thirty thousand fans packed shoulder to shoulder, rooting on the

Western Wildcats football team. Three-fourths of the stadium filled with black and orange is an amazing sight to behold. Football is a religion at Western. Unfortunately, the same can't be said for the women's soccer team. We're lucky if there are a couple of hundred spectators in the stands.

I've come to terms with it.

Sort of.

I keep my gaze trained on the light at the end of the tunnel and push myself faster. As soon as I burst out of the darkness, bright sunlight pours down on me, stroking over the bare skin of my arms and shoulders. It's late August, and summer is still in full swing. A whistle cuts through the silence of the stadium, and my gaze slices to the field. Nick Richards has been head coach of the Wildcats for the last decade. He also happens to be my father.

Two days a week, the guys are up at six in the morning for yoga. Dad is a big believer in flexibility. Even though I'm winded, a smirk lifts the corners of my lips. Watching two-hundred-and-eighty-pound linebackers contort their bodies into Downward-Facing Dog, the Warrior II Pose, and the Cobra is enough to bring a chuckle to my lips. Some of the guys actually like it, but most grumble when they think Dad isn't paying attention. Little do they know that he sees and hears everything.

My father catches sight of me and flashes a quick smile along with a wave in my direction. He has a black ball cap pulled low and aviators covering his eyes. There's a clipboard in one hand as he paces behind the instructor.

When I point to the field, he shakes his head. He might make the guys do yoga, but he refuses to participate. Something about old dogs and new tricks. Every once in a while, I'll tell him that he needs to get out there and set a good example for the team. He usually shoots me a glare in return.

Every Wednesday night, Dad and I get together. Our weekly dinners became a thing when I moved out of the house and into the dorms freshman year. He's busy coaching football, and my schedule is packed tight with school and soccer. Getting together once a week is the best way for us to stay connected. It doesn't matter if we're in the middle of our seasons; we always make time for each other. Especially since Mom lives in sunny California. After eighteen years of marriage, she got fed up with being a distant second to the Western University football program. She packed up her bags and walked out. I hate to say it, but Dad didn't notice her absence for a couple of days. Which only proved her point. Now she's remarried, learning to surf, and is a vegan. I visit for a couple of weeks during the summer before soccer training camp starts up at the end of June.

Even though it's only the two of us, our weekly dinners are set for three people.

I tell myself to stare straight ahead and not glance in his direction.

Don't do it!

Don't you dare do it!

Damn.

My gaze reluctantly zeros in on him like a heat-seeking missile. Long blond hair, bright blue eyes, sun-kissed skin, and muscles for miles. And he's tall, somewhere around six foot three.

I'm describing none other than Rowan Michaels.

Otherwise known as the bane of my existence.

My dad discovered the talented quarterback the summer before we entered high school and took him under his wing. Which has been...aggravating. In the seven years since, Rowan has become an irritatingly permanent fixture in my life. He's the brother I never wanted or asked for. He's the gift I wish I could give back. He's the son my father never had but secretly longed for.

On a campus with over thirty thousand students, one would think that avoidance would be easy to accomplish. That hasn't turned out to be the case. Somehow, we ended up in the same major—Exercise Science. I get stuck in at least one class with the guy each semester. This time it's statistics, which is a requirement. Three times a week, I'm forced to see him. And then there are the weekly dinners at Dad's house.

Every Wednesday, Rowan shows up without fail.

It's so annoying.

No, *he's* annoying!

Our gazes collide, and electricity sizzles through my veins before I immediately snuff it out and pretend it never happened.

I am not attracted to Rowan Michaels.

I am not attracted to Rowan Michaels.

I am not attracted to Rowan Michaels.

Maybe if I repeat the mantra enough times, it'll be true. That's the hope I cling to. I've made it through the last seven years trying to convince myself of this. I only have to get through our final year together, and then we'll go our separate ways—me to graduate school or maybe to the Women's National Soccer League, and Rowan to the NFL. He's one of the most talented quarterbacks in the conference. Hell, probably the country. There is little doubt in my mind that he'll be a first-round draft pick come next spring.

Trust me when I say that Rowan Michaels fever is alive and well at Western University. His fanbase is legendary. The guy is a major player.

Both on and off the field.

Girls fall all over themselves to be with him. They fill the stands at football practice, show up at parties he's rumored to be at, and basically stalk him around campus.

It's a little nauseating. Don't these girls have any self-respect when it comes to a hot guy?

I wince at that unchecked thought.

Fine...I'll begrudgingly admit it; he's good-looking.

I shake my head as if that will banish the insidious thoughts currently invading my brain. Enough about Rowan. It's time to focus on the reason I'm at the stadium at this ungodly hour. I rip my gaze from him as I hit the cement staircase. After half a flight, all thoughts of the blond quarterback vanish from my mind. How could they not when my quads, glutes, and calves are on fire, screaming for mercy as I force myself to the nosebleed section. By the time I finish, my legs are Jell-O, and I still have a two-mile run back to the apartment I share with my best friend off-campus.

I give Dad a half-hearted wave before leaving. It's the most I can muster. His lips quirk at the corners as he shakes his head. He thinks I'm crazy. At the moment, I can't argue with his assessment of the situation. Although, it's the extra training I put in that helps me run circles around the other team in the second half of the game.

The jog home feels like it will last forever. By the time I unlock the apartment door, I'm ready to collapse. I beeline for the shower and jump in before it's fully warm. My skin prickles with goose flesh, but it feels so damn good. Twenty minutes later, I'm dressed and ready to take on the day. My hair has been thrown up in a messy bun, and I'm making a protein smoothie that will fuel me for my morning classes.

Just before taking off, I poke my head into Sydney's room. I know exactly how I'll find her, and that's buried beneath a small mountain of blankets. She doesn't disappoint. We met the summer before freshman year in training camp and have been besties ever since. She's the yin to my yang. The peanut butter to my jelly. The Thelma to my Louise. Where I'm more introverted and cautious, she's loud and bois-terous. She's been known to leap without necessarily looking at what she's jumping into. Every so often, it gets us into trouble. Sydney and I have lived together since sophomore year. I gave up trying to cajole her ass out of bed for a six o'clock run after the first week of us cohabitating when she nearly took my head off with an alarm clock.

"It's that time again," I sing-song obnoxiously, "rise and shine."

There's a grunt and then some shifting from under the blankets that tells me she's alive.

When I chant her name repeatedly, each time escalating in volume, she growls, "Get the fuck out!"

"Awww," I mock, "that's so sweet. I love you, too."

Sydney snorts before a hand snakes out from beneath the blankets to give me a one-fingered salute. Then she grabs a pillow and tosses it in my general vicinity. It falls about five feet short of its mark.

I stare at the dismal attempt. "If you're trying to cause bodily harm, you'll have to do better than that."

"Piss off."

"All right then." I shrug. "See you after class." With that, I close the door behind me.

My farewell is met with another indecipherable mouthful. If this weren't something we went through on the daily, I'd worry she was in the midst of a stroke. Sydney is definitely not a morning person. She's more of an early afternoon person. Another thing I've learned over the years? The action of waking up to a brand-new day is a gradual process. She's like a bear rousing prematurely from hibernation. It's not a pretty sight. She's lucky I don't take her insults personally.

I grab my backpack from the small table crammed into the breakfast nook area along with a coffee before heading out the door. The apartment I share with Sydney is located three blocks from campus, which is highly sought out real estate. We're fortunate Dad is friends with the guy who manages the building. It's probably one of the only perks of having a father who is a head coach of a college football team.

You'd think there would be more, but you'd be wrong. Honestly, being Nick Richard's daughter is more of a hindrance than anything else. People assume you receive special treatment on campus, from professors, or that you have an in with all the football players.

Or worse...

Much worse.

After a bunch of ugly—not to mention untrue—rumors circulated freshman year, I've done my best to distance myself from the Wildcats football team. They're a great bunch of guys, but I don't need all the ugly gossip and speculation that comes along with being friends with them.

As I reach Corbin Hall, the mathematics building for my stats class, my gaze is drawn to a clump of students standing around outside the three-story, red-brick building. In the center of that crowd is Rowan. I don't have to see him physically to know that he's close. The muscles in my belly contract with awareness. It's like a sixth sense. One I wish would go away. He's the last person I want to be cognizant of.

As I jog up the wide stone stairs to the entrance, my gaze fastens on him. A smirk twists the edges of his lips, and my eyes narrow before I drag them away and yank open the door to the building.

Relief rushes through me as I step inside the air conditioning and disappear from sight.

"Hey, Demi, wait up!"

I turn at the sound of my name before slowing my step. The dark-haired guy jogging to catch up smiles before falling in line with me.

Justin Fischer.

He's a baseball player and teammates with Sydney's boyfriend, Ethan. We've been seeing each other for about a month. It's still casual at this point. With school and soccer, I don't have a ton of time to invest in a relationship. He seems to understand that and isn't pushing to be more serious.

When he leans in for a kiss, I angle my head. At the last moment, he tilts in the opposite direction, and we end up bumping teeth instead of locking lips. With a grunt, I pull away and chuckle. My fingers fly to my mouth to make sure I haven't chipped a tooth.

Maybe I've been reluctant to admit it to myself, but that kiss sums up our relationship perfectly.

Awkward and a step out of sync with each other.

"Sorry," he murmurs with a slight smile. I search his face and wait for any telltale sign of sexual chemistry to ping inside me. Unfortunately, my insides remain completely unfazed, which is disappointing but not altogether unexpected. I had a sneaking suspicion when we first got together that it might turn out this way.

"No problem," I say, hoisting my smile and brushing aside those thoughts.

"I haven't seen you for a couple of days," he remarks as we turn a corner and continue walking.

"It's been busy." Which isn't a lie. School might have recently started, but the academics at Western are rigorous. And being a Division I athlete is more like a job. If you're not ready to put in the work, don't bother showing up. There's no half-assing it around this place.

"When's your next game?" he asks.

"Tomorrow at six." My gaze flickers in his direction. Not that I expect him to come, but...

Fine, so maybe I do. If he wants to be my boyfriend, then he needs to show a little support.

His dark brows draw together. "That sucks. I've got a mandatory study hour I have to attend."

I shrug off the disappointment. It's another nail in the coffin of this relationship as far as I'm concerned. "That's cool. It's not a big deal."

"But I'll see you tonight?"

Oh. Right.

Tonight.

Well, damn. In a moment of weakness, I threw out an invitation to join our Wednesday evening dinner. It's one I now regret. If only there were a gracious way to rescind the offer.

"If you're busy, I totally understand—"

"Are you kidding? No way." With a grin, he shakes his head. "I wouldn't miss it for the world. I'm looking forward to meeting Coach Richards."

Great. So this is more about my father than me? Exactly what every girl wants to hear.

I force a brittle smile. "Awesome. He's excited, too."

That might be something of an overstatement.

Justin nods toward the end of the corridor. "I better get moving. Professor Andrews is a real stickler for punctuality."

"Yup. See you later."

This time, when he leans in, our lips align perfectly. The kiss is nothing more than a fleeting caress. There and gone before I can sink into it.

And I'm left feeling...absolutely nothing.

I bury the disappointment where I can't inspect it too closely before giving him a wave as he takes off. For a moment, I stand rooted in the hallway and watch as he disappears through the crowd. There's nothing to distinguish Justin from the thousands of guys who look exactly like him on campus. He's of average height and build with dark hair and espresso-colored eyes. He's nice enough. Although, if I'm completely honest, he's a little self-absorbed. He talks about baseball all the time. If Ethan hadn't introduced us, he's not someone I would have looked twice at. We don't have a ton in common.

As much as I hate to admit it, this relationship has probably reached its expiration date.

Now it's a matter of pulling the plug.

Ugh. I hate breakups. Although, it's doubtful this will end up destroying him. I'll have to make it through tonight and figure out the rest.

With a sigh of resignation, I head to the classroom and find a seat tucked away in the far corner of the small lecture hall. A lanky guy I recognize from a few of my other classes settles beside me. He flashes a dimpled smile as we empty our backpacks.

The tiny hair at the nape of my neck rises seconds before Rowan enters the room. It's like my body knows when he's within a thirty-foot radius. I glance at him from beneath the thick fringe of my lashes before shifting away. Air becomes wedged in my lungs as I wait for him to take a seat. And it won't be next to me because I'm—

"Hey man, would you mind moving?"

Surrounded on both sides.

Damnit. I'm hoping the cutie next to me will tell Rowan to go take a flying leap.

What? It could happen. Not everyone at this university is enamored of the football-playing god. Although I realize the odds aren't stacked in my favor. Rowan is the most recognized athlete on campus. People fall all over themselves to accommodate him.

It's a little sickening.

Okay, maybe more than a little.

"Sure, no problem, Michaels." The guy next to me hastily packs up his books before vacating the desk. Unable to ignore him any longer, I glare as Rowan slides onto the seat next to me.

"Did you really think you could evade me that easily?" Laughter brims in his deep voice. A voice, I might add, that does funny things to my insides.

"One can always hope, right?"

"Oh, answering a question with a question." He leans closer, eating up some of the much-needed distance between us. "I like it."

I roll my eyes as his lips stretch into a satisfied grin. Irritation bubbles up inside me when sexual tension blooms at the bottom of my belly. Or maybe that tension has settled a little lower.

It's definitely lower.

I'm tempted to swear like a sailor. How is it possible that I feel nothing for the guy I'm actually dating, and yet my pulse skitters out of control for someone I don't even like? It's so freaking ironic. It's been this way since we met, and nothing I do stomps it out. I can try to fool myself into believing it's not there, but that doesn't make it any less true.

It's a relief when Professor Peters takes his place at the podium and clears his throat. Once he's captured everyone's attention, he delves headfirst into the probability of dependent and independent events.

Grateful for the excuse to ignore Rowan for the next fifty minutes, I open my textbook and concentrate on the lesson. Just as the blond boy fades into the background, his bare knee bumps into mine. Electricity ricochets through my entire being. I glance at him to see if he's noticed the strange energy we always seem to generate and find his ocean-colored gaze fastened to mine.

My guess is that he does.

Damnation.

Want to read more of Campus Player? Buy the book here -) https://books2read.com/u/mYAxqV

ABOUT THE AUTHOR

Jennifer Sucevic is a USA Today bestselling author who has published nineteen New Adult and Mature Young Adult novels. Her work has been translated into German, Dutch, and Italian. Jen has a bachelor's degree in History and a master's degree in Educational Psychology. Both are from the University of Wisconsin-Milwaukee. She started out her career as a high school counselor, which she loved. She lives in the Midwest with her husband, four kids, and a menagerie of animals. If you would like to receive regular updates regarding new releases, please subscribe to her newsletter here- Jennifer Sucevic Newsletter (subscribepage.com)

Or contact Jen through email, at her website, or on Facebook.

sucevicjennifer@gmail.com

Want to join her reader group? Do it here -)

J Sucevic's Book Boyfriends | Facebook

Social media links-

https://www.tiktok.com/@jennifersucevicauthor

www.jennifersucevic.com

https://www.instagram.com/jennifersucevicauthor

https://www.facebook.com/jennifer.sucevic

Amazon.com: Jennifer Sucevic: Books, Biography, Blog, Audiobooks, Kindle

Jennifer Sucevic Books - BookBub

https://www.tumblr.com/blog/jsucevic

https://www.pinterest.com/jmolitor6/

www.ingramcontent.com/pod-product-compliance
Lightning Source LLC
Chambersburg PA
CBHW051144190726
48290CB00006B/1986